MURDER BY THE BOOK

SHANNON SYMONDS

CONTENTS

Acknowledgements

— · —

ABOUT THE AUTHOR

Shannon Symonds writes in an old house by the sea and in the Utah desert. She is the proud mother of six children and Nana to 18. She loves her Savior, time with her family, writing, laughter, a good mystery, walking the beach, clamming, and bonfires.

Shannon is an indie author and a Cedar Fort Publishing & Media author. Shannon's professional training began at age eight, when she found an Agatha Christie novel and read it on a rainy day at the family beach house. That was it. She was addicted to mysteries.

Shannon worked for over 15 years as an advocate serving survivors of violence alongside law enforcement, and on other causes that she is ridiculously passionate about. In 2018 Shannon was nominated for the Storymakers Whitney Award, she was awarded the Author to Watch Award for her By the Sea Cozy Mystery YA series, and in 2023 her book, Booked for Murder, was a finalist for the Indie Cozy Mystery of the Year award.

Her books and audiobooks have been available at Costco and are still available at Deseret Book, Barnes &

Noble, Audible, Amazon, Target, and other retailers, as well as online.

— · —

OTHER BOOKS ALSO BY SHANNON SYMONDS

To my husband, an editor,
who only corrects me on the page
and loves me with all my misplaced modifiers,
comma splicing, and mixed metaphors.

1

— · —

Hidden Treasure

The old Community Church caretaker woke to the sound of glass breaking. He sat straight up in bed, felt for his glasses in the dark, put them on, and went to investigate. Although he was hard of hearing, he knew every sound the old timbers made during the night, and he knew he'd heard the sound of trouble.

Rain fell lightly outside, pinging against the glass windowpanes. A beautiful stained-glass window on the back door to the church was shattered. The door was closed, but the glass and wet footprints told him someone had descended the stairs that led to his workshop.

The caretaker was born in the church's basement apartment in 1938, on the church's one-hundredth birthday.

The church sat alone, high on the hill above the bay. The light in the bell tower of the historic landmark was a comforting beacon to locals. The unique white stave building was evidence of Balefire Bay's strong Scandinavian heritage and the caretaker's hard work and loving dedication.

He wondered why the intruder was in the workshop when sterling silver candlesticks and other historic pieces were in the chapel.

Slowly, he followed the wet trail in the dark, shuffling softly, knowing well every organized inch of the basement.

A faint light glowed from underneath his workshop door. Glad he kept the hinges oiled, he carefully turned the knob and peered inside. In the far corner of the shop, the door to a large storage room was partially open; light spilled out.

A shadow passed between the light and the door. The sound of wooden crates being moved infuriated him. He'd chased more than one homeless person out of the church. If they thought they were going to move into his perfectly organized storage room, they had another thing coming. It was hard times, but they could use the front door and meet with the pastor like everyone else.

"Hey! Get out of there!" He bellowed. He was old, but his voice was surprisingly loud in the silence of the night. "Get!" He threw the door wide open.

He never saw the blow that killed him. His second-to-last thought as he lay on the cold floor dying was about the old sea chest he and his father kept hidden behind stacks of wooden crates. His last thought was of his father.

2

— • —

IN THE MARKET FOR FUN

Ivy Kelly opened the back of her boss's old Range Rover and peeked inside an ice chest full of her baked goods to make sure they'd survived the drive to town. The scent of lemon bars, marionberry scones, and coffee cake overwhelmed the fishy smell of the saltwater bay. A slow smile spread across her face.

"Well done, Ivy," she said to herself. She knotted her shoulder-length black hair in a bun, adjusted her sunglasses, and shoved her cell phone in her back pocket before hefting the large cooler and kicking the SUV door closed with her foot.

Ivy's seventy-year-old friend, Aggie, had a booth in the small-town's Saturday Market. She'd asked Ivy to help her out by contributing her famous lemon bars and cookies to the Balefire Bay Book and Tea Shop's booth. Aggie offered to pay Ivy, but Ivy wouldn't hear of it. Instead, she told Aggie to use the money to cover the costs of their book club's beverages.

Money didn't drive Ivy's passion for books, baking, or basically anything. Her parents raised her in a small

3

beach town an hour north of Balefire Bay. Working together in their state-of-the-art lab, they'd amassed a fortune patenting their work and investing wisely. Ivy spent her early years doing homework in their basement lab, while they worked, laughed, and invented together.

When her parents recently passed away, she'd inherited enough to retire in her early thirties. Only Ivy's lawyer and a few other very close friends knew about her inheritance and trust fund. She didn't advertise her wealth.

She smiled when she remembered how her parents threw their hands in the air and shouted "Huzzah," when they had a breakthrough. Ivy felt the same way when she toured libraries in Europe. Her parents didn't work. They did what they loved, and so did she.

Their last successful project was creating a living, sentient computer capable of growing and advancing as it learned.

Ivy set the cooler down on the pavement and stood up to catch her breath and relish the view of the bay and ocean. She smiled and said quietly, "Huzzah," grateful for Balefire Bay, her newfound family and work as her favorite, albeit reclusive, mystery writer's assistant, inventorying and appraising antiquarian books.

She picked the cooler up and leaned back as she walked, carrying the heavy container of food and feeling the muscles in her arms work. She made her way down the steep Pelican Way street toward an army of local artists, crafters, and shop owners busily setting up booths.

Hank Howling's Classic Rock Radio Station played sea shanties for the tourists, energizing the mood for the Saturday Market. The crisp spring breeze smelled of fish and gave seagulls a place to float over the bay.

Ivy continued down the block to the Balefire Bay Book and Tea Shop, where her friend Jenny was struggling with and failing to put up a striped lemon-yellow canopy on the sidewalk in front of the shop. Jenny was Ivy's age, in her early thirties, but was a single parent with two adorable girls in elementary school.

"Aggie!" Jenny called. "I need some help."

Aggie, curly, gray hair bouncing, burst through the shop's wooden doors spontaneously river dancing side by side with her business partner, Jessica, to the radio station's current sea shanty. Their support hose and sensible shoes flew like tweens on energy drinks. Aggie's dance skills surprised Ivy. For a stout person, Aggie seemed to know all the moves and was light on her feet.

"A little help, please!" Jenny said. Her mother, Jessica, just laughed and kept up with Aggie's frantic pace, making her glasses bounce on her nose.

Jenny put her hands on her hips, letting the pop-up trade show canopy drop to the pavement, and shook her head. When the music stopped, Jessica and Aggie stopped, bent over with laughter and high fived each other. Pink-cheeked and still laughing, they hugged Jenny. Each occupied a canopy corner: Aggie, on one; Jessica, the other.

"And now, time for another sea shanty! Let's *Blow the Man Down*!" Hank announced.

"Dance with us, girls!" Aggie said.

"Jenny!" Ivy called over the music. Ivy's muscles were burning with the weight of the container.

Jenny left Aggie holding the canopy and quickly walked to Ivy, taking the cooler from her.

"Phew! Thanks. I was afraid I was going to drop it, and it would become a batch of sidewalk sweets for the seagulls." Ivy's arms felt light, like they might float away.

"I'm glad you're here. Maybe you can make those two behave." Jenny laughed, shaking her head, as they both watched Jessica and Aggie giggling as they tried to figure out how to open the legs of a folding table.

"What's the harm in a little silly dancing?" Ivy chuckled.

"Ivy! Just in time to rescue a young woman, namely me." Aggie smiled broadly enough that her eyes were lost in smile lines while her bawdy laughter continued.

Jenny looked at Ivy and rolled her eyes. "Here, hold this for a second." She gave Ivy back her heavy container. Ivy must have looked unstable because Jessica rushed over and opened a folding chair for her to set her ice chest on.

"Isn't Xander supposed to meet us here to help set up?" Ivy asked.

"Yesterday he said he had time to help, but then he texted me and cancelled. Something about his mother, again," Jenny said.

"Oh dear. I haven't met her yet, but I'm impressed with his total dedication to her," Ivy said.

"The question being, is he dedicated out of love or fear?" Jenny winked at Ivy.

"Did you get new tables at the big box store?" Ivy bit her lip, trying not to laugh.

"Yes. They're like an I.Q. test. There's a trick to setting them up."

Jenny expertly laid the plastic table face down on the sidewalk, moved a few rings, and strained to pull the legs up. "Good gravy!" With a loud bang, one side snapped into place, and then another. They set up the canopy and positioned the table.

"Did you hear someone broke into the old church and killed the caretaker last night?" Ivy said.

"By now, everyone in town knows. It was on the social media scanner page," Aggie said.

"Did they arrest anyone?" Ivy asked.

"I heard they arrested the poor homeless man that's been camped out on the hill near the church," Aggie said.

Her brows furrowed and she shook her head. "Really? I want to get the chief's take on the murder. Is the book club meeting this morning? "

"This is why the chief calls you Miss Marple, you know. We all know you love a good murder, but this one is solved," Aggie said. "They found the man sleeping on the docks this morning. He had a small wooden crate from the church in his shopping cart, like no one would notice." She shook her head.

"Maybe the crate was a plant, and he was set up?" Ivy said.

Aggie shrugged. "Maybe, but I know the poor man they arrested. He has some serious mental health issues and has been homeless for years. It's heartbreaking, really, The chief sent him to the Oregon State Hospital in Salem for an evaluation. They are holding him without a release date. It's an open-and-shut case."

"Shouldn't we give it a second look?" Ivy asked.

"To quote the chief, not everything is murder, Miss Marple," Aggie said, smiling with a look of understanding.

Ivy shrugged. "The chief's right. I need to learn to let things go. But I can't stand seeing a mystery without solving it." Ivy looked away from Aggie and at her feet.

"Sometimes it's easier to worry about other people's problems than to work on our own," Aggie said.

Ivy smiled sheepishly. "I began solving mysteries with my friend when we were still in elementary school. We thought we were Nancy Drew."

"Don't you mean Nancy Drew and her sidekick, Bess?" Aggie said.

"No. We both wanted to be Nancy, so we were."

Jenny stood with her hands on her hips, catching her breath. "Only two more tables." Strands of her honey brown hair broke free from her tight ponytail. "I'm getting hot." She took her hoodie off. Her scrunchy came off with the shirt, and her long hair fell wildly down her back. She expertly put her scrunchy back on while lecturing Aggie and Jessica. "Behave you two! We are running out of time, and you're acting like children."

"No commenting on our age!" Aggie chuckled as she went back into the store and returned with purple tablecloths.

"How many people do you think will show up today?" Ivy asked.

"It's spring break in Oregon and Balefire Bay's first Saturday Market. This street will be so packed you will have a hard time walking," Jessica said. "I'll get the books." She went into the store, letting the screen door slam.

"Where do you want me to put the baked goods?" Ivy asked.

Jenny pointed at the corner table. Ivy hefted the cooler onto the table and began unloading her delicious confections.

"Thanks for helping us with the goodies," Aggie said.

"Are you kidding? I love baking and, of course, sampling everything I bake." Ivy wiggled her brows.

Aggie winked at her. "The food will lure the tourists in, then Jessica will seal the deal by selling them her best-selling books for loads of money. Speaking of expensive, what price do you think the lemon bars should be?"

Jessica set a stack of books on the table. "Whatever you charge, I'm buying one."

"Good morning, ladies!" A tall woman with an abnormally small waist and plumped lips came toward them, waving brochures in the air. Her hair was dyed in rainbow colors and had slivers of something that looked like Christmas tinsel in it. Her jumpsuit was light pink with a sequined silver belt.

Jessica froze, mouth open. Ivy, ever the observer, watched Aggie giving Jessica a one-eyebrow-up, puzzled look.

"Hello, ladies. I just had to come over and introduce myself after I caught a whiff of your goodies. I'm Desdemona Dear, yes Dear. It's really my name." She spoke rapidly while they all gawked at her, totally overwhelmed by the speed, the colors, and the unfamiliar face covered in heavy makeup. "I just opened Babes by the Bay Day Spa."

Desdemona handed each of them a hot pink brochure.

"How do you know we're ladies?" Aggie asked.

Desdemona threw her head back and cackled. The sound ran right up Ivy's spine. "I guess that's true. Well, if you'd like to look as good as me, you're welcome to try my new salon using the fifty percent off coupon in my brochure. I can't wait to get to know everyone in town, especially the owners of a shop that sells coffee. I practically live on it."

"You're standing in front of the best coffee and tea shop in town." Ivy smiled and tried not to stare at Desdemona's nails. They were more bedazzled, longer, and pointier than Ivy remembered seeing since she'd left the east coast. *You could kill someone with those, or at least carve their heart out,* Ivy thought.

"I'm having a grand opening party in a few days. All the deets are in the brochure! Now, how about a cup of coffee? Do you make a *Double Shot in the Dark?* Our little coffee shop back home calls it *Black Eyes.*"

10

Aggie belly laughed. "Well, okay if that's..." She made a fist.

Jenny's hand shot out, catching Aggie's fist, cutting her off. She gave Desdemona a demure smile. "If you tell me what that is, I'll make it."

"It's drip coffee with at least two shots of espresso in it. Frankly, I like mine to go nuclear. Add four shots and cream."

Desdemona followed Jenny into the store through the old wooden screen doors. When the doors closed, the booth was temporarily devoid of sound, where sensory overload had been a moment before.

"To each his own. You never know, she might be the most fun this town has seen in a long time," Jessica said.

Aggie's brows rose, and she tipped her head. "She certainly is uniquely pretty. She will bring a lot of energy to the downtown area." Snickering, she shrugged her shoulders. "Back to work. I'll go get the sandwich board and my delicious cinnamon rolls. Can you help Jessica with her new release and children's books?"

"Of course," Ivy said.

Jessica reminded Ivy of Agatha Christie's character, Miss Marple. Jessica's 70-year-old face and short, curly hair didn't fool Ivy. She might try to appear to be a normal senior citizen, but Ivy recognized her genius, no matter how hard Jessica tried to hide it behind her pink reading glasses.

Ivy followed Jessica into the book side of the shop. "How are sales of your latest book, *Falling for Balefire*, going?"

"It just dropped a few notches on the bestsellers list. It was only number one for a week." Jessica pushed a library cart loaded with local authors' books out of her back office. "Some new author, also from the Oregon Coast, passed me up yesterday with a book called *Booked for Murder.*"

"I would be thrilled to have a bestselling book for one hour, much less a week."

Jessica blushed. "It feels almost as good as the day I met Aggie, and we decided to open the shop. Almost." She winked at Ivy. "Tomorrow, I am leaving town for a two-month book tour. I am going to miss you and our book club friends."

Ivy opened her arms and gave Jessica a quick hug. "I will miss you. I know I haven't been in Balefire for a year yet, but you, Aggie, and our group have become like family. I'll help Aggie and Jenny if they need it."

"Ivy, darling, there is something you can do right now to help. Would you go down to Gladys Knot's booth and pick up canning jars of her flowers?" She pointed to a booth in the distance. "Tell Gladys Aggie will pay her in cinnamon rolls."

3

MR. GREEN IN THE GARDEN

Ivy shaded her eyes from the early morning sun as she walked in the direction Jessica said the garden shop was. She watched a woman, whom she decided was Gladys, with gray hair escaping a wide-brimmed gardening hat, holding a selfie stick and beaming at her perched cell phone while talking animatedly.

Ignoring Ivy, she smiled at her phone and spoke to her followers. "Our green family members love the sound of our voices. This is Miss Green, a delightful snake plant. She is over 100 years old! Can you believe it? She doesn't look a day over 29! We talk daily." Gladys laughed gaily, lifted the plant, and kissed a leaf.

The sound of pottery shattering on cement made Ivy and Gladys spin around. A tall, lean strawberry blonde's eyes were as big as daisies. She looked like she was still in high school. Her brows were up so high they were hidden by her bangs. Mouth open, she stood as still as a garden gnome.

The selfie stick came down, as did Gladys' smile. "Pe-tun-ia!" she said, making the single name into a three-syllable word while her face turned red with rage. The girl stepped back, hands out, pushing back, as if she could send Gladys' anger back to Gladys.

Gladys growled, shook her head, and said, "Reginald. Can you please show our daughter how to carry more than one pot at a time? Clean this mess up..."

Concerned for the girl, Ivy moved a little closer to try to interrupt the public scolding unfolding in front of her. "Excuse me."

Gladys whirled around to find Ivy one step behind her. Her red face fell into the same smile she had been filming moments before. "Why hello there. Ivy, isn't it? I've seen you at Aggie's. I do love your name."

Ivy bit her lip. "Is your plant really over one hundred years old?"

"Miss Green? Why, of course, she is. I would never lie to my millions of followers. She belonged to my grandmother. She's been a member of the family since about 1907." Gladys snorted.

"Millions?" Ivy asked.

"Just... three million." Gladys' smile had an edge to it. She wiggled her brows, waiting for Ivy to respond.

"That's impressive. Are you filming live?"

"Oh, heavens no. I am Gladys of Gladiola Gardens. I'm a social media influencer."

"Here in Balefire Bay?"

"That's right. I'm sponsored by Zeke's fertilizer delivery service and Tanner's Tulip Farm. The great thing about social media is anyone anywhere can be famous. I do daily posts with gardening tips and tricks for growing houseplants and other garden delights." Gladys laid down her stick and phone. "I am guessing you're here for Aggie and Jessica's tabletop arrangements. They're right over here."

Ivy followed her around to the back of the booth, where Gladys handed her two-quart jars of pink and yellow tulips with a sprig of lavender and leaves. "These are beautiful. Thank you. Oh, and she said she had arranged your flowers in exchange for tea and food."

"Tell her I'll be by for my favorite cinnamon rolls." Gladys winked. "Reginald! Time for the bakery!" she barked, making Ivy jump. Gladys left Ivy to search for Reginald.

Ivy turned to go and watched Petunia break one of Miss Green's leaves off and put it in her pocket. Petunia glanced up and spotted Ivy watching her. She frowned and her eyes narrowed as she scurried away.

Whoa. She did that deliberately to hurt her mother. Her mother is so abusive, she's getting back at her any way that she can, Ivy thought. Then she closed her eyes and shook her head. *Ivy Kelly*, she said to herself, *you have your own healing to do.*

Ivy had only taken a few steps toward Aggie's booth when she heard Gladys berating her husband again. She paused and looked back at Gladys' booth. "Poor Reginald," Ivy said out loud before she turned, and carefully carried the canning jars of flowers in water back toward Aggie's booth.

"Reginald! Petunia!" Gladys growled.

15

Ivy froze and looked back. The unfolding drama continued. She wanted to look away but couldn't. She realized her hands were shaking, making the water in the jars slosh. Reginald shuffled toward his wife. He reminded Ivy of a sad basset hound, in need of a little patience and love. His shoulders were slumped, and his back was bent. Only a few wisps of hair were carefully combed over his head, while tufts of gray hair grew on his large ears and in his nose. He stared off into space, ignoring the tongue-lashing Gladys was giving Petunia.

The angry woman talked loudly enough for Ivy to hear every word. "Plants are sensitive. Everything we do matters. When a plant dies, we lose money! It's hot out. If you spritz the leaves too much, they will burn at noon. Not enough, and they will burn at noon. Shade is imperative." Gladys' daughter glanced at Reginald and then folded her arms and looked at the ground. Ivy thought, *I bet this happens all the time. She seems unaffected, like she's a pro at tuning out her mother.*

A whiff of perfume distracted Ivy from the conflict. Desdemona was coming her way.

"Oh, my! I just love flowers. I must have some. Wherever did you find them?" Desdemona said. She leaned in and smelled the flowers, overwhelming Ivy with her own scent.

Ivy nodded toward Gladys. "Over there."

Desdemona was off, her arms waving. "Yoohoo!"

4

ALL THE FISH IN THE SEA

By the time Ivy returned, Aggie was busy arranging books on the table, while Jenny was bringing out hot pots of cocoa, tea, and coffee.

Aggie stepped back to admire the books she'd stacked on the table. The sign on their sandwich board read *signed books by local authors* on one side and had a list of baked goods and their prices on the other side. Ivy put the vases on the tables.

"It's a shame we can't sell some of Xander's books," Ivy said.

"It would never do for the general public to know he lives here. If it got out? A famous author in Balefire? None of us would have any peace. It would be the end of the early morning book club," Aggie said.

"Jessica, aren't you a famous author?" Ivy winked at Jessica.

"All the more reason to allow another famous author to hide in plain sight. A lot of wealthy people have hideaways along the coast," Jessica said.

"I think the way the locals let him live and keep his secret is amazing," Ivy said.

"Amen to that," Aggie chimed in. "The poor man deserves a place where he can live a normal life."

"Ha! Poor man? Are you kidding? He will never live a normal life," Jenny said as she rearranged paper cups, plates, napkins and stir sticks. "Seriously. A bestselling author? He's sold millions of books. He is rolling in money. I mean... Just look at his house! It's more of an estate or manor than home." She pointed at Knightley House, sitting below the North Head lighthouse on the end of the peninsula. Ivy had to admit that Xander, her boss, seemed to live a charmed life.

"Yes, but he's a true introvert... very private. It's hard for him," Ivy said.

Jenny shook her head no. "Hard for him? You work for him, and you're going out with him. You should know better than anyone else that 'poor man' is absolutely the worst description of Alexander Knightly, author and world famous bazillionaire. The man has his own butler, cook, and housekeeper in one—Anderson. I would love to have an Anderson in my life."

"Stop it," Ivy said. She looked over her shoulder. "Someone will hear you. And how much is a bazillion, anyway? Is that even a word?" She chuckled.

They worked quickly, side by side, plating Ivy's baked goods on Blue Willow platters.

"Are you ladies open yet?" Conner, Aggie's son and a local police officer, picked up one of his mom's cinnamon rolls, completely ruining Jenny's display. A long piece of his dark hair fell into the sticky frosting, and he grimaced while he took a napkin and fruitlessly tried to wipe off the icing, which dripped unceremoniously down his uniform.

"Hey!" Jenny slapped his hand playfully. He smiled, gave Ivy a quick buddy hug, and strolled away to patrol the festival and keep the tourists under control.

"He loves working patrol at the Saturday Market. It's like getting paid to eat everything in sight and shoot the breeze with all the locals. By the way." Jenny stopped what she was doing and looked directly into Ivy's eyes until she had her full attention. "When are you going to choose between those two? It's killing me, and I know Conner is a wreck. At least tell him that you're dating Xander."

"Choose?" Ivy's brows rose.

"Don't look all innocent. You have two men that love and adore you, Conner and Xander, but you keep putting them both off. None of us can figure out why."

Ivy winced. "None of you? You've been talking about it?" She smiled, weakly. "I don't know why that surprises me. What are you worried about?" Not sure she wanted the answer, she folded her arms tightly around her middle and looked at her feet,

"You haven't officially committed to Xander. You keep telling me that you're friends. It doesn't make sense. And because Conner is my brother from another mother, and I can't stand to see his puppy dog eyes looking at you anymore. He hasn't asked anyone else out since you came to town."

19

Ivy bit her lip, knowing Jenny was right. "I'm kind of dating Xander, but he hasn't asked me to be his one and only date. I don't know."

Jenny's mouth fell open. "Kind of dating? Xander outright spoils you. He is either the sweetest man on earth or the worst boss ever. He gave you the Range Rover to drive, for pity's sake."

"It's really rusty and..."

"Seriously?" Jenny's voice and brows rose to astronomical heights.

Ivy looked around to see if Jessica and Aggie were listening or anyone else was within a few hundred feet. She sighed. "I refuse to jump into anything. I tried that once. I'm not sure I'll ever be able to truly trust anyone again. My ex cost me my parents and almost cost you your life. What if I pick the wrong man, again?"

"You picked Xander just fine. Now let everyone know you're officially dating," Jenny raised one brow to astronomical heights.

"I'm not ready to say that until he uses the L word and asks to make it official. Besides, Conner is just a good friend. Honestly, it's my picker. It's broken."

Jenny waved her mom-style pointer finger in Ivy's face. "Oh, no it's not. You've picked the only two eligible bachelors in town with jobs, driver's licenses, and all their own teeth. There are a few local women our age that want to eat you for breakfast."

"Oh, come on. There are a lot of men in town with teeth."

"You are not going to derail this conversation. I love you Ivy, but if you hurt Conner as bad as I think you're going to, I... I... don't know what I'll do, but it will be painful." Jenny folded her arms and tapped her foot.

Ivy stood up to her full four-foot-eleven-inch height. "I'm not leading them on. I promise. I just don't trust my own judgment. I can't even decide what car to buy because owning one is too big of a commitment. I get sick just thinking about it. My ex-husband worked for a black ops organization, and I had no idea. I missed every single sign that he was a homicidal maniac while we dated and then I married him. How much more broken can a woman's picker be?" She spoke as low and as rapidly as she could, hoping no one was listening in.

"I don't know why you're whispering. The whole town knows what he did. But he's dead. We're sure of it. Seriously, you made the state and local papers and Hank's news on the radio station. It's not a secret that he was a jerk. Besides, you met in the middle of Covid. We were all vulnerable during the lockdown. Most of us completely understand. A handsome face can be distracting and hide a lot."

Ivy saw Xander heading their way. "Shush," Ivy said. Her eyes widened. "There's Xander. I don't want him to hear you."

Alexander Knightly, Ivy's employer, and the number one bestselling mystery suspense writer in the country, wore a baseball hat over his thick, shoulder-length brown hair and Ray-Bans, looking like a movie star avoiding the paparazzi.

Jenny's eyes followed Ivy's gaze. "I wonder if he thinks that's a disguise?" Jenny asked, chuckling. "You know, like every celebrity on the planet and Superman? They put on a pair of thick glasses or sunglasses and a hat, and they think no one will recognize them?"

Xander was at a booth run by the new About Time Antique Mall's owner. Ivy didn't know his name. She'd nicknamed him the Crow. Possibly due to his age, he had a dowager's hump under the long black raincoat he usually wore, making him look to Ivy as if he was hiding wings. She wasn't sure why, but he made her shiver, like a cold wind, when he passed by.

"Did you hear about the break-in at the Victorian just up the coast?" Ivy asked Jenny.

"Yeah. Who hasn't? It's on social media," Jenny said.

"Do you see the new antique shop owner with Xander? Do you know his name? I call him the Crow. Some local storage units were also burgled. I've wondered if he's the thief. I never see him move new merchandise into his shop, and yet it keeps filling up." Ivy chewed her bottom lip, thinking.

Jenny shook her head. "Rude! Look, I know you and your friends when you were growing up were some kind of super sleuths, but seriously, you see crime and criminals everywhere. Okay, he makes my skin crawl, but not every Johnny Cash fan in black is a killer," Jenny said.

The local grocery clerk interrupted their conversation. "I want two lemon bars, please."

As the clerk walked away, Ivy, who was still watching Xander and the Crow, said, "Sometimes thieves wear black. I've been right."

"Yes. But most people in town are good, even if they dress in black," Jenny said.

Ivy nodded. "You're right."

The Crow's booth had stacks of books and knick-knacks that appeared to be old and valuable. There was one sign on the table, and it read, "Don't touch! Ask for help." Xander was touching everything. Ivy wondered if someone in town had clued in the Crow, revealing Xander's identity and the town's unspoken agreement to give him his privacy.

As if Xander could feel them staring at him, his head jerked up, and he flashed one of his world-famous smiles, his dazzling white teeth glinting in the sun. He put down the book he was holding and said something to the Crow before he made his way toward Ivy.

Shoppers were already wandering between booths, even though several were still being organized and arranged. Ivy wondered how anyone could walk by Xander and not recognize him, but apparently his disguise was working.

He walked right up to Ivy and pulled her into a quick but tight hug. Leaving his arm draped over her shoulder, he said, "How are my favorite ladies in the world?"

"Ladies?" Aggie said.

Aggie and Jessica said in unison, "Ladies never make history!" They dissolved into peals of laughter.

"I feel more like a gray goddess," Aggie said.

Xander belly laughed. He gave Jenny's shoulder a buddy punch, like one old friend to another. One of Jenny's brows rose, and she gave Ivy the stink eye.

Ivy tried to step away from Xander, but he put his arm around her shoulder and gave her a sideways squeeze.

"I'm sorry I wasn't here helping you set up this morning, but my mother texted and needed me to wire her more money," Xander said.

"Didn't you send some last week?" Ivy asked.

"Yes, but she's my mom. I take care of her," Xander said. He looked down at Ivy. "How much are your beautiful lemon bars? I want two." Xander pulled a money clip out of his pocket.

"Xander!" Conner called to him, waving as he walked briskly back to their booth. "Xander!"

"Conner!" Xander waited, smiling.

"My new boat is being delivered this week. It's a forty-footer. A little longer than my last boat and better for tuna fishing. I am hoping you, Ivy, and everyone in the book club will come on my maiden voyage. I'm going to christen her," Conner said. "I've hired a new crewman and will be ready to let anyone fish that wants to."

Xander clapped him on the back, knocking him a little off balance. "I would be honored! What will you name her?"

"You'll see. I want all of you to come," Conner looked at everyone, including Ivy.

Ivy quickly looked away from Conner and Jenny. *Friends. We are all friends. Right?*

"Of course we'll come. I'm sure everyone in the book club will be there." Xander answered for her and everyone there.

Speaking for Ivy annoyed her. She absolutely wanted to go, but it felt like he'd just ordered shrimp for her dinner without asking if she liked it or had a shellfish allergy.

His arm fell from Ivy's shoulder. He and Conner walked away from the booth without looking back or saying goodbye. Hank's radio station was playing *I'm Shipping Up to Boston* by Dropkick Murphys over the loudspeaker. People lined up for coffee and Ivy's enticing desserts.

Ivy watched as Conner pulled his cell phone out of his pocket, unlocked it, and handed it to Xander, who appeared to be swiping through photos she guessed were of his new love, a boat.

5

---·---

DOWN THE GARDEN PATH

Ivy drove the winding road up the hill to the church and garden. She'd never seen the garden before. The homeless man being arrested for the caretaker's murder felt wrong. She could see a man wanting to get out of the rain being startled and lashing out, but dragging a wooden crate in a grocery cart down the steep hill made no sense to her at all.

There was a long set of wooden stairs that led from the last road on the bayside of the hill to the church. Being tired from working at the market made them look more daunting to Ivy than they were. She climbed them slowly.

Halfway up the stairs, she turned around to look at the bay and quickly grabbed the handrail. The view was breathtaking. The stairs were old and didn't feel safe.

She pictured the homeless man parking his grocery cart at the bottom of the stairs, leaving it unattended, and then go to the church. *He didn't do it.* Then as she climbed, she tried to picture him carrying a full wooden crate down these stairs without falling to his death. He wouldn't. He would have unpacked it and left the crate. They had the wrong man.

The chief clung to the belief that nothing happened in Balefire Bay. Once again, wanting his town in order, he'd arrested the wrong person.

I guess this is a book club conversation. The chief and Ivy's friends met most mornings in the Bookshop taking their places by the fire. They rarely got around to sharing what they were reading, although they were all voracious readers. They were more likely to gossip about the goings on in Balefire. More than anything, they loved true crime and solving local mysteries.

She thought about going back down and driving home without seeing the church, but she'd gone this far. She decided to press on.

The view at the top made the climb worth it. She'd seen the church from a distance but never stopped to admire its beauty. The wooden church must have been built by skilled Scandinavian craftsmen who put their hearts into the work. It was bigger than she expected. The stained-glass windows had newer frames, but other than that, it looked original.

What really surprised her was the garden to the left of the church. It was larger than she had expected. About two acres of flowers in full bloom followed the natural lines of the mountain. There was a white wooden trellis covered in flowering clematis at the entrance closest to the church.

Reverently, she walked into the garden and followed the path created by multi-colored bricks. It wound around trees and flower beds filled with a wide variety of large and small flowers like hydrangea, dahlias, and rhododendrons.

She was so charmed by what she saw that she was startled when she came around a corner and almost tripped over an older woman who was on her knees, weeding.

"Oh, hello," the woman said. She smiled and grunted as she stood up and took off her gardening gloves. She wore a large straw hat to shade herself from the sun, but her cheeks were still bright pink. "I didn't mean to startle you." She stepped aside to give Ivy room to continue walking.

"Your flowers are amazing," Ivy said.

"They aren't my flowers. Do you live here?"

"I do," Ivy said.

"Then you probably heard what happened to our caretaker. I'm the pastor's wife. I wanted to keep the gardens up until we found a new caretaker. It's harder work than I expected."

"Can you tell me about your caretaker? What was he like?" Ivy asked.

"I can if we sit down." Ivy followed the pastor's wife a little farther down the path to a stone bench sitting between two large blue hydrangeas. "Ah..." The woman sat down and closed her eyes. "That's better." She patted the bench next to her. Ivy sat beside her.

"Did you ever meet our caretaker?" The pastor's wife asked.

"No."

"Well, he was something special. His name was Angelo, but his mother and the congregation called him Angel. It was a fitting name. He was raised right here in the gardens and lived in an apartment in the basement of the church."

"Was he old?" Ivy asked.

She nodded. "He was 87, a little slower but still very strong after a lifetime of working in the gardens as well as working on the church. He was also as bright and smart as ever. That's why the whole thing doesn't make sense."

"Do you mind telling me what happened?"

She sighed and looked at Ivy. "I keep thinking about it. I found him, you know."

"I am so sorry. If it's too hard to talk about it, I understand," Ivy said.

"It might actually do me some good. Get my thoughts sorted and stop them from spinning a web of confusion. There is an office, and kitchen at the back of the church. It's cozy. When I made breakfast, Angel usually joined us. When he didn't come up, I called him. He didn't answer, so I went down to check on him.

"That's when I found him lying on the storeroom floor on his back. That's the part that doesn't make sense. The thief could have easily gone to the chapel and taken two large sterling silver candlesticks, or any number of valuable things the church has had for almost two hundred years. Instead, they went downstairs, walked past Angel's power tools, also worth selling, and opened an unmarked door to the storeroom that looks like a broom closet. You might not notice it if you didn't know it was there."

"Do many people know it's there?"

"Some locals that helped Angel with things like the roof or repairs that were too physical for his older body, but not many. People we hired. We just had the bell tower and roof repaired recently. The contractor and his men were in and out of the shop."

"What would be of value in the storeroom?"

"I honestly don't know. It's full of old crates. Some of them date back to the early eighteen-hundreds. None of them are marked very well. I think they are full of old books, linens, and decorations used in the church over the years. I know our Christmas and Easter decorations were by the door and labeled. Angel knew what was in every box. If I asked, he'd bring them up," the pastor's wife said. "I better get back to work. Adam left the Garden of Eden and left us in a world of weeds."

"I am so sorry for your loss. He sounds like a lovely man and a true friend." Ivy stood up and offered her a hand, pulling her up beside her.

"By the way, I didn't hear your car pull into the parking lot. Did you walk?"

"Parking lot?" Ivy's brows rose and she covered her mouth, hiding her smile. "I took the stairs up. Where's the parking lot?"

"There is a road that comes pretty straight up the south side of the hill and takes you behind the church. You can park there. At least you picked a nice day for a walk."

"And a nice day for a stroll in your garden. Thank you for telling me about your caretaker. I can't tell you how sad it makes me feel to know the man who created all of this is gone before his time."

"He was an Angel."

6

STORM ON THE HORIZON

Ivy woke earlier than usual, thinking about her conversation with the pastor's wife and about Angel. She opened her cabin door and enjoyed the view from its deck. She held Judy, a small Cavalier King Charles Spaniel, whose whole body wiggled with delight. Judy knew they were going on a walk.

Ivy fell in love with Judy when she came to work with Xander. The feeling was mutual.

"You know all my secrets. Don't you girl?" Ivy said. "Here's another. You're the only person in the world I trust to love me no matter what."

Holding Judy gave Ivy a sense of peace. Xander was dog-sitting for his mother while she was overseas, traveling. Ivy hoped his mother would keep on traveling and forget to come back for Judy.

Her cabin, the Crow's Nest, sat on the North Head, high above the town and below Knightly House and Xander's lighthouse. It hung over the bay, on the edge of a nine-hundred-foot cliff, giving her a breathtaking view of the bay and ocean. The cabin was hers as long

32

as she worked as his personal assistant as well as in the Knightly House library. His generosity was sometimes overwhelming.

"Come on, girl. We don't want to be late. Let's see what Anderson made you for breakfast." She put down the small black-and-white dog, who looked at her with intelligent eyes that had just a hint of mischief and arrogance. Judy ran happy circles around Ivy while they walked over to the house.

Ivy tried to keep things at work professional, but no matter how many deep breaths she took, her pulse still raced when Xander was in the room. One minute she'd catch herself with a silly grin on her face and the next she was mad at herself for picking apart every interaction, looking for reasons not to run away without risking love again. Aggie warned her that if she didn't risk trusting him soon, she would sabotage her relationship with him.

A chance encounter on a bus with Aggie led her—no, Aggie begged and manipulated her to pass up Portland and go with her to Balefire Bay.

"Let's go, Judy." Judy barked and sprinted ahead of Ivy across the expansive lawn to the main house. Ivy opened the back door and followed Judy into the entryway, which held Judy's mini dog shower, towels, bowls for her food, and various doggy coats hanging on hooks. Just beyond Judy's mud room was the house's magnificent kitchen.

"Wipe her feet," Anderson said, without looking up. He was a muscular ex-Marine in his fifties who still looked good enough to put on the cover of a romance novel. He was more than Xander's assistant, more than the manager of Knightly House and the Sanctuary—or estate. He was like a father to Xander and a wise friend Ivy could talk to as well as have a laugh with.

Beads of sweat gathered on Anderson's forehead as he vigorously polished the large island in the center of the cooking area with butcher's oil.

Ivy knelt, rinsed Judy's feet in the tiny shower and dried her with one of the navy-blue towels stacked on a bench. She held Judy wrapped in the towel and waited for Anderson's usual smile of approval.

The kitchen was Anderson's domain, where he was happiest. Polished copper and stainless-steel pots and pans hung over his head. A talented Dutch artist had carved a three-masted sailing ship on the side of the island. Recently, at Anderson's request, Xander replaced the quartz top with a butcher block counter. He was oiling it energetically, if not frantically.

Ivy had to bite her lip so she wouldn't laugh. "Careful. If you keep polishing like that, you might start a fire." She smiled at him. He didn't look up. His brows were drawn together over a serious frown. He wiped sweat off his forehead using the back of his hand.

"Are you okay?" Ivy asked.

"Okay? Okay? Not on your life. Xander's mother, Rhoda, called last night and said she is coming out with friends. They should be here any minute."

"You're kidding. He didn't tell me his mother was going to visit. When did you find out she was coming?"

"Yesterday, at nine p.m. She texted Xander telling him she was on her way after they arrived in D.C. from London, then she called while they were waiting to board their flight to Portland and told him to come pick her up early this morning."

"She didn't give you much notice. Is that normal?"

"Nothing is ever normal when she's here. Every time she returns to Knightly House, it's unplanned."

"Anderson?" Ivy said.

He paused for a minute and looked at her expectantly.

"I don't think I have ever seen you afraid before or rattled. You didn't so much as break into a sweat when someone broke into the house," Ivy said.

Anderson's chin pulled in, and he glared at her. "I'm not afraid. You think I'm afraid? Afraid?"

"Not even just a little?" Ivy raised one brow and put her hand over her smiling mouth.

"Never." He deflated. "It's a long story."

"I've got time," Ivy said.

He didn't respond. Finally, she said, "I can't wait to meet her."

"You can't wait to meet her? Trust me. Yes. Yes, you can. I've known her for years. Normal is not a word I would use to describe her. Unless making decisions on a whim and going full speed ahead without a thought for the consequences is normal. Every time she visits, she ends up in the middle of some drama she's created. Last time she was here, she sued Gladys Knot for posting a selfie with Xander in the background; and won, even though his back was turned to the camera."

"Ouch. Can she really be that bad," Ivy said. "You're scaring me."

He stopped polishing and tossed his cleaning cloth on the counter by the sink. "Good. You should be terrified. Her name is Rhoda. If you move fast, you can quit your job and make it out of town before she arrives."

Ivy bit her lip, unsuccessfully trying to hold back a snicker.

"Laugh it up, buttercup. You better dust the library, toot sweet."

"I am Xander's assistant. Dusting isn't in my job description. Besides, I'm sure it's fine," Ivy said. It was Anderson's turn to laugh, deep and loud. He was still laughing when Ivy left the kitchen.

Ivy's phone vibrated in her pocket.

Text from Xander: *Sorry! Back soon. Picked up Mom. Stopped for gas and wanted to warn you. Make sure the library is clean and dust free.*

Warn me?

Judy ran down the hall, her nails clicking on the stone floor. She put her feet up on the large wooden library door and looked at Ivy.

Ivy punched her code into the lock and pushed the heavy door open, letting Judy in. The black iron hinges squeaked like the house was haunted. "I know Judy. I should oil the hinges before she arrives, but I love that sound. It fits."

The library looked like it was plucked from a castle, right down to the stone fireplace. Her brows drew together, and she put her hands on her hips. She had

36

never noticed the dust moats floating in the sun that poured through the floor-to-ceiling windows. Beyond the windows, a squadron of pelicans followed each other toward shore.

"I told you it was dusty," Anderson said, making her jump.

"You scared me. You are seriously stealthy," Ivy said.

"I came to help." He handed Ivy a feather duster, polish, and a rag before he plugged in his industrial vacuum.

She went up the carved spiral staircase that led to the mezzanine, walked thirty feet to the south end of the library and climbed the rolling ladder to start on the top shelves.

"I can't believe how much dust is on the empty shelves," Ivy said.

"Don't worry, Xander will fill them soon enough."

"They'll still get dusty." She smiled, remembering Xander's boyish excitement when he acquired a first edition, or any book, really.

The library had floor-to-ceiling dark, oak bookshelves on the walls, on the mezzanine, and on the main floor. The moldings were carved to look like they belonged in a wizarding school. Anderson opened the French doors by the fireplace, blowing ash onto the small oriental rug in front of it.

Looking down at the ash on the rug, Anderson said, "I'll vacuum."

He vacuumed like he scrubbed, aggressively. Smiling, she turned on the music using her cell phone and connected it to the room speakers. She played The Cranberries singing one of her favorite songs, *Linger.*

He looked up at her and shook his head. She sighed, turned her music off, and put on a classical music playlist. He smiled broadly, showing his perfect teeth.

An hour later, she was dusting the last of the shelves inside the north turret. She climbed on a bench to reach the top shelf.

"What are you doing up there?" Anderson called from across the room.

"Dusting?" She shouted over the music.

Before she could step off the bench, he ran over, picked her up, and put her on the floor.

"Girl. You could have fallen out the window." He pointed at the small-paned windows inside the turret.

"I'm fine."

"You are clearly not as anxious and alarmed as you should be. I think we're done here. I'll bring you some decaf chai tea."

She smiled at him and gave him a quick hug. "Thanks, Dad."

"I may be old, but I am not that old." He gathered his cleaning supplies and shut the door behind himself.

She turned off the music and closed her eyes. The room wasn't silent. The sound of the ocean and gulls had become the sound of home. Ivy's heart slowed down and matched the pace of the waves.

Judy was sleeping in a dog basket by the fireplace. Ivy sat down on the brown leather sofa that faced the sea and watched a single cloud on the horizon.

"It looks like a storm is blowing in, Judy," Ivy whispered.

It wasn't long before the hinges squeaked, and Anderson was back with her chai. "What? Are you sitting down?"

"Just watching a storm blow in."

"There is a storm coming all right, and you had better batten down the hatches."

"Hellooo..." a female voice called from the entryway, loud and long.

"It's too late." Anderson looked down the hall and then back at Ivy, his mouth pressed into a straight line. He shrugged.

"I didn't see any flying monkeys," Ivy said softly. His head snapped around and he stood as if at attention. She knew the storm had arrived.

A stately woman with platinum blonde hair, manicured hot pink nails, and wearing a matching pink tracksuit held her arms out wide, came at Anderson and gathered his stiff body in a hug.

"Anderson, darling, I missed you so much," Rhoda said.

Still at attention, Anderson nodded, "Rhoda."

Rhoda pushed Anderson playfully. "Oh, you."

Xander entered the library after her. His shoulder-length brown hair was in a ponytail, and he had bloodshot eyes with dark circles under them. She'd never seen him look this way, even when he was racing a publishing deadline.

Xander joined Ivy at the window. "Mom, let me introduce..."

Rhoda held her hand up, interrupting his introduction. "When Ashley and I got married, I insisted he bring me home so you could meet his family. And I wanted Ashley and his daughter, Charlotte, to see your fabulous house. First, I want to introduce you to my husband, Ashley. Ashley! Ashley!"

A fit-looking man with a closely trimmed silver beard and short, thick silver hair strode into the room. Ivy thought the best way to describe him was a proper Englishman. He focused on Rhoda and failed to look around the magnificent room, which was a different response from the usual first-time visitor. The library seemed to be a universal jaw dropping experience, followed by a string of adjectives and explicatives.

"Ashley, dear, this is Anderson. I've told you all about him," Rhoda said.

Ashley gave Anderson a little nod. "Good to meet you." His very British accent went well with his tweed jacket and wool scarf.

Rhoda strode to the library door. "Charlotte! George! Come meet Anderson! Brett darling, would you bring the bags in?"

Just Anderson? Interesting, Ivy thought.

"I should get breakfast started," Anderson said. He tried to get around Rhoda, but she put a hand on his chest. "We are going to Aggie's to eat some of those heavenly cinnamon rolls."

Xander leaned over and said softly to Ivy, "I know I should have warned you, but I had no idea they were coming. I could have called before I left for the airport, but didn't want to wake you up. I tried from the mountain, but there isn't good cell service between here and the city..." Rhoda interrupted him.

"Kids, Anderson." She leaned on Anderson's muscular arm. "Anderson, this is Charlotte, Ashley's daughter, and George, her companion."

Ivy looked up at Xander, one brow raised, and whispered, "Companion?" *What is this? A Jane Austen story?*

"I am her husband." George corrected Rhoda, who ignored him.

Charlotte stood next to him, arms folded, head down. Her auburn, curly hair hid her face. When she looked up and her and Ivy's eyes connected, Ivy gave her a little wave. She waved back. *It might be nice to have another woman who is close to my age in the house for a while.*

A young black man walked in. Ivy guessed he was high school age and had graduated or was close to graduation. *This must be the Brett that Rhoda asked to bring in the bags.* He was dressed like he'd just stepped out of a very expensive sporting goods store. Every piece of his clothing, including his white running shoes, had a logo on it.

Brett smiled broadly, but his eyes still looked tired. He opened his arms wide and met Anderson for a hug that could only be described as the kind of hug best friends give each other after being apart for a long time.

"Mom," Xander said. She ignored him.

Ivy smiled at Xander and softly said, "It's alright."

"Let's go to Aggies!" Rhoda announced. "Xander, will you drive us?"

"Let me take you," Anderson said.

He was fast to volunteer. A few minutes ago, he was terrified about Rhoda's return.

"Oh! There's my baby. You have a baby sister on the way." Rhoda knelt at Ivy's feet and scooped up Judy, who licked her chin.

Ivy's heart fell all the way to the bottom of her stomach. She knew Judy belonged to Xander's mother, but she'd completely fallen in love with Judy. Ivy realized she wasn't breathing, and tears were pooling in her eyes.

Xander put a hand on her shoulder. "Mom, this is Ivy."

Ivy was silent, trying to remain calm all the while wanting to take Judy away from Rhoda and run for the hills.

"I heard you did a good job of taking care of my tiny Miss Judy." Rhoda pulled a hundred-dollar bill out of her pocket and tried to give it to Ivy, who waved her hands, refusing the money wordlessly.

Ivy wanted to say something polite but couldn't move.

Rhoda shrugged and turned toward the door. "Anderson, Ashley. Kids, let's go," Rhoda ordered the little group like a drill sergeant.

Anderson looked back at Ivy and mouthed the words, I told you so.

And as quickly as they blew in, they were gone.

"I can't tell you how sorry I am," Xander said. "You're coming to breakfast."

"Am I?" she asked and then hiccupped.

"We've stressed you out."

"No. Hiccup." She took a deep breath and held it, mentally counting to ten.

"You always hiccup when you're anxious."

"I do not," she lied.

For a brief second, he smiled. Then, looking concerned, he searched her face. "Please. Don't leave me alone with this mess." Xander rubbed the back of his neck and winced sheepishly. He took her in his arms for a gentle hug before holding her hand and walking with her to the front door.

"What was that? Is that normal, and who's Brett?" Ivy asked.

"That was classic Rhoda. Brett is my younger half-brother."

7

NOTHING TO BE GLAD ABOUT

Xander and Ivy took the beat-up Range Rover to town. Ivy's arms were folded tightly, and her legs were crossed. She looked out the open passenger window, trying to distract herself. Tiny pieces of hair escaped from her hair clip as they bounced down the gravel drive. The gates to the Sanctuary were closing behind them before either of them spoke.

"Look, I know..." Xander started to say, while at the same time Ivy said, "What does..."

"You go first," Xander said.

She studied his handsome face. He looked straight ahead, hands at ten and two.

Ivy turned to face him. "I know it's none of my business, but when your mom calls Charlotte's husband a companion, it's odd. And Brett? This is the first I've heard of him. You don't have to tell me anything, but your half-brother is so young."

He stopped temporarily while a large elk from the local wild herd sauntered across the road as they moved from field to field. They were big and would charge at

44

you or your car if they thought you were dangerous. There was nothing to do but wait.

He glanced at her. "She probably doesn't like George. You might as well know. Mom can be..." He thought for a minute. "Don't get me wrong. She's my mom, you know? But she can be a bit much, large in charge. Well, not that she's large. She's more medium."

Ivy put her hand over her mouth to hide her smile while she listened to Xander try to describe what she had already witnessed. "She obviously loves you and Anderson."

He nodded his head, eyes on the road. "She does. Can you believe it? She married Ashley. Not a word or warning."

Ivy opened her mouth to respond. He went on.

"I give her money, as much money as she wants. She doesn't need anything. Why would she get married without calling me? And why keep it a secret? If I find out he's using her, I'll... I'll... I don't know, but I'll do something."

Ivy was surprised to hear that his mother was a much bigger part of his life than she expected.

She'd been taught by her best friend's Grandmother to see how a man treats his mother to know how he would treat her. She remembered Grandma telling them that if they married the man, they married his family. Up until today, she hadn't understood how much of Xander's time was spent caring for them. *Is he a kind and caring son, or should their mother-son relationship be the subject of research?*

Ivy had a hundred questions about Rhoda, but he was anxiously running his hand through his hair over and over again, making a bigger and bigger mess of it. He was so tightly wound; she was afraid to reach out and touch him. He stared straight ahead, his hands still at ten and two, gripping the steering wheel.

She decided a positive perspective might help. "The way you support her and the time you give her says a lot about how much you care about her," Ivy said.

"Care? I don't care? You can't care about my mother. It's like trying to care about the wind. All you can do is witness the chaos and clean up after it's over. She'll leave soon. She always does." His voice rose slightly, and the elk froze, his head swung around, and he took one step toward the car and examined them.

They sat silently. It was a standoff. Finally, the elk turned and took a step towards the rest of the herd, waiting in the woods.

"It must be difficult," Ivy said softly.

"Difficult?" He hissed. "When I was a kid, after my dad died, I never knew when she was going to take off with someone new and move us again. If Anderson hadn't been in my life, I'd be a very different man."

"Aren't you worried that Ashley is after her money?" Ivy asked.

He talked softly, but his tone still had an edge. "Ashley's the one who should be worried about her spending all his money. He probably doesn't know, or she hasn't told him that her money comes from me. I gave her and Brett money before they left to tour Europe. I paid for

46

the trip. I wanted them to experience its history, not find another husband."

"You couldn't have predicted that would happen. Don't blame yourself," Ivy said.

"Of course I blame myself. I should have gone with them. She probably flaunted her Amex and money in front of Ashley and led him on, or he probably wouldn't have been interested in her."

"What can you do?" Ivy asked.

"Nothing," he said through clenched teeth. "Absolutely nothing. She never said a word about him. In fact, this is the first I've heard anything from her other than 'send money' in over a month and they're married?" He ran a hand through his hair, making a mess of it without making eye contact. Ivy watched his eyes cloud over.

Xander noisily changed gears as they were rolling down the winding road to the highway.

"I don't blame you for being angry. Why don't you let me do what I do best and research him?" Ivy said.

Xander talked through clenched teeth. "Who's angry? I don't care what she does. She never had the time for me, why should I worry about her?"

Ivy couldn't let it go. "I hope you don't mind if I check him out. Even if you don't care, I do. He'll be in the house while I work." Ivy hiccupped. His face told her she'd pushed too hard. Eyes wide, she leaned closer to the door.

He glanced at her, deflated, and squeezed her hand, but his sad eyes let her know that she'd overwhelmed him.

He chewed his lower lip. "I'm sorry. I don't know why I let her get to me like this." Ivy didn't know how to respond.

"I haven't seen Brett in a while. She talks to him like he's one of her dogs or a plaything. I offered to let him stay with me so I could give him some stability, but he didn't want that. I've been a better parent to him than she has. In fact, Anderson has been more of a parent to both of us than my own mother." He turned the blinker on and waited while a line of cars with out-of-state plates and a UPS truck passed.

"Brett seems nice," Ivy said.

"He's spoiled. I ruined him. Whatever Brett wants, he gets. She makes sure of that. I just wanted to give him a better childhood than I had. I mean, don't get me wrong, I love him, and frankly, my need to support Mom and Brett drove me to take a risk and send my first book to a publisher."

"Ashley appears to be smitten. He never took his eyes off of her. Maybe he really loves her," Ivy said.

"Mom? Rhoda?" He squinted, like it was too much for him to comprehend.

Ivy felt like everything she'd said and did was wrong. She needed time to digest the raw feelings he'd just shared. They sat in silence, while he wandered, lost in his past.

8

— · —

STORM IN A TEACUP

Xander parked in an empty space in front of Aggie's shop. Jenny had recently decorated the windows with children's picture books whose covers were illustrations of children going to the seaside, whales, bonfires, and all things beach.

Anderson, Rhoda, and her group were already inside. She could hear Rhoda talking loudly through the screen door. It was time for the morning book club. A young couple was going out of the shop as they went in. The man was frowning and listening to the woman's complaints about how loud and busy things had suddenly become.

Xander stopped and stood, arms folded, by the door. Ivy stood by him. She glanced up at him and buried her hands deep in her hoodie pocket.

The bookshop was on the left of the large open space. The tea shop and eclectic collection of vintage tables and chairs were on the right.

The bookshop felt very Agatha Christie. Aggie sat next to the fire in her favorite chair, knitting.

49

The book club had gathered. Ivy looked from face to face at Balefire Bay's real crime fanatics, who spent most mornings gossiping about local crime. Right after Ivy arrived at Balefire Bay, she'd worked with her new book club friends to identify a killer, prevent two other murders, and solve a mystery.

The police chief occupied a comfortable chair opposite Aggie. His hat was in his lap, and he was wiping his scalp with a cloth handkerchief. He took his aviator glasses off and cleaned them with the same hanky. He was obviously entertained by Rhoda. His handlebar mustache was turned up at the corners by his hidden smile.

Rhoda stood outside the circle chatting rapidly with Ashley.

Conner, Aggie's son, wearing his police uniform sat next to the chief. His black hair was trying to escape the ponytail the chief made him wear while he was on duty. His dark eyes caught hers and he smiled.

Vera, another officer who was also wearing a uniform, sat close to Conner. They often worked the same shift. She was a curly red headed, gum chewing southerner. She and Ivy were new friends. She had a constant smile and a sarcastic sense of humor.

A jolt ran through Ivy and the hair stood on end. The Crow sat silently on Vera's other side. This was the first time Ivy had seen him sitting in the circle with the morning book club. When Ivy watched him talk to Xander at the Saturday Market, she'd guessed he wanted to sell something to Xander. He played nervously with the used paperback he held, fanning the pages of the well-worn book. Little did he know that this circle was more about local gossip and crime in Balefire.

Rhoda reminded Ivy of the Queen of Hearts, holding court. She pointed her manicured finger at the chief. "So, this is the chief of police, a very important man. Conner is Aggie's son." She pointed at Aggie, who smiled and left the circle to work on the tea side of the building.

Xander plopped himself down in Aggie's chair.

"Next we have... Oh, and who might you be?" Rhoda asked.

"Vera. Pleased to meet you."

"Are you a meter-maid?" Rhoda asked.

Conner cleared his throat. "Vera is one of the best officers on the force. I'm the other one." His dimpled face broke into a smile, his dark brown eyes twinkled.

Rhoda pointed at the Crow, who sat next to Vera. "And who are you?" He glanced up at her. His deep wrinkles changed from a valley of seriousness between his eyes to a spiderweb of less exercised smile lines. His grey hair and pallor had Ivy guessing he was at least sixty years old.

The Crow stood and bowed. "I just moved to Balefire and recently opened the antique mall down the road."

Rhoda shrugged. "Oh. Well, isn't that nice for you? Ashley and I are dying to have one of Aggie's rolls. We'll be back after rolls and coffee." She turned, waved a hand like a tour guide, directing the group toward Aggie.

Vera said softly, "We're walking, we're walking." Ivy and Conner snickered. Rhoda glanced back, put her nose in the air and turned her back on them.

Xander stayed by the warm fire. His head was laid back on the soft chair, his mouth hung open, and his eyes were closed. Ivy wasn't surprised that he was napping after a sleepless night and early morning drive to the airport. *He is still handsome.* At that moment, a little line of drool made its way down his chin.

Aggie waited to take Rhoda's order behind her marble counter and the bakery's glass display.

"Five of your famous cinnamon rolls and proper English tea for our group." Rhoda paid, pointed her manicured finger at a nearby table, and said, "Sit." Some of her entourage complied with her order by sitting close to the counter. Brett and Charlotte sat at one table. Anderson sat at the other. Ashley and George were huddled, arms folded, and heads close together. George was doing all the talking. Ashley scowled when George added gestures and an energy that made Ivy wonder what they were talking about.

Jenny's laughter caught Ivy's attention. Jenny was talking to Conner. Jenny looked up, noticed Ivy watching her, smiled and stuck her tongue out before sitting behind the bookstore counter. In the mornings, she manned the register. On most mornings, Ivy found her leaning against the counter, entertained by the book club's chatter.

Brett got up from the table while Rhoda was distracted. He walked to Jenny and said something quietly to her. Ivy strained to hear what was being said, without success. He sauntered back to the counter, defying his mom's order to sit down.

Ivy had just decided to give Aggie a hand when Gladys, the owner of the local garden shop, came in the side door of the tea shop with her husband and daughter, Petunia. Brett perked right up. He used his cell phone camera to check his hair and waved at Petunia, who looked at him and then quickly looked away.

"Morning, Aggie," Gladys said. Without making eye contact with Rhoda, she said, "I can't believe you let that woman eat here. She'll sue you like she did me."

"I won, you... you...influencer," Rhoda said. Both of her arms were locked at her side and her hands were tightly clenched fists.

Gladys turned her nose up, and still completely ignoring Rhoda, responded to her, loudly. "That's right. I am the most popular influencer in Balefire Bay, and don't you forget it!"

You had to give it to Gladys. She has an amazing set of lungs and a voice that could carry for miles. She seemed to only have one volume: loud.

Ivy put on an apron and went behind the counter to help Aggie.

Gladys stepped in front of Rhoda, who scowled and clenched her jaw. For a minute, Ivy wondered if there was about to be a brawl.

Gladys stood at the counter, facing Aggie, feet spread, hands on her hips, looking at today's menu on the wall and blocking anyone else from getting to the counter. "I'll have a black cup of coffee," Gladys said.

"Would you like cream, sugar, whipped cream, or sprinkles?" Aggie asked. Her mouth twitched as she suppressed a smile.

"Now Aggie, you know me. All business. This beautiful body doesn't need any sweetening or red dye forty."

Aggie bit her lip, but one of her brows rose. Her look of incredulity was obvious.

Gladys glanced over her shoulder and barked. "Reginald! Petunia! Get a table." Her husband and daughter looked like a couple of scared birds, ready to fly. They didn't move. Their eyes were glued on Gladys. "Reginald!"

Petunia stepped back behind her father. Her shoulders were slumped, and her chin was down, like she was trying to fold her entire body into as small a space as it could occupy. Her father put his arm around her shoulder and gently walked her to the table next to Rhoda, Ashley, and Anderson. Ivy couldn't hear what Petunia was saying to her father, but her tone was clearly upset and a little angry.

"I'll take one cinnamon roll and two muffins," Gladys announced.

"I just sold my last cinnamon roll. I'm so sorry. Would you like three muffins? Coffee cake?" Aggie offered. A young woman pushing a sleeping baby in a stroller came in and was looking over the menu posted on the wall.

"I suppose you're saving the rolls for your chummy book club," Gladys said. She leaned over the counter, eyes narrowed and tried to stare down Aggie, who didn't flinch.

Gladys pointed at Rhoda's group. "One of them should go without a roll. We eat here all the time. Did that woman order your last rolls?"

Gladys was so loud she woke the baby in the other customer's stroller. Eyes wide, the mother made a hasty exit with her crying baby.

"I also have scones," Aggie said. Cool as a cucumber, she waited.

"Give me a scone. Take it off what you owe me." Gladys yanked her chair out and sat down with her family, complaining loudly.

Ivy looked back at Xander who was awake and focused entirely on his mother, but still resting by the fire. Ivy didn't blame him for staying with the club and avoiding the shouting match. Anderson sat by him reading the local newspaper.

Anderson was right. Rhoda was like a storm at sea that blew you over with waves as big as mountains and left you exhausted and tied to the mainsail. All you can do is hang on for the wild ride.

"How can I help?" Ivy said to Aggie, who gave her a quick squeeze.

"You're an angel. Could you plate the cinnamon rolls as they come out of the warming oven for me?" Aggie said. "After the three in the oven are done, there are another two that will need to be plated and delivered to Rhoda's guests.

Ivy lined up five plates and put a paper doily on each one. Using large tongs, she pulled three oversized rolls out of the oven and drizzled frosting on them before putting them on the plates. She moved the three rolls to the counter and went back to work on Gladys' order. Her stomach growled.

"Are those my mom's?"

Ivy turned to see Brett at the counter. "Yup. You can take them, and I'll get the rest ready," Ivy said. Brett took two of the three rolls. She turned back around, finished the last two rolls and took the scones out of the oven.

She was putting a scone on a plate when she heard George say, "Let me help, mate."

"Dude!" Brett said.

The sound of breaking plates made Ivy whip around. Brett and George were bent over the remains of two of the rolls. Ashley and Rhoda stood over Brett and George, clearly annoyed.

"Thirty second rule," Brett said.

"What? Here, this one stayed on the paper. Do you want me to give this one to Charlotte?" George said. He picked up a roll from the floor next to Brett and took it to his table. Ivy wanted to stop him, but didn't want to get in the middle of the chaos.

"I'm not hungry." Charlotte grabbed a napkin from the holder on their table and joined Brett, on the ground, trying to wipe up the mess. Ivy went to the backroom and came back with a broom and sanitary wipes.

"That's so nice of you, but I have it, Charlotte. You enjoy your breakfast," Ivy said.

Charlotte made eye contact with Ivy and breathed a sigh of relief. "Thank you. I'm sorry for the mess."

Ivy smiled at her. "No worries. I look forward to getting to know you."

"Coffee, black," Gladys said loudly.

Glass shards were under the table and the counter. Ivy bent over, trying to get to the pieces under the counter with the broom.

"Where are the rest of the rolls?" Rhoda said.

Ivy glanced up and saw her at the empty counter.

"Two of them are right there." Aggie pointed at Ivy, who was sweeping up bits of a roll mixed with glass shards. "You have two at the table."

"Yes, but we're missing one roll," Rhoda said.

Ivy squatted down and used bleach wipes to scrub the sticky sugar mess.

"Are you sure?" Aggie said.

Ivy glanced up at Aggie, while cleaning, and said, "They dropped two, George picked up one, and I thought the other three were still on the counter."

"Gladys!" Reginald roared. There was a loud crash and thud.

By the time Ivy jumped up, Gladys was on the floor. It looked like her chair had fallen back. Her arms were spread wide, and her eyes were open. She made a gurgling sound. A broken plate was on the ground next to her and a half eaten cinnamon roll must have rolled out of her open hand and ended its journey amongst the broken China. The scones sat untouched on the table.

"Gladys!" Reginald dropped to his knees.

"Call 911!" Ivy shouted at Aggie, who stood with her eyes and mouth wide open. Ivy dropped down to see if Gladys had a pulse. She felt something. It was a thready, barely perceptible, rapid pulse and then it was gone. Her lips were blue and there was foam on one side of her mouth. Her pupils were pinpoint, and her skin was clammy. Ivy tried to take a pulse using Gladys' wrist. Nothing. Oddly, she noticed her fingernails were blue.

Ivy glanced up to see Charlotte, looking green and holding her hand over her mouth, running for the back door, while everyone in the store stood in a circle looking at Gladys.

Conner dropped on the floor next to Ivy. "Mom! Do you have a defibrillator?" He got up on his knees, the palms of his hands stacked over her sternum. "One, two." He counted while Reginald watched wide-eyed and wringing his hat in his hands.

"We need an ambulance at Aggie's tea shop!" The chief barked into his radio. "Vera, I'm going out to meet the ambulance. Holler if you need me."

"Will do. Excuse me, sweetie." Vera touched Ivy's shoulder and knelt on the floor next to Conner, holding a plastic mouth guard for life saving breaths.

"Be careful, Vera, I think she's been poisoned," Ivy said. Vera and Conner didn't acknowledge her. She looked up at Reginald and decided not to repeat herself.

"Twenty-nine, thirty," Conner said. He pulled his hands back and Vera applied two ventilation breaths, causing Gladys' chest to rise and fall.

"It almost looks like a..." Vera leaned closer to Conner and said something quietly into his bouncing ear.

"It... couldn't... hurt," Conner said, emphasizing every word with an attempt to start Gladys' heart before going back to counting.

Vera jumped up and yelled. "Aggie! Do you have a first aid kit? Narcan?"

Reginald sat down hard in a chair and groaned.

Aggie took a step back, put a hand on Reginald's, and stared wide-eyed, frozen with the shock of what was unfolding before her.

"Jenny!" Vera barked. "We need Narcan. Get my first aid kit, in my squad car." She threw Jenny her keys. "Reginald! What meds does she take?"

Reginald didn't move. He looked frozen with fear.

"I have it!" Jenny pushed her way through the gathering crowd. "Excuse me. Excuse me!"

Ivy stood and tried to step back, to give Vera room. She noticed the broken plate and baked goods were being walked on and spread around Gladys. If Gladys was poisoned the crime scene was definitely contaminated.

Ivy shivered, frozen. She knew she needed to help but had no idea how. The blueish look of Gladys' skin and the little line of foam and frosting dripping from Gladys' mouth didn't bode well.

Vera found the Narcan in her first aid bag and fearlessly administered the shot.

9

NOBODY MOVE

The medics worked rapidly. Ivy couldn't look away. She heard the blood rushing in her ears as she listened to Vera and the ambulance crew shout instructions while they strapped Gladys to a gurney.

A medic straddled Gladys on the gurney and continued compressions. They raised the gurney and moved as a team toward the doors.

The team rolled her into the back of the ambulance. The ambulance driver held the door open and called out to Conner over the chaos. "Conner. If her husband wants to go, you'll have to help him get into the ambulance." The medic working on Gladys didn't miss a beat. He continued counting compressions while another worked on breaths with a bag-mask device.

Conner helped Reginald climb into the ambulance to ride with Gladys. The medic didn't stop trying to resuscitate Gladys. It was obvious that even if Ivy thought she was gone, they were going to give it their all. One shouted into a radio, prepping the hospital, while another hung I.V. fluid on a pole. Breathing hard, Conner, hands on his hips, still red in the face from exertion, stood next to Vera, watching the drama play out inside the ambulance.

"I've got a pulse," the EMT providing CPR shouted. The driver slammed the doors shut, ran to the front, turned on the lights and sirens and raced down the center of the highway.

"I hope she makes it," Ivy said. She looked up at Xander's ashen face. Members of the book club stood outside and silently watched the ambulance speed south. Ivy realized that other people had emerged from shops and gathered in groups, watching and whispering.

"Xander? How far is it to the nearest hospital?" Ivy asked.

When the ambulance rounded the bend and was out of sight, it broke his trance. "I don't know," he said.

People loitering on the sidewalk shook their heads and talked quietly as they made their way back to the little pharmacy, the flower shop, and other small shops on the street. The Crow stayed across the street, watching from the door to his store.

The chief put a gentle hand on Ivy's shoulder. She looked up at him. He took off his aviators, exposing his watery blue eyes. "They'll get there as fast as possible. Don't lose hope."

"I don't think she'll make it. She wasn't sick, Chief. I think she was poisoned. Her lips and nails were blue, she had foam coming from her mouth, and she had pinpoint-sized pupils," Ivy said.

He smiled sadly. "Not everything is murder. Gladys wasn't in the best of shape. Who knows, maybe she's a diabetic and that was her last cinnamon roll, or she had a massive stroke?"

Ivy's brows shot up, and she tipped her head, lips compressed, hands on her hips. She looked incredulously at the chief.

He deflated and shook his head from side to side. "But if it makes you feel any better, I plan on questioning everyone who was in the bakery."

"Petunia ran out the back door when her mother went down," Ivy said, frustrated that the chief had already written off Gladys.

"She is a quiet little thing. You know, shy. She must have been terrified. Conner! Vera!" the chief called while walking back into the shop.

Xander leaned over and said quietly, "We should go. I should take Brett out of..."

Before he could finish, Rhoda pushed through the screen door. "Xander! Let's go. Brett! Anderson, Ashley." Everyone except Xander followed her onto the sidewalk.

"Rhoda!" Vera burst through the door onto the sidewalk, waving her pocket notebook at Xander's mother. "Don't you run off. The chief wants your contact information. We're going to need a statement from everyone that was in the building."

Rhoda pointed at Ivy and kept walking. "She knows where to find us."

Vera passed Ivy. "Don't make me take you to jail." Vera trotted in front of Rhoda and used her whistle to stop the parade.

"Do you know who I am?" Rhoda asked.

"Yes, but do you know who I am?" She pointed at her badge. "I am giving you the opportunity to do the right thing rather than arresting you for being rude and arrogant, as usual!" Vera barked.

Rhoda spun around. "Xander!"

"Mother, you have to stay and work with Vera." Xander put an arm around Rhoda, who was still complaining loudly while her cohort stood by, waiting for a decision to be made.

Ivy saw a chance to go inside unobserved and get her hands on evidence that would prove that Gladys was poisoned, as she suspected. She wanted a piece of roll she'd seen on the floor before it was trampled to pieces. Rhoda and Vera continued keeping everyone entertained while she quietly opened the double screen doors, wincing when the rusty hinges creaked. She froze. No one reacted, so she slipped inside.

Aggie and Desdemona stood by the fireplace, leaning toward each other, entirely engrossed in their conversation. Jenny was at the cash register. Her arms were folded, and her face was cloudy as she talked to the chief while Conner took notes.

The tea side of the shop was eerily empty. Unnoticed, Ivy stayed close to the bookstore shelves and out of view while she snuck quietly into Aggie's back room to retrieve a small baggie from a box on the shelf.

"What are you doing, little lady?" Vera said. She blocked the door to the pantry.

Ivy jumped. "Vera!" she lowered her voice. "This isn't an accident. She ate the wrong roll!"

Vera's eyes narrowed. "The wrong roll?"

"I think it was meant for Rhoda." Ivy said, louder than she wanted to, frustration oozing out with every word.

The conversation in the bookshop with Rhoda got louder.

"I wouldn't be surprised if someone wanted to kill Rhoda. I know I do, right now," Vera said.

The chief barked, "Will you please be quiet! Sit down!"

"I will not sit down. I know my rights," Rhoda shouted, emphasizing every word, using her pointer finger to poke him in the chest.

Vera walked away.

"Vera! Listen. You have to believe me."

Vera looked over her shoulder. "I hear you," Vera said and went to help the chief.

Quickly, Ivy scanned the floor. She spotted a small piece of cinnamon roll the broom had missed under the counter. Hoping it was part of the roll that she believed killed Gladys, she used the baggie, putting it on her hand like she did with the bags she collected Judy's morning offerings in. When she knelt to pick it up, someone bumped into her causing her to drop the baggie. Before she could look up to see who ran into her and retrieve the baggie, Vera barked orders.

"Ivy! People, stay out of the bakery!" Vera's sharp voice made Ivy jump. She picked up the baggie, unnoticed.

"Excuse me," Petunia said. She bumped Ivy lightly while she passed, knocking the baggie from Ivy's hands and kicking it across the floor.

Ivy watched Gladys' daughter, Petunia, cool as a cucumber, get her coat from the back of her chair and put it on.

"Ivy!" Vera said. She shook her head at Ivy and pointed, directing her to join the group at the fireplace. "Wait over there." Rhoda and her entourage all stared at Vera.

"Can I grab something to eat? I'm starving." Ivy put her hand over her stomach.

Vera stood frozen, pointing at the chair she wanted Ivy to occupy. Before joining the group, Ivy glanced over her shoulder. Petunia and her coat were gone. Ivy quickly scanned the floor for the baggie but couldn't see it. She joined everyone sitting by the fireplace.

Vera growled and wagged her pointer finger back and forth in Ivy's direction before going back to arguing with Rhoda. "Enough of this chaos, little miss! Quiet down or I will drag you by your dyed hair to the station!"

"Well, I never..."

"I don't care!" Vera's voice was so loud the entire room was mesmerized.

Ivy's stomach growled loudly. *See, I am hungry,* reasoned her inner good girl.

Rhoda threw herself down onto one of the furthest chairs from the fireplace, arms folded, scowling.

Jenny watched the entertainment from the bookstore checkout counter, with an odd smile on her face. Rhoda was as entertaining as an afternoon soap opera.

Jenny had a bowl of chocolate kisses for their customers next to the register. Ivy had an idea. She could move closer to the chief and listen to the interviews if she was offering everyone some chocolate. She retrieved the bowl and handed Desdemona the first piece of candy.

"Why, thank you, darlin'," Desdemona said. She took a handful of kisses out of the bowl.

Wishing she had tea or water, Ivy was finishing a piece of candy when Rhoda's voice escalated, and Rhoda pushed her way past Vera and out the door. She was followed by Xander and the rest of her entourage.

Stunned, eyes and mouth opened wide, Ivy walked to Vera. "What was that?"

"A whole lot of arrogance stuffed into spandex, fluffed, and full of herself." Vera passed Ivy before she looked back over her shoulder, reached back for a chocolate, and said, "Come on, Miss Marple. Someone has got to encourage the chief to call an attempted murder, an attempted murder."

"Vera, shouldn't we save a piece of the roll Gladys was eating as evidence?" Ivy said.

"We'll find a piece when we process the scene. Now, do a girl a favor and follow the chief's directions," Vera said.

Ivy put the bowl of candy back on the counter and pulled her little wallet out of her back pocket to pay

Jenny for the chocolate. A piece of torn white paper fluttered to the floor. It must have been in her pocket with her wallet. She picked it up and turned it over. It said, "*Stop or die.*"

10

LEAVE THE LIBRARIAN BEHIND

The chief and local officers were the only people in the bakery. Ivy was the last to leave.

"Xander, wait!" Ivy called. Xander was in the Range Rover with his mother, who was still complaining rather vociferously. Before she could get his attention, he drove away, following Anderson and the others. Ivy guessed that in all the chaos, he forgot that he had brought her to town.

"Cheese and rice!" Ivy folded her arms and stomped her foot. Then she looked around to see if anyone had witnessed her tantrum. Deflated, she glanced back toward the store. Everyone she knew was gone. Only a few onlookers were still gossiping on the corner.

The Crow was down the street, standing by the About Time Antique Mall entrance, looking at her. He gave her a small wave, locked the door to his business, and crossed the road walking toward her. Warily, she took a step back, brows knit.

"Ivy! It is Ivy, isn't it?" the Crow said.

She nodded.

"I have been wanting to take something to Mr. Knightly. Would you like a ride home? It would allow me to give it to you. You can deliver it to Xander, can't you?"

"For Xander? What is it? Is he expecting it? I can walk," Ivy said, before she realized how rude she sounded. All her defenses were up after what happened to Gladys.

At that moment, a drop of rain hit the pavement.

He smiled, nodded, and turned around.

"Wait. I'll take the ride, and I'm happy to deliver your package," Ivy said.

"I'm parked in the public parking lot. If you want to wait there, I'll get what I need and swing back around to pick you up." The Crow smiled, but his piercing eyes didn't match the grin on his face.

Ivy thought that for the short time she had known him, he'd had a perpetually sad expression. One side of his face was radically different from the other. One brow always looked surprised. The same side of his face had frown lines around his mouth, while the other side of his mouth turned up. He went through the back door to his business and came back out with a package wrapped in white butcher paper.

His black station wagon reminded Ivy of a hearse. He held the passenger side door open while she got in. She rolled her window down enough that she could make a quick escape if she needed to. Ivy imagined herself jumping out of the window and rolling, like a stunt woman in a major motion picture. Instead, she hugged the passenger door.

He started the car and pulled onto the highway. "Before the moderator shut down the comments that had Gladys' name in them, a comment on the social media scanner page said that Gladys might make it."

"You've already joined the Coho County scanner pages?" Ivy asked.

He nodded and smiled down at her. "I am also on the Village Rants and Raves, and the Straight out of Balefire group." He chuckled softly. "Balefire has a wonderful game of grapevine going all day long." He belly laughed at his own joke.

When he stopped at the Sanctuary gate, Ivy got out.

"Can you give this to Xander? He was looking at it during the Saturday Market. He knows what to do." The Crow handed her the package, waved, and waited while Ivy used her code to open the gate. When she was behind the closing gate, he turned the car around and left.

She exhaled loudly.

11

— • —

NEVER AGAIN, AGAIN

Ivy's cell phone alarm went off at 4 am. She pulled her duvet over her head and covered her ears. The phone vibrated and played, the Beatles singing *Good Day Sunshine* until she sat up and hit the stop button. She moaned and rubbed her eyes.

Rhoda and her entourage had only been at the Knightly House for a little over a week, and already Ivy was over it. Rhoda kept her hopping. Ivy's new nickname was Coffee Girl.

"I wonder how many cups of coffee she'll drink today," Ivy said to the empty room. She missed Judy. She was only able to snuggle with Judy when the little spaniel managed to escape the house.

Tiny paws scratched outside Ivy's bedroom's French doors. A slow smile spread across Ivy's face. She pushed back the covers, slipped on her flip-flops, and opened the doors to the deck. Judy slid in with a misty breeze. Ivy quickly closed the door, shutting out the cold, and scooped up Judy, giving her a kiss and hug.

"Judy. You naughty and wonderful dog. We don't have time to lie in bed or do yoga on the deck. Today, we're going fishing on Conner's new boat."

There was no point in showering or doing her hair. She had been on boats enough to know that she needed to wear layers and tie up her hair. She put on jeans, a t-shirt, a fisherman's sweater, a down coat, a down vest, and braided her hair before she put on a knit cap.

She layered up the socks on her feet and slipped on rubber boots Xander had purchased for her last month on a shopping trip to Portland. She made him stop at a thrift store that allowed you to buy by the pound from bins. At the bottom of the last bin, she'd found her new favorite red hunter boots.

She put her cell phone in a plastic sandwich bag and into her zippered coat pocket. "Someday, I should patent my genius waterproof cell phone bag. Come on, Judy."

After turning the lights off, she carried Judy up the slight incline toward the Knightly House. The sun had yet to rise, but the stars and moon lit her way. The rhythm of the surf against the rocky cliff and her boots sloshing through the wet grass were the only sounds.

Lights were on in the kitchen and some of the bedrooms in the house. The door opened and Anderson came out with an ice chest and a full grocery sack.

"Good morning," Ivy said softly.

"Is it?" He frowned as he put the cooler and bag in the back of Xander's SUV. "Her royal highness is upset with her breakfast. She wants a latte, croissants, and an omelet in the next ten minutes. At this rate, we'll miss the boat."

Ivy shook her head, put her hand over her mouth, and tried not to laugh. Clearly, Anderson was very serious. "Are you going to take all that?"

"I tossed cold bottled coffees in the cooler and granola bars in the bag, along with pretzels. There are some water bottles for anyone who decides to be healthy. Just for you, I snuck in apples."

"Cosmic Crisps?"

"Of course. Nothing but the best for you, Coffee Girl."

She laughed softly. "You're the best."

"Yes, I am. It's a miracle I haven't murdered her yet." He hustled back into the house.

"There you are! Mommy has been looking for you," Rhoda said, loudly. Ending the quiet morning and making a bird fly from a nearby tree. Rhoda took Judy from Ivy's arms and snuggled her along with her new Cavalier King Charles Spaniel, Sandy. "Really, Coffee Girl? I've had quite enough of your fixation with Judy. You may be a good dog sitter, but you do not own her. She's going back to the manor in Britain with me."

Ivy's stomach lurched as it did every time Rhoda repeated her threat.

Xander turned on the porch lights and joined the group by the SUV and old Range Rover. "Let's load up. We're already late."

"Really. The fish aren't even awake. Ashley, open the door for me," Rhoda said.

"Of course, my love," Ashley replied.

Xander's brother, Brett, shook his head and made eye contact with Ivy, who shrugged.

The BMW's dome lights came on as Rhoda climbed into the front seat. Ivy hiccupped.

"Now what?" Rhoda said.

"Sorry," Ivy said.

"I should think so."

Ivy had been shocked by the dark circles under Xander's bloodshot eyes. His usually groomed hair was in a knot of tangles at the back of his head, and he had a five o'clock shadow that was rapidly becoming a beard. She'd never seen him look so tired. He turned in his seat and nodded at her.

Sad was the only word she could use to describe his eyes.

"Where's Charlotte? Have you seen her, Ashley?" Rhoda asked.

"I'll get her, my dear." He trotted back into the house. A minute later, Charlotte joined them. She looked like she'd walked out of a fishing fashion magazine. She and Rhoda had gone on a shopping trip to prepare for the adventure. She even had on a fishing vest over her fisherman's sweater.

"You're going to be cold," Ivy said to Charlotte.

Charlotte looked at Ivy and smiled. "Don't be silly. She batted her eyelashes, turned on her heels, and joined Brett and Anderson in the Range Rover.

The streetlights in Balefire shone on closed businesses and empty sidewalks. They passed the closed book and tea shop, drove south, and around the tiny bay to a parking lot near the boat launch and dry dock.

Fishermen quietly loaded gear, readied their boats, and helped customers board and prep for a day of deep-sea fishing.

A gleaming white vessel stood out from the crowd. There was no doubt it was newer than its ragtag neighbors. The name *Fool me Twice* decorated the stern of the boat.

"Cap!" Conner's new crewman called. "They're here." His back was to Ivy as he cut bait on a board attached to the stern. He looked taller than Xander, well over six feet. His shoulders were broad underneath his plaid flannel shirt and overalls. Steam raised from his hard-working body.

Conner came out of the boat's cabin and, with one hand on the starboard rail, leapt easily onto the dock. "Join me at the bow." They followed him to the front of the boat.

"While we're waiting for a few more passengers," Conner said. He motioned to Ivy to come closer. He leaned in and whispered. "I wanted to tell you something I probably shouldn't."

She stepped closer to him.

"Gladys was declared dead last night." He looked over her shoulder and waved at someone else buried in a large coat and hat walking down the short pier to join them. Ivy realized it was Aggie.

Ivy was surprised by the sad knot in her stomach when Conner gave her the news.

"Sorry. But I thought you should know," Conner said.

"Morning." Aggie hugged Conner.

"Is Jenny coming?" Ivy whispered to Aggie.

"She has to take her girls to school, then she'll run the shop," Aggie said. "How do you christen a boat?"

Ivy shrugged and shook her head. "No clue."

Conner reached into a wooden crate on the dock and held up a bottle of champagne and small, clear plastic cups. "Is everyone here?" He studied the quiet group. "Gather around." He gave each person a cup and a little bubbly.

Ivy held her cup, knowing she wouldn't drink it. After her failed marriage, she never wanted to drink again.

"As we all know, we're lucky to be alive and blessed to live in Balefire with friends who are truly like family. Thank you for joining me. I am about to christen my new boat, before taking her out on her maiden voyage." He took a three-by-five card out of his pocket and looked at it. Although he held it, he never looked at it again.

Conner raised his glass. "Today we've come together to name this lady, *Fool Me Twice*, and send her to sea to be cared for, and for her to care for our Balefire Bay family. We ask the sailors of old and the mood of God that is the sea to accept *Fool Me Twice* as her name, to help her through her passages, and return us to shore safely. A toast to the sea, and the sailors that came before us, and to *Fool Me Twice*."

Conner emptied his cup. The group's cheer shattered the quiet morning. He took a full bottle out of the box and broke it on a cleat on the side of the boat. Then he placed a spray of greenery on the bow of the large boat.

12

—·—

GOOD CATCH

Most of their group huddled inside the main cabin of the forty-foot boat. Conner was up top in the wheelhouse, navigating between buoys and taking them out to sea. Ivy stood alone astern, watching the North Head shrink in the distance as the sun rose slowly over the mountains in the east.

The sky was a striking salmon and azure blue before a ray of light shot over the mountain and lit up dolphins swimming in the chum caused by the deckhand cutting and prepping bait. Ivy couldn't remember ever seeing anything more beautiful.

She held tightly to the rail as they sped further out to sea.

"How far out will we go?" Ivy shouted over the motor to the crew member.

He didn't turn around or answer her questions. He remained hunched over, working rapidly while fish blood from cutting the bait spilled onto the deck and out to the ocean. His brown, unkept, wavy hair hung past his shoulders. He had on a bright orange knit hat. He turned his back to her and pulled his hoodie up over his hair and his hat. She wasn't able to see his face but occasionally caught a glimpse of his chin and a short beard. There was something about him. She couldn't quite put her finger on it.

"How far out will we go?" Ivy shouted louder. He shrugged, still ignoring her. She folded her arms and rolled her eyes. After a few minutes, her arms dropped to her side, and she consciously willed herself not to be irritated and ruin the beautiful morning.

As the sun continued to rise, a dozen bottlenose dolphins suddenly broke the wake, jumping for the chum. Their sleek bodies jumping over and over again against the ocean backdrop took Ivy's breath away.

"Look! Porpoise!" George called, breaking the spell.

Once the sun was fully up, Rhoda, Ashley, Brett, George, and Charlotte watched the choppy sea with her on the main deck. The deckhand prepped fishing poles, placing each one in a rod holder mounted on the gunnel or handrail. Xander, Aggie, and Anderson could be seen through the cabin window pouring coffee, chatting, and eating cinnamon rolls from Aggie's shop.

"I think I'm going to be sick." Charlotte bumped into Ivy as she pushed her way past her to the stern railing and threw up over the side. "Daddy, I need my sea sickness pills."

Ivy watched Ashley enter the cabin, go into Charlotte's purse. Ivy went back to searching the water for the dolphins, but they were gone.

Charlotte shrieked. Ivy spun around. Every hair on Ivy's neck and head stood on end. Charlotte was wailing and pointing out to sea where Rhoda was flailing in the waves, getting a mouth full of sea water every time she yelled for help.

Conner's deckhand pushed past her with a life ring in his hands. He dropped the ring, ripped off his coat, tossed his rubber boots aside, took off his Grunden overalls, picked the ring back up, and dove beautifully into the ocean.

Ivy ran to the rail watching helplessly as Rhoda and the crewman struggled to survive.

Charlotte was clutching her father and crying hysterically. Brett took his boots off and was taking off his coat.

"Brett, no!" Ivy said. "He obviously knows what he's doing."

Brett's eye darted back and forth from the water to Ivy.

"Brett, get down." Xander pulled him off the rail on his way to Ivy.

He put his arm around her, and they stood side by side, clutching the stern rail, watching the deckhand brave the swells and the icy Pacific to reach Rhoda, while they both drifted further and further from the boat.

"Man overboard! Man overboard!" Anderson bellowed. His call reached Conner on the bridge. The boat turned sharply, heading back toward Rhoda and the deckhand. Anderson was already headed up to the helm and Conner. Unable to look away, Ivy felt helpless.

Xander's face was twisted in anguish, watching his mother try to reach the ring. He pulled Ivy to him, she put her arms around his waist and hugged him, watching, wishing she could do something, anything more.

"Mom! Swim!" Xander yelled before he squeezed Ivy's shoulders hard enough to hurt.

Anderson bellowed from the wheelhouse. "No one else goes in the water!" Ivy followed Anderson's line of sight. Once again, Brett had one hand on the rail and a leg over the side. Anderson slid down the ladder, hands and feet hugging the outside, took Brett by his collar and yanked him back onto the deck, hard.

The sound of the motor changed. They were idling. Conner joined them on the main deck and unlatched a swim deck or platform aft.

A cry in the distance brought her back to the unfolding scene at sea. The deckhand was screaming something. He had the rope from the life ring tied over his shoulder and under one arm. He stroked and fought the current, heading their direction, dragging Rhoda behind him, holding onto the ring.

"He needs another ring!" Anderson yelled loud enough to be heard by Conner.

"They're inside the bench!" Conner shouted back. Aggie opened a bench next to the cabin door for Anderson to retrieve out a ring and rope.

After Conner tied the ring to the rail, Anderson threw it like a frisbee to the deckhand, who reached it after only a few strokes.

Conner climbed onto the swim deck and waited for the deckhand to reach the platform. The crewman was a strong swimmer. Holding onto the rope tied to Rhoda's life ring, the deckhand pulled Rhoda up to the deck, where he handed Conner the rope to tie it off using a cleat.

Conner strained; his face turned red with effort as he tried to pull Rhoda onto the deck. The crewman took a handful of Rhoda's pants and shoved her on her belly onto the platform, while her weight pushed him under. Her legs dragged behind the ship.

Rhoda was shivering uncontrollably as Conner pulled her to her feet and gracelessly pushed her over the gunnel into Anderson's waiting arms. Her hair hung in her face in wet, stringy clumps.

"This is your fault! You hired this man, and he pushed me overboard," Rhoda shouted.

Ivy couldn't believe what she was hearing. "Why would he push you overboard and then save you?"

"My deckhand did not push you overboard," Conner said firmly but calmly.

"What do you really know about him? And if it wasn't him, who was it?" Rhoda whipped around pointing at them all, stopping at George. Charlotte stepped back, looking at George, then Rhoda, and back again.

George pulled Charlotte away from the group. Anderson reached out and gathered Rhoda into his arms. Xander went to her and put a reassuring hand on her shoulder.

Ashley stood still, his brows knit, frowning, and letting Anderson comfort her. *Is he frozen with fear? What is wrong with him? Did he push her overboard?*

"Ashley," Anderson said, firmly.

Ashley jolted and seemed to wake up. He gently pulled Rhoda away from Anderson. She fell into his and Xander's arms.

"Take me to the cabin!" Rhoda barked. Ashley sighed, put his arm around her and led her toward the cabin, where Aggie met them with a blanket for Rhoda.

Ivy was only distracted by Rhoda's drama for a moment. She went to the back of the boat to make sure the deckhand was on board.

She watched him surface, his long dark hair tangled in his face. He easily lifted himself onto the deck, over the rail, and landed softly on bare feet. His skin was bright red. He was in his underwear and shaking violently. She couldn't imagine how cold he was. He pushed his tangled hair out of his face, and Ivy gasped.

Suddenly, her worlds collided. Her childhood, her teen years, Harvard, Ian's violence, and her first love.

"Nephi," Ivy said softly. He squinted and looked at her, tipping his head. Then his eyes widened, his mouth fell open, and a look of stunned recognition crossed his face for just a moment. Instantly, his mouth shut and his eyes narrowed. Nephi stepped back as she reached out. He pushed past her and ran for the boat's cabin.

She followed him into the cabin but wasn't fast enough to catch him before he went past the galley and into the captain's bedroom and slammed the door. Just as she got to the door, she heard the lock click into place.

Shocked, she sat down hard on the stairs that led to the rooms below. *What just happened? Have I lost my mind? It can't be. He looks so different. I must be seeing things.* She wrestled with reality until she jumped to her feet and banged her fist on the door.

"Hello?"

Nothing.

Bang, bang, bang... Nothing. "Hello? Is that you?"

The door swung open, and his angry face met hers. "Leave me alone, Sophie." He almost ripped the door off the hinges when he shut and locked it.

"Ivy! My name is Ivy!" she yelled at the door as she closed her eyes, unable to hold back tears, memories, a collision of emotions powerful enough to make her drop to her knees, cover her face, and hiccup.

Wanting Xander to hold her, she looked up. He and Ashley were completely engrossed in his mother's tirade.

13

— · —

FISH OUT OF WATER!

Ivy stood on deck, once again seeking peace and watching the wake behind the boat. Conner was taking them back to shore. The boat was planed out and cutting through the waves like butter. She zipped her coat up, not because she was cold, but because she desperately wanted to be held and talk to Xander. He was still completely focused on his mother and hadn't noticed how distressed she was.

If she ever doubted she had PTSD, all doubts were gone. Her thoughts tumbled erratically through her mind. She knew adrenaline was coursing through her body. She was disconnected, running in and out of the past, the present, and trying without success to make sense of what had just happened.

Flashes of Nephi and her childhood best friend tumbled through Ivy's mind. The three of them were practically inseparable. Practically, because Ivy had a massive crush on him while he had a massive crush on the prettiest girl in school. Her friendship with Esther and Nephi was the birthplace of her love for solving mysteries, starting when their friend went missing.

Aggie joined Ivy at the rail, touched her hand, and startled her. "How are you doing?"

"Don't be nice to me. Why would you ask me that?" Ivy wiped her eyes with her sleeve. "Here I am trying to be strong and you're being nice." She giggled nervously.

Aggie gave her a motherly hug. "You don't always have to be strong and do everything alone."

"Don't I?" Ivy said.

"I heard your reunion," Aggie said.

"I'm sorry. I kind of lost control."

Aggie smiled at her, "Kind of? Who is he and why did he call you Sophie?"

"I grew up in Necanicum. Do you know the town?" Ivy said.

"I know it isn't very big, but it is in one of the prettiest spots on the Oregon Coast."

"Conner's deckhand was my best friend's young uncle. He and my best friend lived a few houses down in an old Victorian. I was the only child of two scientists and lived in a very modern house on the beach with my dog, Spam and my fish, the Angel of Death. Esther lived with her mother, her grandmother Mable, Mary, her annoying little sister, Nephi, and her cat, Molly. It was constant chaos, and I loved it. It was so different from my family's quiet house."

"Was Sophie your name before your divorce and coming to Balefire Bay?"

Ivy nodded. "I chose the name Ivy because it grew outside Esther's second story bedroom window. I can't tell you how many times I risked my life climbing in that window when I should have been home in bed."

"Ivy is strong. But it also clings to where it grows. I'm surprised I haven't seen him or any of your friends if they only live a few hours away," Aggie said.

Ivy took in a deep breath and let it out slowly, struggling to gain control of her emotions. "I had a massive crush on Nephi. He had a massive crush on a pretty girl. My best friend ended up dating the pretty girl's twin brother. I was the only one with no one and on top of that, in love with someone who saw me as a little sister."

"Ouch. That sounds painful."

"Sometimes. But sometimes it was magical. I gained my thirst for solving mysteries when the pretty girl disappeared. The three of us found her and saved her from being killed by her stalker."

"So that's how it all began," Aggie said. She smiled down at Ivy.

"That and my parents, who were both brilliant scientists, and always drilled into me the importance of research, asking questions, and solving the mysteries of the universe."

"That makes a lot of sense," Aggie said. "Scientists organize and make sense of our world as well as try to make it a better place to live. Now I know why you are driven to solve any mystery that comes your way."

"Why? What do you mean?" Ivy asked.

"When the world is dangerous and life is messy, solving the mystery of it all organizes it and means there is an order to the universe," Aggie said.

"Absolutely. If we don't know how everything works or organize our lives, everything feels like chaos to me," Ivy said.

"What if your life refuses to be organized? What can we really control?" Aggie asked.

Ivy thought for a moment. "The whole world is in chaos. I guess solving mysteries or making sure people get justice, even people I don't particularly like, like Gladys, makes the world feel safer. You know? When everything is in its place and I understand it, I am no longer afraid of it."

"I know what you're telling me, but love won't be organized. It is chaotic. Glorious chaos."

Ivy nodded, "You're right."

"It sounds like Nephi's family was really important to you. Why did you lose touch?" Aggie asked.

Ivy grimaced and cleared her throat before looking away from Aggie. "I am sure I've told you. Besides hiding from my ex..."

"...Who the town believes is now dead."

Ivy nodded and sighed. "I didn't want anyone to know what a mess my life had become. I blamed myself for getting married so fast during the quarantine . But the truth is, it was hard to watch Nephi and Esther get married and have their 'happily ever afters.' I was left behind, and isolated at Harvard—a small-town fish in a big pond—and they were living the dream. Besides, I had feelings for Nephi while he only had eyes for his wife; as any good husband should. When Nephi and Esther's families went to England to live, I thought the distance would help, but it didn't."

"What did you do?"

"It was about then the quarantine started. I was so lonely; I married the first handsome man to ask me out. Sadly, he was a homicidal trained killer," Ivy said.

"Almost every person I know has a husband or boyfriend they regret."

"It isn't regret that keeps me from going home, it's shame. I didn't want any of them to know what a mess my life was when they had everything. I'm smart. I should never have fallen for what my ex was peddling. What's worse is, because of my need to fix everything, I hung on far too long," Ivy said. "I'm still mad at myself even though reason tells me it wasn't my fault."

"Listen to reason," Aggie said. "I don't know where Nephi was before, but when I met him, he said he was divorced."

Ivy's head snapped up. "Divorced?"

Aggie nodded. "I asked if he was going to visit family. He said he didn't have any."

"No... That can't be."

"I don't know about you, but there are people in my life that I really care about. I would offer my home to them, travel to see them, and love them as much as I love you. I can't think of anything you've told me that would make me love or care about you less. I bet they are all worried sick about you," Aggie said.

"I thought they were all so happy, no one would notice I was gone," Ivy said.

"Really? People don't stay organized on a shelf. Whatever happened in their lives, Nephi is hiding like you. I can't imagine how worried his mother is." Aggie gave her another hug before pointing at the horizon. "Look."

Ivy spotted Balefire Bay's lighthouse overshadowing Xander's property when a 32-foot Coast Guard skiff rounded the head, leaving a wake behind it.

Conner's boat slowed enough to let the skiff run alongside. Conner waved at the boat from his position at the helm. It was clear Conner had notified the Coast Guard, probably as soon as Rhoda fell overboard. He'd known the boat was coming.

One of the men on the skiff put a bull horn to his mouth and said, "Prepare to be boarded."

Conner climbed down from the upper deck and walked briskly to the rail. He dropped an aluminum ladder over the side for one of the three seamen dressed in navy blue to come aboard. The stoutest seaman, with grey hair escaping his cap, boarded first. By the bling on his uniform, she guessed he was a Marine Law Enforcement Officer, but didn't know enough to be sure.

Conner leaned toward the sailor, turning his back to his passengers, and spoke softly enough she couldn't hear him over the idling motors. The man followed him inside the cabin while everyone stayed on deck. Brett, George, and Charlotte closed ranks and were talking quietly.

It felt like they were inside forever. Ivy was making her way to Brett's group when Anderson stopped her with a look. There was no mistaking his feelings. His eyes were narrowed over his clenched jaw and he was giving off dark energy that could only be described as rolling fury. With a brisk nod to the left, he led her around the cabin and out of sight of the small group.

"It's just like a bunch of rich snobs to look for someone to blame that can't defend himself," he barked.

"Who are they blaming?" Ivy asked.

"The deckhand that you apparently know," Anderson said. "Rhoda claims he pushed her overboard."

A jolt of shock ran through Ivy, leaving her eyes and mouth wide open for a short moment. "What? He didn't do it. He saved her! Besides, I do know him. He would never..."

"What do you know about him?" Anderson's head jerked back. "When was the last time you saw him? Wait." Anderson looked past her. "The Coasties must think he did it."

"Coasties?" Ivy followed his gaze. The sailor followed Nephi out of the cabin. Nephi's face was hidden in his wavy hair.

Nephi stopped. "I didn't do it!"

"Over the side, son." The sailor's voice was firm. He pushed Nephi forward.

Nephi's shoulders dropped, and he exhaled loudly. He glanced at the seaman, put one hand on the rail and landed lightly on the skiff like a cat—a big cat with its shoulders hunched. A sailor on the Coast Guard boat took one of Nephi's wrists and pulled it behind his broad back. Nephi's hands rolled into fists when they pulled his other arm behind his back, but he allowed himself to be cuffed.

Ivy folded her arms tightly around her middle, her eyes narrowed, and she struggled to contain dark emotions. "Where are they taking him?" Ivy's voice broke, and she hiccupped once.

"I don't know," Anderson said.

The skiff peeled off and headed back the way it came.

"How do you know him?" Anderson asked again.

"I had a crush on him when I was just a girl, which lasted all the way through high school and beyond, until he married someone else."

She felt a hand on her shoulder and glanced up. Xander was standing behind her. She wondered how much he'd heard.

"What was that?" he asked.

"I know him. He wouldn't ever hurt anyone," Ivy said.

His brows came together, his eyes narrowed. "How well do you know him?"

Ivy matched his stare with a furrowed brow and looked straight into his eyes. "I know what you're insinuating, and you've got it all wrong. Your mom wants someone to blame. What lengths will you go to make her happy? I know I'm right about him. Don't you trust me?"

The anger she'd seen in his eyes melted into sadness as his features softened. "Don't you trust me?" he said softly. Xander's hand fell to his side and his shoulders dropped as he walked away.

Ivy was immediately sorry for how emotional she was and the way she snapped at him. "Xander," Ivy called.

He stopped but didn't turn around. She took his hand and faced him. "I'm sorry. I shouldn't have snapped at you. I know there's no excuse, but I was shocked to see someone from my past here." She waved a hand, indicating everything.

He gave her a quick hug and whispered in her ear. "I trust you."

Rhoda came out of the cabin, nose in the air, arms folded and still wrapped in a blanket. Ashley and Conner stood by her side. Xander joined them. *Why didn't I say it back? I trust him. I do.* Her stomach was in knots.

Anderson crossed the deck to her, folded his arms and studied her face. "So, you do know him and you're sure he wouldn't have pushed Rhoda?" Anderson asked.

Ivy cleared her throat. "I'm sure. His name is Nephi James. His home was my favorite place to be in high school, besides my parent's lab."

Where is his wife? Why is he here?

Hiccup.

14

OLD HISTORY, NEW MYSTERY

Chatter and gossip filled the final leg of the ride back to the dock. Everyone on board had an opinion about the deckhand. Some thought it was an accident, and he didn't mean to push her. Instead, he just ran into her. Others believed he did it. Another theory was that he wasn't guilty of anything. Someone else bumped into Rhoda and knocked her overboard.

The boat's engine was loud enough that Ivy only caught bits and pieces of the conversations floating around her.

"Does Balefire have a decent pub? I could use a drink," George said.

"Go to The Crews Quarters," Brett said.

"How do you know, young man? Isn't it illegal for young people to consume alcohol in America?" Charlotte said. She glowered at him.

Brett's eyes narrowed, and he folded his arms. "They have a restaurant side. All the poker machines and booze are on the bar side."

"Sounds perfect," George said.

Charlotte turned around to George. Ivy waited for her to say whatever was bringing her eyes together and creating the frown on her face. She unfolded her arms and balled her hands into fists.

George looked back at her with one brow raised and a half smile. For a microsecond, Charlotte's eyes widened and her mouth fell open as she stepped back. Just for a moment, but long enough for Ivy to see fear in Charlotte's expression and body language. Charlotte pushed her way to her father and stood by him.

Ivy stored each tidbit of opinion or information away, knowing she would remember it long past the day's adventure. In fact, she was certain she would never forget Nephi's face when he saw hers. He looked wet, fierce, and shocked, followed by definite anger with a flicker of sadness in his eyes.

Charlotte's quiet, but urgent voice interrupted her thoughts. George towered over Charlotte, who looked at her feet as she spoke, her lower lip jutting out and her arms wrapped around herself.

"You told me you wouldn't do it again," Charlotte said.

"Do what? Gamble?" George chuckled. "We're in America, darling. It's a new day. But if you care so much, I won't. I just need some time alone and the pub sounds like the perfect place." This time, he walked away. Charlotte stood still as he brushed past her, then her arms fell.

Ivy went to her side and said, "I couldn't help but overhear. Are you alright?"

"Yes," Charlotte said. She folded her arms and looked at her shoes.

"I'm here if you need someone to talk to," Ivy said.

"Thanks," Charlotte said softly. Her arms dropped, she turned on her heel and followed George across the deck.

When the boat docked, Conner leapt softly from the boat onto the dock. Xander threw a ball tied to a rope to him. Conner caught the ball and used the rope to tie the boat securely to the cleats on the dock. Still stunned, everyone gathered their things.

Conner returned to the boat and put the stairs up. As people disembarked, Aggie took a hold of her son and gathered him into a warm embrace. She kissed him on the cheek.

"It will all be fine," Aggie said. She reassured him as if he was still her little boy. He fell into her hug, then quickly stepped back and regained his composure.

"Not in front of everyone, Mom." He winked at Aggie.

The others patted him on the back or stopped long enough to tell Conner how sorry they were to end the day like this and how much they wanted to go out with him again some other time. Anderson patted his shoulder fondly and said he was a great captain, and he knew the charter boat would be a success.

Conner was quiet. Ivy noticed he was chewing on his bottom lip. He frowned with his entire face as he began cleaning up the boat and putting away the poles.

She called up to him. "Can I help you?"

Hard at work, he called over his shoulder. "No. I've got it."

She didn't blame him for wanting to be alone and decompress. Sometimes cooking and cleaning were just the thing to take care of her own anxiety or stress. She joined Xander and his family on the dock. They huddled in a group that opened to make room for her. They speculated around her while Rhoda insisted she was right.

"That slimy deckhand pushed me. I could have died. He was trying to kill me. First the cinnamon roll and now this?" Rhoda's nose ran and her wet mascara mixed with her runny base makeup under her bedraggled hair. She used her sleeve to wipe her nose.

Xander's shoulders dropped, and he rubbed his eyes. "Mom, I don't think..."

"You don't believe me?" Rhoda's voice rose a full octave.

"No. It's not that. Of course I believe you, I just don't think..."

She folded her arms and stuck her chin out. "You don't have to think. I know he pushed me."

Xander closed his eyes and sighed. Ivy recognized that ever since Xander's mother arrived, he'd more often than not had a somber expression on his face. *He is definitely more detached or maybe overwhelmed.*

After they met, they spent all their free time together, joking, laughing, hugging, and sharing meals with Anderson. She couldn't remember feeling more comfortable with someone, other than Nephi. She and Xander had worked in the library together, gone to the book club, and she had cheered him during a book signing in Vancouver, Washington.

The thing she loved best was the time he'd asked her to read his manuscript out loud as it progressed. They sat in the library, snuggled together around his laptop on the couch facing the floor-to-ceiling view of the ocean. She would read his work out loud to him. He would stop her and make corrections when he didn't like the way it flowed or caught an error in the story.

Since Xander's mother and brother returned she hadn't spent any time alone with him.

Brett climbed onto the dock. Xander helped Ashley and they both steadied Rhoda as she climbed off the boat. Charlotte and her husband walked closely behind them.

Charlotte was still upset and talking rapidly and quietly to George. This time, her brows were up, and tears pooled in her eyes. It looked more like pleading to Ivy. Her voice was so soft, Ivy couldn't hear her. She obviously didn't want to share her feelings with the group. George towered over her, his arm draped around her shoulder, frowning.

She pulled away from him. He grabbed her arm and forcefully pulled her back. Ivy gasped. *He is abusive! No, I am a mess and like the chief says, seeing murder, mysteries, and problems everywhere.*

Ivy watched them leave the dock without looking back. A cold breeze was strong enough to tug at her black hair and to make her take a wide stance and brace herself against it.

"Ivy," Anderson said.

Startled, she jumped and then turned to face him.

"I need to know more about your friend, Nephi, the deckhand. Rhoda is sure she was pushed and the target, but any person in our group could've been a target," Anderson said. "Why would he do it? Was it planned?"

"He would never do anything like that. He's a good man. Maybe it was just plain dumb luck, an accident." Ivy folded her arms.

"Well, this is a first. I thought you would totally accept the idea of foul play. Why don't you think he pushed Rhoda overboard?" Anderson folded his arms and raised one brow, looking down his nose at her slight frame.

Ivy took a deep breath and blew it out slowly while she decided what she wanted to share or what was safe to share without creating more problems for Nephi. "There are plenty of people who would like to push that woman overboard."

"Hah!" Anderson laughed and then bit his lip, squelching a smile. "True. But annoyance, even hatred, isn't enough of a motive for tossing someone in the Pacific, in my opinion."

"Nephi comes from a wonderful and religious family. His niece was my best friend, Esther James."

"The philanthropist?"

Ivy's brows rose. She glanced up at him. "The philanthropist? I guess so. She has done so many amazing things. I took care of myself and went to Harvard like my parents expected. She married her boyfriend, Parker, and they became a power couple serving others all over the world."

"Where did Nephi go after school?" Anderson asked.

"His wife is a twin to Parker. The four of them returned to the Stewart Estate, or one of their houses, in England. I visited once. It's straight out of Downton Abbey, but with bad Wi-Fi and cell service."

"And now?" Anderson tilted his head and examined her face.

Ivy shrugged. "Do I still have feelings for him?"

Anderson smiled. "No. That's not what I'm asking. I mean, what has he been doing since the last time you saw him? But now that you mention it, do you still have feelings for him?"

"No," she lied. "We lost touch. I really have no idea. When I saw his face, it sent me boomeranging through time. You know? I can't remember the last time we spoke."

Anderson was stone-faced. No response, no tell.

He must play a mean game of cards, Ivy thought. "Look, something has obviously happened to him. He looks different. He has a tattoo, for heaven's sake."

"What does a tattoo have to do with anything?" Anderson asked.

"He's changed. Something is wrong. He has always been a nice guy, like a giant Clark Kent with Superman's strength. Good, through and through." She looked up at Anderson and searched his face for some understanding.

He looked down at her with narrowed eyes and lips pressed tight. She could feel his judgment and skepticism raining down on her.

"If he was really like that, something terrible must have happened," Anderson said.

"To him?" Ivy asked. She shook her head as she thought of how he looked today compared to Nephi's all-American boy look of long ago. "Things have happened to all of us."

Ivy needed Anderson to understand. If he believed in Nephi, maybe Xander would, too. "He had a great sense of humor, but he had a larger sense of right and wrong and would always stand up for me, even when I didn't deserve it. He's tough, protective and, well...honest. He is as honest as you can be. He's smart but doesn't flaunt it."

Anderson's mouth twitched, one corner turned up, and his eyes smiled. He belly laughed. "Whoa. You really got it bad. You do like him, don't you?"

Realizing she'd said too much, she stood as tall as she could, threw her shoulders back and looked him in the eyes. "I... I..." she groaned and deflated. "I did. I am an adult now and don't choose to. I am going out with Xander."

"The heart wants what it wants," Anderson said and shrugged. "Trust me."

"Well, my heart doesn't get what it wants, ever. Besides, I am already surrounded by gorgeous men, engaged in chocolate therapy, and trying to yoga away all the feels. I don't need more drama. Rhoda is over the top."

Anderson threw his head back and roared with laughter.

Ivy contemplated kicking him in the shins with her size six sandal but wasn't sure he would notice, or that a kick would deliver the message she wanted to convey.

"Look, Anderson. Rhoda is a spoiled... batch... of brownies," Ivy said.

Anderson shook his head and looked into her eyes, still suppressing a smile. "Agreed. But what if she is telling the truth?"

Ivy shook her head no. "Whatever she is saying is going to be done with maximum drama and very little thought for the people around her. We don't know if she was the intended target. Because she made a major fuss, no one collected any evidence or looked to see if there were any cameras onboard."

"That's a good question." Anderson turned and climbed back onto the boat. "Conner," he bellowed.

Conner poked his head out of the helm window. "Yo."

"Do you have any security cameras?" Anderson asked.

"I have two, but only one was on. I am required by maritime law to have one observing the helm or me, so it won't help. The second camera is only on at night or when I am away from the boat for security. Did anyone actually see Nephi push her overboard?" Conner asked.

"I didn't see anyone push her," Ivy barked.

"Me either, but I believe we should err on the side of caution and be vigilant while she is in Balefire. I can think of dozens of people she has offended," Anderson said.

Conner nodded and chuckled to himself while he climbed down the bridge ladder to the main deck. "If offending people made murder justifiable, someone would have killed you long ago. Maybe you two should stay on the dock and I'll ask the chief to send a forensic team out," Conner said.

"You know what he is going to say, don't you?" Ivy said.

"Yes. Nothing ever happens in Balefire Bay. It was an accident." Conner's phone vibrated. He took it out of his pocket. "Yes. Chief? I see. No, I don't have a problem with it. Okay."

Conner looked from Anderson to Ivy. "Well, that's that. The chief called the Coast Guard and told them about his recent run in with Rhoda and how difficult she is, and they are releasing Nephi, pending further investigation—which likely means it will go nowhere. I guess I better go pick him up."

"Did he say it?" Ivy asked.

"Say what?" Conner asked.

"Nothing ever..." Ivy began.

Conner finished her sentence. "... happens in Balefire Bay."

Anderson laughed deep and long. Ivy rolled her eyes, and Conner shrugged.

"The chief wants him to stay in town in case they decide to question him again, or something comes up in his background check," Conner said. "Can he bunk in one of Xander's cabins?" He asked Ivy and Anderson.

Anderson put his hands in his jeans pockets and sighed. "I say yes, but I can't predict Xander's decisions when his mother is involved," Anderson said. "I guess we better go find out. Why don't you call us after you pick him up? We should know by then. Come on Ivy. We'd better check the drama levels at the house and ask."

"Me? Why me? I think you can handle this on your own."

"Oh, no. You're not getting out of this. If I have to suffer, you're suffering with me. Let's go into the lion's den together."

Ivy stopped and looked back at Conner. "What if someone else pushed her and it's like at the tea shop and that same someone is out to get Rhoda?"

Conner chuckled and shook his head. "The chief also told me you would think it was murder. I was to remind you that not everything is."

15

RESEARCH LIBRARIAN OR STALKER?

When Ivy got home, she did what came naturally. She googled Nephi to see where he had been and if anything had happened to him. The first thing that came up was from a United Kingdom newspaper. The story title read; *Heiress Paisley Stewart James divorces her American husband.* Family friends, the Thornycroft-Woosters, reported they were not surprised.

"What do you expect of a vulgar American after an accident like that," Bitsy Vandercroft told Fox News. Although he was never charged in America, friends and family expressed concern.

"We just hope he is safe and sober." The caption read Lord Stewart. It was Paisley's father. What did he mean, sober? Nephi wouldn't drink, no matter how many times friends of his had encouraged him to drink. He always said it was a choice, but Ivy knew his religion discouraged alcohol use.

Accident? Ivy wasn't surprised to see the article didn't include basic facts, like what accident, when, who, and why that would lead to divorce. The family was well known enough. It may have been recently covered. Still, it wasn't great reporting.

She went back through the news. She found another article dated about nine months before the divorce. It read, "Lord Stewart asked for privacy at this time of great loss. They ask instead that mourners donate to the Ormond Hospital." Later in the article, they report that Joseph Stewart-James, Nephi's son, died and Paisley was gravely injured in a car accident in the United States.

She searched obituaries by the same name to find out more. "Joseph Stewart-James, born on Christmas Eve, a gift to his parents, passed one year to the day on December 24th. Private services will be held January 20th, on the estate." The obituary listed both Nephi and Paisley as surviving parents. *Paisley lived. Where is she?*

Joseph was an infant. He died at age one during an accident. Ivy's heart was breaking. She realized she was crying and blew her nose. *No wonder he is a shadow of himself. I wouldn't have survived the pain.* Lost in thought, she rubbed her chest just above her heart, as if she could rub away the pain and tightness she was feeling.

Ivy's phone chimed. She had a text from Anderson.

Anderson texted: *Bringing your friend back to the Sanctuary.*

Ivy replied: *What did Rhoda say?*

Anderson said: *I can't use words like that. I am about thirty minutes out.*

16

THE HOUSE GUEST

Ivy watched Anderson and Nephi cross the Sanctuary lawn from the Knightly House towards her cabin. Judy was jumping playfully at Nephi's feet. If he noticed, he didn't respond. He looked so different to her, yet he still gave her a light flutter, like butterflies filled her.

Ivy knelt down and said, "Judy!" That was all it took. The small dog knocked her backwards and covered her face in kisses.

"I see you finally found love," Nephi said.

"Rude," Ivy said, falling right into their childhood banter. She looked up, way up. His six-foot six-inch frame towered over her. She caught a bit of relief in Nephi's green eyes. He gave her a small, crooked smile, with a single dimple in the stubble on his left cheek.

"Listen shorty, if I find love, you will be the last to know." She laughed and hugged his waist. He still smelled wonderful. She wondered whether it was soap or fabric softener. He lifted her off her feet. "Hey. Put me down."

"Make me."

She playfully pinched his arm. He put her down feigning a major injury.

"You're still mean," Nephi said.

"Tough. I prefer the word tough," Ivy said. A warm and familiar feeling washed over her. It radiated from her heart to her pink cheeks. It was a feeling she hadn't felt in a long time.

He smiled at her, but his eyes didn't join the smile. They seemed to turn down, trying and failing to mask something dark like despair.

"Can you take him to the cabin that's closest to you? The Lookout? Show him where everything is?" Anderson asked. "I have to get back. Rhoda doesn't want him on the property, and she was letting Xander know in no uncertain terms when we pulled up. Can I talk to you for a second, alone?"

She followed Anderson onto the deck. "Listen, after I talked to you, I talked to Conner and Aggie. I can't see why he would push Rhoda overboard, so I talked to Xander. When he heard you'd known him a long time and you trusted him, he felt bad about Rhoda's behavior."

"I was stunned when I saw you coming. Did Xander want to do this or was he pressured into it? You know he'll do anything you ask," Ivy said.

"He thinks it was an accident. He offered to give him a cabin because he has been ordered to stay in town until this is worked out. He was sleeping on the boat, but Conner has charters scheduled. He hired another fisherman to go out with him until Nephi can."

Ivy nodded. "Okay. Is Rhoda really going to allow this?"

Anderson rubbed the back of his neck. "To make her happy, Xander voluntold me to make sushi, her favorite, for dinner. She bought a sushi mat and a knife, so now she is an expert Itamee or Sushi Chef." He wiggled his brows. "I get to be the Itamee's Sous Chef and move the first aid kit onto the counter."

"Oh my. Can you video it all for me?" Ivy asked.

"Not on your life!" Anderson said. They walked back to Nephi. "I'm sure they will get it worked out before too long, and you will soon be back to fishing. In the meantime, Ivy will help you get settled."

"Thanks, man," Nephi said. He shook Anderson's hand.

Ivy realized if she'd seen Nephi in town, she would have made all kinds of assumptions about him. She may have wondered if he had a home.

"No worries. Just steer clear of Rhoda." Anderson turned, scooped up Judy, and walked back to the house. Judy squirmed in his arms and whined, looking back at her over Anderson's shoulder, making Ivy sad and angry all at the same time.

"Come on. I'll show you where you will be bunking." Ivy took a hold of his arm at the elbow. Every part of her wanted to hug and cry with him. Instead, they walked quietly, side by side, to the Lookout, a log cabin like hers that was hidden in the trees just east of her cabin. She took the key off a hook under the porch, opened the door, and then turned on the light.

It smelled musty. She walked through the great room to the French doors, opened the curtains, and walked out onto the deck, taking a deep breath of fresh air and closing her eyes for a moment to listen to the sound of the waves against the cliff.

She turned around and leaned back on the deck rail. Nephi had set his backpack on a small kitchen table and was standing in front of the empty fridge, staring.

"Wishing won't fill that fridge up," Ivy called.

He looked up, smiled sadly, and walked to her side, put both hands on the rail and looked as mesmerized as she always was with the stunning view from the cliff's edge.

"I'll take us to town for groceries," Ivy said. She opened the door to the bathroom and the bedroom's French doors, letting the stale air out and the sea air in, then knelt and looked for the bedlinen that she knew she'd find underneath the bed. She pulled a tote with sheets and towels in it from there.

Ivy had often cleaned cabins and readied them for Xander and his friends. She started with the bed. She put the corner of the sheet with the tag on the bed and tried to stretch the sheet to the next corner. It wouldn't go. She took it off and started again.

The bed was up against the wall. The worst place for a bed to be, in her opinion. She finally got the bottom corners on and then climbed on the bed and stretched the cotton sheet toward the top left corner, pressed up against the wall and under the window. She just about had it on when one of the bottom corners popped off.

Out of habit, she stretched out, trying to keep it from getting away, and finished the corner she was working on, turned on her knees and put the bottom corner back on. Flushed, she pushed her hair out of her eyes and looked up.

Nephi's face was beetroot red, and his hand was over his mouth. He laughed. "Need some help?"

Ivy got up on her knees and fell right into her high school stubborn self. She put her hands on her hips, nose in the air, and said, "No."

He easily pulled the bed away from the wall, folded his arms, and smiled while she walked around the bed and finished making it.

"You didn't have to make the bed. I could have done it," Nephi said. He brought his pack to the chest of drawers, opened the top drawer, took his wallet out of the pack, put it in his back pocket, and dropped the rest of his belongings into the drawer.

"Let's go to town. I could eat a whale," Nephi said. "And if I remember correctly, so could you. I'm buying."

It was true. Ivy could eat and burn her weight in food every day. She'd try to count calories and then would end the day by baking a chocolate cake and eating a quarter of it before bed.

"I still do yoga. It burns a lot of calories," Ivy said.

"Right. Do you have a vehicle?"

"Don't you?" Ivy asked.

"I don't drive." He'd made the statement with absolute finality and without any eye contact.

Ivy knew better than to question him or to let him know she had been Google stalking him. "Come on. Let's go up to Knightly House and get the keys to the Range Rover."

"Nice. Is that your car?" Nephi asked.

"I thought so." She shrugged.

Ivy glanced at Nephi while trying to keep her eyes on the road. He'd rolled down the window on the Rover, leaned on the door and let the wind blow his long, curly hair into knots. She rounded the last bend before Highway 101 and stopped for a herd of elk who grazed lazily, without caring where she was going or when she needed to be there.

"I missed the smell of the trees and the ocean," Nephi said.

Her brow furrowed. "Where have you been?"

No answer. The minutes stretched on silently, slowly.

"Do you want to go to a restaurant or grocery store?" Ivy said.

"Is there any good food in town?" Nephi asked.

"There is a new Thai restaurant. You used to like Thai. Would that work?"

He nodded.

This is like walking on Legos barefoot. Ivy thought. She hiccupped.

"Nervous?" Nephi asked.

"No," Ivy said, firmly.

It started to rain, so she turned on the wipers. *Grey day, cold wind, and rain. Perfect.*

A waitress in jeans and a sweater with a tag that read Flo had an apron tied tightly around her small waist. She sat them at a window booth and left them with glossy menus. From where they were, they could see the ocean on the south spit.

Out of habit, Ivy searched the choppy sea for whales, hoping to catch one breaching. She looked up and caught Nephi's gaze before he quickly looked down at his menu.

The waitress returned with water. "Would you like something to drink first?"

One of Ivy's brows lifted, and she peaked over her menu, waiting to see what Nephi would order. She'd known him long enough to know every restaurant meal started with a diet soda.

"Diet Coke. Keep them coming." Nephi closed his menu.

"And you?" She turned her middle-aged face to Ivy and smiled.

"Water is fine."

"Don't make me drink alone." He smiled ever so slightly.

Ivy sighed. "Diet Coke. Make it a double."

"Do you know what you want to order?" the waitress asked.

"Chicken Pad Thai," they said at the same time.

"Jinx," they said, together. Then it happened. Laughter, as if they'd never been separated.

The waitress cackled, collecting menus, then entered the kitchen to place the order.

Silently, they studied each other's faces.

"You look the same," Nephi said.

"I do not! I am older and... and... I think I've grown. I'm taller," Ivy said.

His eyes twinkled. "You wish." They studied each other's faces.

"You're still pretty," Nephi said.

Her mouth fell open, and she sat back in her seat. He'd never said that to her before. She would have died and gone to heaven to hear a compliment like that when she was a teenager.

"Well, you're still... You still have dimples and wear flannel," Ivy said.

He grinned. "Yes, I do."

Silence again.

"I," they both said. She laughed nervously.

"You first," Ivy said. "I heard about the divorce. I'm sorry."

"Don't be." His shoulders dropped, and any light that was shining out of his eyes went out. He looked past her. Saltwater tears pooled in his eyes. "She was done with me."

"What do you mean, done with you?" Knowing full well what it meant. She realized, by his response, she shouldn't have asked as soon as the words slipped out. His eyes darkened and his jaw flexed as he ground his teeth loud enough it made her cringe.

She wanted to take the conversation back to what they were a minute ago, laughing, like they were still young, and still best friends. But she sat silently, waiting for the storm to pass from his face.

"Listen, after you and Esther married and seemed to have it all together, my entire life became a train wreck. I've avoided you and everyone else, because I was embarrassed about what a mess my life was," Ivy said softly.

His brow furrowed and he chewed on the corner of his lip.

"In other words, I have no right to judge you or anyone else." He was looking directly into her eyes. She looked down at her hands on the table.

After a moment, he took in a deep breath and let it out slowly. "I might as well tell you." He fell back in his seat. "After what happened today, if there is an investigation, it's bound to come out. But don't share it with Conner, okay? I like working with him. I want to keep my job."

"Pinky promise," Ivy said.

"I did something awful, and we weren't able to get past it. She wouldn't forgive me, and I can't forgive myself."

A million questions raced through Ivy's mind, but she remained silent, studying his face as memories washed across his eyes, leaving tears pooled in the corners.

She remembered his easy laughter, driving her and Esther to the beach instead of class, singing by a bonfire. Then they parted ways to go to different universities. She never dreamed that one day she would be so wounded that she would hide from them.

Looking at Nephi, she understood that she'd been so into her own problems, she'd lost touch. All she knew was that they'd had a baby last year sometime. *Why did I suppose I was the only one struggling? They needed me as much as I needed them.*

"I insisted on coming home to the coast for Christmas to show Mom our new son, Joseph. He was named after Joe Hart?" He paused for a moment, not breathing, a faraway look in his eyes. When he finally took a deep breath, he looked down, closed his eyes, and with his jaw set and shoulders back, he went on. "We had an accident on Highway 26."

Her heart skipped a beat.

"We ran into unexpected winter snow. You know, the kind that comes on fast and hard. One minute the mountain roads were fine, the next, they were a nightmare. They were a solid sheet of black ice when we passed the midway point. The storm was relentless. I was way too confident. I was sure turning around was as dangerous as going forward. She begged me to just pull off the road, but I thought I could make it. I was so stupid."

The pain surrounded him like waves of dark energy. He was silent. Ivy reached across the table, wishing she could touch him, comfort him somehow. He sat back, folded in on himself.

She knew all too well how quickly Highway 26, from the city to the coast, could become deadly. It didn't even have to be storming or snowing. When it is just cold and clear, you could drive around one curve on dry pavement, go around the next bend in the road and find a solid sheet of black ice.

He bit his lip and looked up at her with wet eyes.

"What happened? Is Paisley okay?" Ivy asked. Her heart was pounding so hard, blood was rushing in her ears. She knew who he'd lost, but he talked like Paisley was dead.

He shook his head. "Paisley made it, but she was critically injured." He took a deep, jagged breath and wiped his eyes again with the back of his hand. "I can't talk about this—here."

"I am so sorry. I can't even imagine how awful it is for you. I should have been there for your family. You were always there for me when we were young. I spent more time with you than my parents in high school."

They sat quietly for a moment.

"How is Paisley now?"

"She wasn't walking when I left."

Ivy gasped.

"She didn't even want to look at me. When she heard our son, Joseph, was gone, she became angry at me and angry with God." He fell back in his chair and finally looked at her, frowning, arms folded, studying her face with narrowed eyes. "And so did I."

Where there had been butterflies, there was a vice tightening its grip on her heart. An unwelcome tear escaped her eye, and her nose began to run. She tried to talk. She opened her mouth, but didn't know what to say, where to begin.

She reached across the table with both hands, not knowing what to say, but wanting to hold him, touch him.

He yanked his hands back and jumped up. "I have to get groceries." He stood up and almost ran into the waitress carrying their food as he left the restaurant.

With both plates in her hands, the waitress watched him leave and then asked Ivy, "Do you want boxes with this?"

"Yes, please," Ivy said quietly, wiping her eyes with her napkin.

After paying the bill, Ivy sat in the Rover for a moment, overwhelmed by tears. She gulped air, tugged her long sleeves down ,and used them to wipe her eyes while she tried to calm herself by taking deep breaths.

After several minutes, despite her red nose and blotchy face, she pulled away from the curb to see if she could find him. She didn't know what she would say, but she wasn't leaving him to walk home while he was still raw and hurting.

She rolled all the windows down, hoping the evening air would cool her hot face and hide her distress.

I cut ties with my lifetime friends because I had imag-
ined they were all having their happy endings and their
lives were perfect. I pushed them away because I didn't
want to share what was happening to me. I was sure I
didn't need them. I never dreamed they might need me.

It didn't take long. She caught up with Nephi at the grocery store. They walked silently side by side up and down the aisles. She knew her nose was red, and she hiccupped sporadically and threw all the ingredients for every dessert she knew how to make into her cart. Meanwhile, he didn't look much better. He was like a brick wall trying to contain emotion that randomly leaked out and made him wipe the corner of his eye or sniff.

Nephi put what she considered to be the worst food choices possible in his shopping cart, mac and cheese, canned chili, ramen noodles, 3 cases of diet cola, a brick of mild cheddar cheese, and two gallons of whole milk.

At the check-out stand, she watched him pull money out of his wallet and change out of his pocket and feed it into the self-checkout cash register, right down to his last dime.

No one broke the silence. She certainly didn't know what to say. *How do you respond to someone you've known most of your life, but isn't the same person you knew anymore? He probably doesn't know what to say to me, either.*

He's a prisoner of his own guilt and shame, he's his own jailer, meting out his punishment; just like me.

The only sound on the drive home was the ocean through his open window. When they pulled up and parked by the Crow's Nest, they separated the groceries without speaking and walked toward their separate cabins. She was at her door before she realized she had his box of Pad Thai. She held it, looking back over her shoulder at his retreating figure, and then went inside and put Nephi's boxed food in the fridge.

After putting a warm black sweater on with her shorts, she put an apron on, and she gathered the ingredients she needed for chocolate cake. She carefully measured cocoa and sugar into the mixing bowl. She didn't need a recipe card to make her grandmother's cake. She was baking while thoughts of her friend Paisley's certain grief, her vibrant body in pain, and the magnitude of the loss of their child stormed in her head.

She put the cake in the oven and her teapot on the stove to boil. Then she sat down and googled how to talk to a grieving parent, searching desperately for something, anything to say that might give Nephi some comfort. For the first time in her memory, she didn't know what to say.

There were millions of references to grief and websites suggesting things to say to people when they were grieving, but everything she found sounded trite.

She also found an article about the accident and wished she hadn't.

An hour and a half later, Ivy squared her shoulders and carried a German Chocolate cake on a plate, along with Pad Thai and ice cream in a grocery bag to The Lookout. Conner's new, but used, black truck eclipsed Nephi's cabin. She couldn't figure out how to knock with everything in her hands. Rather than put anything down, she kicked the door with her foot.

Aggie opened the door, grinning, and winked. "Bring that delicious cake in here!"

Ivy smiled back, instantly warmed inside and out by Aggie's welcome.

Conner got up from the table and took the grocery sack from her, a lock of his dark hair falling over his brown eyes while his smile calmed her. Nephi gave her a quick nod.

After Ivy's arms were emptied, Aggie enveloped Ivy in a tight hug. "How is our girl? What a day, huh? How did you know we needed cake?"

"Doesn't everyone need cake all the time?" Ivy took a step back. "You're busy. I just came to bring Nephi his Thai food and a cake to welcome him to the Sanctuary. I can come back later."

"You made the cake yourself?" Nephi asked. His brows were up, and he tipped his head. "Really?"

"Really." She felt twelve again. Her hands were on her hips before she noticed. "It's just science, you know?

121

Baking is a scientific experiment that brings natural ingredients together to create something new, and in my case, amazing," Ivy said. She followed Conner to the table. "Nephi? Do you want me to warm up your Pad Thai?"

Nephi shook his head, no. "Dessert before dinner."

Aggie opened Nephi's cupboards and drawers, searching until she found plates and forks.

"Aggie, what brings you here?" Ivy asked.

Aggie sat next to Conner and passed out plates, paper towels, and silverware. "When I met Nephi on the Coast Bus, I knew that he was good people."

"Wait. What? You met him on the bus? You brought him here?" Ivy asked.

Aggie giggled, "Of course I did. Conner needed help."

"Why am I surprised?" Ivy said.

"I have no clue, Love," Aggie said.

"Okay, back to business," Aggie said. "He didn't do it. No one asked us, but I was looking straight at Rhoda's bunch when she went overboard. I don't think Nephi was close enough to her."

"I wish we had a photo or video," Conner said.

Aggie pointed the cake cutter at the group. "My integrity is all I have. They should believe me. If she was pushed, it was someone else."

"I believe you," Nephi said.

"Yes, but we need everyone else to believe you and me. Rhoda's family was all around her when she went over. Then she blames the man who saves her? She probably tripped over her own ego." Aggie finally took a breath and smiled sheepishly. "Can you tell I am a little wound up?"

Conner rolled his eyes. "Mom is a serious mother bear."

"What about the theory that it was an accident?" Ivy asked. The whole room went completely silent, and all wide eyes were on her and all mouths were open for a moment of silence.

Aggie was the first to break the silence. She jumped to her feet and leaned over the table, emphasizing her words with her pointer finger. "I'm surprised that you, of all people, believe that annoying woman going over the rail on my son's boat into an ocean that is cold enough to kill anyone in ten minutes was an accident. Why didn't someone else fall overboard when we crossed the choppy waves at the bar? Frankly, we are lucky Nephi made it back onboard in one piece."

Ivy deflated. "You're right."

Smiling triumphantly, Aggie patted Nephi's shoulder. "Young man, you need some people with good common sense to sort this out before the chief puts you back in jail just to get Rhoda off his back."

"Where are you going to find people with common sense?" Conner asked. He smiled and winked at Ivy.

"And my son needs help on his ship." Aggie sat down and cut the cake.

"Boat, Mom," Conner said. Color rose up his neck and moved to his cheeks. He chuckled and shook his head.

Aggie pointed at Nephi for emphasis. "He slept on the boat the night before the trip. Having Nephi onboard kept it safe and sound. He's polite, honest, and hard working. If he was going to do something criminal, he had a chance that first night to steal the boat, or worse."

"There is also the fact that I introduced him to Rhoda. He'd never met her before," Conner said.

Aggie laughed heartily while serving Ivy a piece of cake.

Conner leaned toward Nephi. "My mother collects people. Whenever she takes a long bus ride to visit her sister, she meets someone. Occasionally, they come to town to stay, like Ivy did. She says she knows good people when she meets them."

Nephi looked at Ivy and smiled with one brow raised. "Really?"

She ignored him. "Okay, let's focus on the important facts," Ivy said. "Aggie, you think Nephi wasn't close enough to Rhoda to push her and Nephi is dependent on the boat for income and housing." Turning to Conner, she asked, "What possible motivation could he have had to push Rhoda overboard?"

Conner shook his head. "Maybe he was trying to save us all from her annoying demands, like providing a heater on the deck. She drives me crazy. She always has."

"Did you meet her before?" Ivy asked.

"Well sure," Aggie answered. "She and Xander lived here off and on before he built his home. But Conner probably didn't like her because of the way she treated Xander when he was young. She wasn't the same woman. She was a mousy little thing with unkempt hair and no figure. She bought her looks later. She was much kinder when she was struggling like the rest of us. Once she hosted a birthday bonfire for Xander, and brought him to a potluck at the store, and other small-town things."

"Was she a book club member?" Ivy asked.

Aggie nodded. "She loved true crime, mystery novels, and a bit of drama in her life. Now she seems to love a lot of drama and create small mysteries."

Ivy put her hand over her mouth, suppressing a laugh. *I love Xander. I shouldn't diss his mom, but holy crumpets. She is an enigma.* "What changed her into the Rhoda we are surviving now?" Ivy asked.

"Money. Xander was young when we met. They didn't have much the first time I met them. She cleaned vacation rentals. They would be in town for a while before she'd move on with a new boyfriend," Aggie said.

"Then they'd come back when her relationships ended," Conner said. "The rental company kept tiny beach houses in a campground for their summer employees, making living here more affordable than other places. They still provide housing for some of their employees."

"When did Xander fall in love with Balefire Bay?" Ivy said.

"I honestly don't know," Conner said. "All I know is it was one of my favorite summers. We found a dory abandoned on the beach with a hole in it. We went to the library and learned how to patch it and make it waterproof. We didn't have enough money for tools or what we needed, so we tried every restaurant in town and begged to take their pop cans so we could recycle them. We worked hard." He laughed lightly. "It sank on its maiden voyage."

"So, you've sunk two vessels? Should I be worried?" Nephi's eyes twinkled above a broad smile.

"Hey, I didn't sink the last one. Ivy's ex sank it," Conner said, laughing.

Ivy's heart fell to the bottom of her stomach. Her head snapped around to see Nephi's reaction to Conner's casual drop of a subject she hadn't discussed with any of her friends outside Balefire. The book club members had helped her when she arrived in town and her ex showed up. Her history was common knowledge, but rarely came up. She made big eyes at Conner and shook her head no. He shrugged.

I'm the worst. The first thing I do is make him unload his history and avoid sharing mine.

"Apparently, we have a lot more catching up to do than I realized." Nephi smiled, but his eyes were narrowed, and she knew he wouldn't let this one go.

"Conner. Why is this the first I am hearing about your first shipwreck?" Aggie asked, "Hm?" She sat up to her full height and folded her arms over her ample chest.

Conner laughed loudly and Nephi joined him. "Boat, mom, boat. The dory was a boat, and we were kids. If I told you every hair brained thing I did as a boy, you would have locked me in my room for life!"

"I can't believe this is the first I've heard of Xander living here before he was an author," Ivy said. "No wonder the locals aren't fazed when they see him."

"He wasn't really a resident. They came and went, like the many visitors who pass through for a season.

"Back to motive," Aggie said. "The last time Rhoda was here, she sued Gladys and won. Gladys posted a selfie with Rhoda that showed Xander, with his back to the camera. She won the suit and Gladys had to pay up and take the photo down. Rhoda benefited. I can't see a clear motive. If Ivy is right, the cinnamon roll that killed Gladys was meant for Rhoda and today was a second attempt. We just narrowed our suspect list to anyone on the boat. It would also reduce Gladys' death to an awful mistake."

"Poor Petunia," Ivy said. "I watched her intentionally damage Gladys' favorite plant. Gladys was overbearing and bossy. But is that a motive for murder?"

"Maybe the accident freed Reginald and Petunia," Conner said. "Maybe Reginald wanted out."

The room was quiet until Ivy broke the silence. "Money, love, and revenge are all good motives. Rhoda certainly appears to have a lot of money, or at least acts like she does. But the truth is, someone may have accidentally bumped into her, or she could have accidentally fallen overboard. That would mean that Rhoda's little dip in the ocean has nothing to do with what I believe was a real attempt on her life at the bakery. And what about the caretaker's death?"

Conner groaned. "We found the caretaker's killer. He is in the care of the Oregon Mental Health system. He was stealing from the crates, the caretaker walked in, and he pushed him. He hit his head and died. Case closed."

"Did you know the caretaker?" Ivy said.

"I'm not a regular church-going man," Conner said.

"I talked to the pastor's wife. He was a lovely man. What she described to me wasn't the act of a homeless person trying to get out of the rain," Ivy said.

"What has this got to do with Gladys?" Conner asked.

"I don't know. But the caretaker deserves justice too," Ivy said.

"Why don't we focus on what happened to Gladys and on the boat right now? Those are the crimes we witnessed," Aggie said.

Ivy rubbed her forehead and closed her eyes in frustration. "Maybe Gladys died of natural causes. Maybe the man you have in custody killed the caretaker. I know you want what happened to Rhoda to be an accident. I don't think the water was choppy enough to cause her to fall. The rails are high enough to keep her on deck in normal weather. Maybe the deaths aren't related at all."

"If we charged him, he did it. Plain and simple. He had a crate in his cart," Conner said.

"I have another theory. Have you thought about the antique shop owner? There is something about him," Ivy said.

"This is Oregon, where 'Keep Portland Weird' is a saying you see on bumper stickers and signs everywhere. "

"Laugh it up officer, but there is something about him I can't quite put my finger on. All the break-ins have been in older homes or high-end summer houses, besides the church. That doesn't sound like the work of a man living out of a shopping cart. Where would he store the stolen goods and how would he sell them? If there is another break-in at a home with valuable antiques, will you reopen the case?"

"That's up to the chief, but you can ask him," Conner said. He was still grinning.

Ivy deflated. Her shoulders dropped. She chewed her lip, looking beyond Nephi, wishing she had answers. She liked the chief, but the local police were too quick to believe the obvious without questioning it, and after her visit to the church and her talk with the pastor's wife, she was positive the police were wrong. *I need to find a way to protect Nephi from the possibility of being charged with attempted murder.*

"How much money does Rhoda have?" Nephi asked.

"I think Ivy has more than she does. Heck, I have more money tied up in my boat than she does," Conner smiled at Ivy, knowing full well she didn't want him to talk about her money. She kicked his foot under the table and acted like she was zipping her lips in his direction, but it was too late.

Nephi leaned back in his chair and stared at her through narrowed eyes.

Ivy ignored him, got up and took the cake knife to the sink and washed it vigorously.

"Alright, Ivy, if someone wants to kill Rhoda, money is the most likely motive. That's my guess," Conner said.

Aggie got up, filled a kettle, and put it on to boil. "We should follow the money. How do any of the people on the boat stand to profit by Rhoda's death? Who profits from Gladys' death or did her husband kill her?"

"More importantly, does Ashley's family know most of Rhoda's money is actually Xander's? I wouldn't put it past her to exaggerate what she has," Conner said.

"Xander gave her a sizable chunk of money for their trip to Europe. The most common suspect is usually the lover or spouse, but I remember Ashley going toward the cabin to get Charlotte's sea-sickness pills, which means he wasn't close enough to Rhoda to push her. It appears that Ashley has money and doesn't need hers, but appearances can be deceiving," Ivy said.

Ivy found a pen with the cabin instructions notebook and sticky notes. She tested the pen on a sticky note while going on.

Ivy wrote George's name on a sticky note. "George was arguing with Charlotte about going to a bar with video poker machines and gambling. We need to check him out and see if there is a way George benefits from Rhoda's death."

"Charlotte," Agnes said and got a faraway look in her eyes. "Maybe she hates Rhoda. She's probably been daddy's little girl. Now she has to share the throne with Rhoda and a new stepbrother, Brett."

"Maybe she thinks that Rhoda could inherit all or part of her inheritance and maybe even her title," Ivy said. "If they are married long enough, he might leave something to Brett, reducing her inheritance."

"What do we know about Ashley's finances?" Aggie asked.

Ivy tore a blank page out of the back of the cabin notebook. She wrote down "Money" and underlined the word. Under it, she listed Rhoda and Ashley and their children. They needed to know who stood to gain the most by Rhoda's death.

"What if Rhoda wasn't the target and just got in the way? Who else profits from the death of anyone on the ship?" Aggie said.

"Boat. Brett," Conner said.

"How does Brett profit?" Ivy asked.

Conner leaned forward and counted off three reasons on his fingers. "His brother becomes his full-time guardian. If he doesn't want to go to England where he doesn't have any friends, he wouldn't have to live with his overbearing mother. Rhoda's death would be a way out. Maybe living with Rhoda is worse than we imagine, and he would rather live at the Sanctuary with his very generous brother. Also, without Rhoda, he becomes Xander's only heir."

Ivy put down her pen for a moment. "Ouch. He doesn't look that calculating to me. I mean, I know killers are often the nice boy next door, but he seems so young and sweet."

"Brett?" Conner chuckled. "I don't remember much about him. All I remember was his whining when his mother wouldn't let him go out and play on the beach with us. She had him under her thumb."

"Some people think that rules and supervision are evidence of a mother's love," Aggie said.

"Well, then I am glad you didn't love me that much," Conner said with a half-smile.

Nephi yawned, big. Ivy looked at the dark circles under his red eyes and unwashed hair and said, "We should call it a night."

"Okay, but let's meet at the Book and Tea shop with the book club tomorrow so we can keep working on this and free Nephi from all suspicion," Aggie said. "We need to focus on what happened on the boat first, in my opinion."

"I'm going to make a virtual murder board to organize our thoughts," Ivy said. "I'll be there early."

"What about work?" Nephi said. "And your car? Do you have to ask to use it?"

"What about work? I've become a glorified coffee girl instead of a high paid research librarian. As an added bonus, I get to share the car." She gave him a brisk hug. "Keep the cake. See you in the morning. I do yoga at sunrise and then I'll drive us down at eight."

They all said their goodnights. Ivy walked back to the cabin without hearing the ocean or the crunch of the gravel on the trail under her feet. Her head was swimming. She had a one-track mind and tonight the track had switched to sleuth. She was sure they had three murders to solve. Nephi was counting on them.

17

A GIRL CAN BUY ANYTHING ONLINE

Ivy woke at 5 am. She tried to go back to sleep, but her mind was switched on and already thinking about the attempted murder. Like it or not, there would be no more sleep for her.

Anxious about having to go to the house to ask for the keys to the Rover and being called Coffee Girl, Ivy thought she should at least try to look competent.

She went to the bathroom and tried to tame her messy hair while practicing her sales pitch. She said to the mirror, "Xander, can I use the Rover? I know your family needs it, but I am going to the book club to talk about your mother and why everyone wants to kill her."

Nope, that won't work. She smiled in the mirror, trying to look confident. "Xander? Can we agree that you told me I could use the Range Rover anytime I needed it, and it should be parked at my cabin?" *Wrong again.* "Xander, I think your mother's a monster and I am not that worried about her, but I am worried about having a car at my disposal to help my first love. I know I'm going out with you, but for some reason, I can't let Nephi go down for the attempted murder of your mother. He still makes my knees weak."

She leaned forward and rested her forehead on the cold glass of the mirror. She closed her eyes. *I am so bad. Jenny's right. I need to make up my mind and stop wanting three different people. Could we mash them into one person?* She took a deep breath and blew it out noisily. *I need to go to a church or something and repent. Hello Father, I am here to confess. I've given my heart to three good men. Do I want them all—yes. Every single one.*

"Argh." *The fact that I work for Xander only makes it worse. I hate being dependent on anyone. Wait. I'm not dependent. Conner's right. I have money, I just don't spend it. One sweater works, right?*

She knew what she had to do but argued with herself. She hated flaunting the money her parents had left her, but not having her own car had become unbearable. *I am dependent. Even worse, I'm in love with a man that might be so busy with his mother, he doesn't have time for me. He's been so caught up with his family, he hasn't called me or texted me.* She checked her phone for the tenth time that day. *He hasn't stopped by for sunrise cacao, yoga, and a morning kiss since they arrived. It's like he's ashamed of me.*

I've been eclipsed by his mother, which can only mean one thing. Whatever we had wasn't love. "Or am I just trying to talk myself into chasing a dream I already chased without success all through school: Nephi," she said out loud to no one.

Still wearing pajamas, she decided to do what any Millennial would do, shop online. She found the bag of chocolate kisses she'd hidden in the back of her closet and carried it onto the back deck, where she sat in her favorite Adirondack. She scrolled.

She ordered a used, but new-to-her Jeep, blue paint with a matte finish, leather seats, soft top, hitch, and a roof rack to be delivered by that evening to the gate of the Sanctuary. She was happy with herself for not going all hog wild with her inheritance. *The Jeep is practical, right?*

Retail therapy. I forgot how good it feels.

A used car is practical. It costs more than a new one because of all the added features and the lift kit. Besides, it's cute. I love the picture of Mount Hood on the spare tire cover. I won't have to ask to borrow anything Rhoda might want again, hopefully. Well, maybe Judy. I could surely use a Judy hug right now.

And then a little thought hit her in the gut. She would feel safer driving it in the mountain passes during the winter. *I wish we were still kids, and Nephi was driving us around in his beat-up truck.*

After paying the Portland Dealership online and adding a costly same day delivery, she sat back and breathed a sigh of relief. She didn't realize how much she had missed the freedom of a dependable vehicle until that moment.

Ivy's phone chimed. She had an email from the dealership.

"Crumpets," she said out loud. She got back online and shopped for car insurance.

When she was done, she lay in bed, tossing and turning until she gave up. She brought her laptop to bed with her and created a spreadsheet that included suspects, motives, and means.

By the time she was finished, the sun was rising. She put on her yoga pants and t-shirt and took her yoga mat out to the deck. She checked the horizon for her favorite couple, Mr. and Mrs. Bald Eagle. Dad was high in the sky looking for an unsuspecting fish.

She turned on soft Celtic coffee house music and lost herself to measured breaths, stretches and joy. *Sweat, sun, music, and a new used car. These are a few of my favorite things.*

Ivy was in child's pose, on her knees, her forehead on the mat, arms outstretched in front of her, sweat trickling through her hair, drool running down her chin, snoring when steps on the stairs to the deck woke her. She sat up and looked around. Nephi was standing in front of her on one leg, hands in front of him, doing a perfect tree pose.

"Nice. Do you do yoga now?" Ivy asked, smiling. She stopped the music playing on her phone.

"I know many things. I will demonstrate." He smirked and wiggled his eyebrows. She sat back and laughed.

136

"Here is my cool dude pose." Nephi put his arms up and flexed his muscles. "Breathe in two, three, four, push your chest out, two, three, four, breathe out, two, three, four."

Ivy laughed so loudly; she covered her mouth to regain some dignity. "I suppose you're here to ride with me to the book club?" She reached up and touched her forehead. The yoga mat had a pattern that was now pressed firmly into her forehead.

He nodded.

"I'll make us some cocao to drink."

"Cocoa," He corrected her.

"Nope. I am making pumpkin spice cocao. This is something much, much better. Trust me, it's like cocao only better, much better." Ivy smiled broadly.

"What I need is soda or caffeine," he said.

"Me too. Honestly, just trust me. This chocolate comes with a kick."

She put a quarter cup of ground cacao in her French press, heated the water in her teapot until it whistled, and poured the boiling water over the grounds. Leaving their drinks on the counter to steep, she took a quick shower, re-messed her messy bun, and put her phone and small wallet in her jeans pocket.

A few minutes later, she handed Nephi a warm cup of cacao with cream and settled into the Adirondack next to him, enjoying the feeling of her warm mug.

"This is really good," he said.

She nodded, smiling, and turned her attention to the bay, the gulls, the sound of the ocean, and tried to soak in this peaceful moment.

Nephi gulped his cup down. "Okay. Let's get this show on the road. How are we getting to the bookstore?"

Ivy took another slow sip. "I have no idea."

"What? No Rover? How do you get down the mountain?" Nephi asked. He sat forward, scratched the stubble on his face and watched her, waiting for an answer.

"I need to text Anderson and see if we can borrow the Range Rover."

"I thought the Rover was yours to drive?" Nephi asked.

"I did too." Ivy shrugged, took her cell phone out of her back pocket, and sent a text to Anderson. By the time she stood to put her mug in the sink, he'd replied. "We can use the Rover. They've already left this morning, and he isn't planning on going anywhere today."

Ivy typed another short text. She only had to wait a short moment before her phone vibrated. "He changed his mind. He wants to go with us and talk about what happened on the boat."

"You mean solve a murder mystery, right?" Nephi asked with one brow raised.

She left him hanging and chuckled. She nodded her head towards Knightly House, and he followed her across the lawn to the garage. Anderson joined them. He sat in the driver's seat, and she suppressed a smile. *One more day without a car.*

18

JUST PEACHY

Nephi held the screen door to the Balefire Bay Book and Tea Shop open for Ivy. The door squeaked like the Knightly House Library door before slamming shut behind her. She loved that sound. It had become the sound of coming home to family.

"Hey," Jenny called from behind the bookstore counter. "Do you want me to light a fire?"

"I can do it." Ivy smiled at Nephi. "Watch me now." She walked through the circle of overstuffed chairs to the stone fireplace, reached behind a plant on the mantle and flipped a switch, lighting the gas log. "Tah dah!"

He smiled with his eyes. Anderson called from Aggie's tea counter. "The usual?" She nodded. "Nephi, what will you have?"

"I'm good." He sat in the chair closest to the fire.

Aggie brought Nephi a plate with a large piping hot cinnamon roll. "Fresh from the oven."

"Is it safe? Do you have a royal taster?" Nephi asked.

Aggie huffed, took the plate out of his hands, and handed the plate to Ivy.

Butter and frosting were melting on top.

"Oh! I smell something new," Ivy said. She sniffed loudly, holding the warm plate tightly and looking at Nephi out of the corner of her eye. "Peach! Did you add peaches to the frosting and filling?"

Nephi snatched the plate, roll and all, from Ivy's hands. "Mine."

"I just wanted to see it," Ivy laughed.

"I call it a peach cobbler roll." Aggie smiled proudly and sat down across from the fire next to Anderson.

"I want the recipe," Ivy said.

"Over my... well. No." Aggie threw her head back and laughed. "I am thrilled to have baked something that will keep you up at night guessing."

"You are torturing me." Ivy shook her head.

"Aren't I just!" Aggie said.

"What brings this group of trouble together today?" Jenny asked.

"Murder," Aggie said.

Jenny's brows raised. "Are you sure? After all, Gladys could have grabbed the wrong roll. Rhoda was the target, in my opinion, and I don't think Conner's handsome deckhand pushed anyone over."

Ivy spoke up. "I agree. And yes, I tend to be a murder magnet or see it everywhere, but this time I am right. If someone pushed Rhoda overboard, we need to figure out who that person is before they try again and succeed at murder, or before Nephi gets blamed for something he didn't do."

"Pushing Rhoda? Do we need to stop them, really?" Nephi asked. He raised one brow and tipped his head. Aggie laughed right out loud. Most of the group snickered.

"Come on now." Anderson cleared his throat. He spoke so rarely in a group setting; it silenced the room. "People need means, motive and opportunity to commit murder. Does it really matter whether someone deserves it or not? And if that isn't the case, who is on the official murder committee and when are they going to vote to do away with me due to bad cooking or an overdue library book?"

"You have an overdue library book? No! Not you?" Aggie said, laughing at her own joke. Anderson rolled his eyes, remaining serious. "Conner. Can you tell us where everything stands with Gladys' death?"

"Not a fair question. You know I can't talk about an open investigation. Read her obituary," Conner said.

Vera plopped into a chair without her usual smile. She adjusted her duty belt, pushed her red curls back and said, "Well, I'll tell you."

"Vera," Conner said.

Vera put her nose in the air. "What? There is no investigation. The family flat refused to let the medical examiner do an autopsy and the judge said there wasn't enough evidence to sign a search warrant or order an autopsy, especially in light of Gladys' health history. We also didn't collect roll pieces. The investigation is as dead as Gladys."

"Will they process the other evidence from the scene?" Ivy asked.

Vera shrugged and shook her head.

Frustration knotted Ivy's stomach. "Reginald and Petunia said no to an autopsy? Why wouldn't they want to know what happened to her? I don't believe it. They aren't strong enough to stand up in a stiff wind! Why? Were they threatened?"

Vera frowned and shook her head in agreement with Ivy. "I don't know, but I wondered the same thing, myself. Only a few days after Gladys died, Reginald bought a nice extended cab truck for the flower shop from the owner of the gas station."

Ivy tried to picture Reginald driving a big truck. All she could envision was arthritic knuckles clutching the wheel. "When is the funeral?"

"Ain't gonna be one," Vera said. "She's already been cremated, and her ashes were spread in her garden and around her beloved one-hundred-year-old plant. Her online social media accounts were also closed."

"She was paid from her social media account. Would Reginald or Petunia know how to close social media accounts, and why didn't they just make them memorial accounts?" Ivy asked.

"If they had help buying the truck, closing accounts, and the like, we need to look closer," Aggie said.

"Agreed," Ivy said. "Does anyone feel comfortable talking to Petunia?"

The room was silent.

"Oh, for heaven's sake. Ivy and I will." Aggie sat back.

Ivy held colorful spreadsheets. "Can everyone agree not to share what I am about to give you with anyone?"

They all nodded in agreement before she passed them around the circle.

"I thought we needed a murder board. I couldn't sleep last night, so I put this together. It only took a few minutes. I can share what we know so far. Then, if we all pool our knowledge, we might know more than we think we do."

"You just whipped this out?" Vera said.

Ivy shrugged. "I am sending you all a link to the document on a drive. That will allow you to add what you know." She copied and texted the link in a group text. "I have the names of people with motives at the top of each column. Their motive is below their name, and what we know about them in relation to the cinnamon roll in brown ink, the boat in blue, and miscellaneous in black." She looked up to see if they were following.

Aggie's eyes were big and round. "How do you do that on your phone? You have an app?"

"Well, kind of. Does anyone want me to help them set up their drive?" Ivy asked. Almost every hand shot up. She sighed and forced a smile. "No problem."

She gave the group a minute to look blankly at their spreadsheets. "Let's stick with paper for now. I can make notes on mine. Reginald is up first because the spouse is usually the culprit. What would his motive be?" Ivy said.

Vera raised her hand.

"You don't need to raise your hand," Ivy snickered.

Vera put her gum in a tissue and thought for a moment. "I believe she was a very hard woman to live with. From what I know, she verbally and emotionally abused him one hundred percent of the time. I don't think I ever saw her have a kind word to say to or about poor Reginald. Is that a motive?"

Ivy looked around the room.

"I couldn't live with her, and I doubt many could, but wouldn't he just leave her?" Anderson asked.

"Who controlled the family's money?" Ivy asked.

"I can answer that one," Jenny offered from her seat at the register. A tourist walked into the bookstore. They all waited, silently, until they disappeared in the stacks. "Sometimes, when I would run a deposit to the bank for the store, I would run into Gladys in the bank. I saw her deposit slip and noticed they were business checks printed over a photo of a field of daisies. I asked her if Reginald was okay using flowery checks. She said he wasn't on her account and that she had to do everything for him. She ran things and what he liked didn't matter."

"Maybe he didn't want to manage their money," Conner said.

"He might not have known how. Money is a motive. What do you all think?" Ivy asked.

"I should let the chief know," Conner said.

Vera put a new piece of gum in her mouth. "He already knows. A little while after the incident, I did an extensive interview with Reginald. He said he was having trouble getting their money out of the bank because the shop's money and their account were both in her name. He was using a credit card he'd found with her name on it when the bank called him. He didn't know what to do. I gave him the phone number of a few attorneys that might be able to help him."

"That's rough," Nephi said.

"And now he has a new truck? Not too rough," Ivy said. "Even though men are most likely to commit murder. Statistically, poison is a weapon women use more than men. Are there any other women in his life? Other than Petunia?"

"He doesn't have that much energy," Vera said.

"Hey now. Play nice," Aggie said.

"I don't believe Reginald is a cold-blooded killer, and he wasn't on the boat. Aren't we looking for someone who was in both places?" Anderson asked.

Ivy chewed her lip for a moment. "Only if the incidents are related. If the boat is an accident or not related, he is still a suspect. That's what complicates everything. I think we need to look at both incidents equally. What do you all think?"

"I agree one hundred percent. We need to gather all the information before we come to any conclusions and not ignore either incident. I just wish the chief felt the same way," Conner said.

"Money and emotional abuse are motives." Ivy chewed on her pen, thinking, until she realized what she was doing, and blushed. "I say we keep Reginald on the board until we find a legitimate reason for him to decline the autopsy and an explanation for the new truck." Ivy made a note. "Next, he was only in one location. Does he seem like the type to poison his wife? Is there a will and life insurance policy? We need to find answers to these questions." Her chair felt like it was swallowing her. She moved to the edge and crossed her legs, pulling a book off the coffee table to use in her lap as a desk so she could take notes.

"You have everyone on here, but you don't have Xander or yourself," Vera said.

"Did I miss the morning murder club?"

Ivy's head snapped up when she heard the familiar voice of the chief. He had Conner's paper in his hands and stood over him, frowning.

Conner looked at his feet while his neck turned red. Vera didn't flinch. The room was silent.

The chief looked from face to face. "I know you think I don't care, but I do. Two things have deeply shifted my opinion. One. The money Reginald seems to have found prior to his wife's life insurance policy paying out and his refusal to do an autopsy. Two. The fact that Xander and Rhoda were just run off the road by a black SUV.

Ivy and Anderson jumped to their feet. The chief used one hand to motion them to sit back down. "Now. Now. Xander is fine. He's just a little black and blue. We think Rhoda may have a broken leg. They got a partial plate number that belongs to a rental. They are on the way to the hospital by ambulance."

Ivy dropped back into her seat; her heart was pounding in her ears. Here she is with friends and the man that was so good to her was in pain in an ambulance. She looked around the room at the wide-eyed faces and open mouths. "I feel so helpless. I wish I was at the hospital."

The chief took his hat off and looked at Ivy. "I understand, but by the time you drove the two hours to get there, they would be on their way back. But the accident is more evidence that Rhoda is the target."

"Conner, you and I will talk later," the chief said.

Conner slid down in his seat, red faced.

"He didn't do nothing, Chief. I told them about the autopsy, but there wasn't an open investigation, so why does it matter?" Vera said.

The chief sat down and leaned toward Vera. "Well, I'd talk to you, Vera, but it wouldn't change a thing." Conner chuckled but stopped when the chief gave him a sharp look. "Well now. Let's take a look at your spreadsheet." He took a pen out of his shirt pocket.

"We'll start with Xander. The boy hasn't got a motive, other than fear of an overbearing mother, and today he was with Rhoda and could have been killed." He ran a line down Xander's column. "And you, Ivy? You've taken far more abuse in your previous life than Rhoda has dished out so far. I doubt it's you. It would take more than Rhoda to set off Miss Marple here, right Ivy? Do you have a motive we don't know about?"

Ivy suppressed a smile. "If I did have a motive, I wouldn't tell you, Chief."

"Next, we have Petunia. She is like a wilted flower. Do you really think she has it in her?" He crossed Petunia off the list.

"I've seen Petunia and Brett together a few times," Jenny said.

"Okay, I'll make a note and Conner, you talk to Brett today."

"But it's Conner's day off," Vera said.

"He should have thought of that before he joined your little murder meeting," the chief said with a wink and a smile at Conner. "Next we have Ashley, his daughter, and George." The chief looked around the room. "This is where I think we should focus. They have the most to gain and they were at both locations. Now, the car accident is an open investigation. The next step is for me to talk to the rental company and get the name of the person who rented the car."

Feeling sheepish about not letting the chief know the book club was meeting–he was usually right in the middle of things with the book club–Ivy waited silently for instructions.

"Well, what do you think we should do, Miss Marple?" He looked directly at Ivy.

Ivy squirmed. *Well, here it goes. Miss Marple isn't pulling back. Give it to him straight.* "I have something to add. Someone slipped me a threat on torn paper into my back pocket during the chaos on the day Gladys was murdered. It said, *stop or die*. It's in my wallet." She took out her wallet and handed the paper to the chief.

The chief rubbed the back of his neck, sighed deeply, and said, "Why didn't you give it to us earlier?" He examined it front and back for a moment. "It's so tiny, I doubt we can pull a full print, unless it is mine or yours after handling it. The print is uniform and nondescript, like the person who wrote it tried to make the handwriting unidentifiable. It won't help, but it might have changed my mind sooner."

"I'm sorry, Chief. Everything was chaos when Gladys died. I wanted to. I should have," Ivy said.

The room was silent.

She squared her shoulders, determined to go on. "I know I made a mistake, but I have an idea. I think I should offer Charlotte some moral support. She was arguing with her husband, George, about his issues with gambling. I bet she can fill me in on George's and her father's financial status and what happens when he dies? And I think Nephi or Conner should confess their gambling addiction to George and invite him to a poker game. Maybe you could get them to talk about Rhoda,"

Nephi smiled at her. "Just what poker game is that?"

"The one you put together," Ivy said.

"I'll play poker. I'm not very good at it, but I want to help," Aggie said.

"She wins every time," Jenny said, chuckling.

Ivy smiled, knowing Aggie's little gray-haired lady look hid one of the sharpest minds in the room. "Hopefully, the conversation and planning will tell us all we need to know before we have to host an illegal game. Is gambling on poker illegal in Oregon?" She turned in her seat to face the chief and raised one eyebrow, using her best poker face.

He threw himself back in his chair and belly laughed. "I'll let you know when I'm ready to retire and you can

149

be the next chief, Miss Marple. Does it matter? We are not hosting a backroom poker game. We're setting a trap for a murderer."

19

ONCE UPON A TIME

"Miss Marple?" Nephi was still laughing as they walked with Anderson to the Range Rover.

Anderson was two steps ahead of them and looking at the phone in his hand. "I have dozens of texts. I am going to need to use the car to pick up Rhoda and Xander from the hospital. They're going to release them today. I'll run you home first."

"Just drop us at the bottom of the hill and we can walk," Ivy said.

Nephi's brows raised. "We can?"

"Or we could run and see who gets there first."

"I wouldn't want you to be left behind in the woods," Nephi gave her a buddy push and grabbed her waist before she went over. "Sorry. I forget you're a lightweight."

She punched him in the arm.

"Ow. And how pointy your knuckles are." Nephi's smile was contagious.

"Children. Get in and let's get going." Anderson climbed into the SUV and started the motor. Quietly, they squeezed into the car.

Anderson dropped them at the bottom of the winding gravel road that ran up the hill to the Sanctuary.

Nephi and Ivy stood side by side, looking up the steep drive to the cabins and homes on the point overshadowed by the lighthouse. Pine trees, ferns, and white spring daisies lined the dark road. Ivy looked up at Nephi and he looked down at her.

"Lions, tigers, and bears." Nephi quoted The Wizard of Oz with a straight face.

Ivy didn't miss a beat. "Oh, my."

They walked in silence for the first few minutes.

"I hate being without a car," Nephi said.

"I love walking."

One of his brows rose, and he narrowed his eyes as he studied her face. "You have a great poker face."

She laughed lightly. "Don't worry, hope is on the horizon, or coming from Portland."

"What do you mean?"

"You're just going to have to wait and see," Ivy said, smiling widely, with a glint in her eyes.

"I hate mysteries and surprises. Lately, it feels like life is one mystery after another," Nephi said.

She chuckled. "Yes, it does. Especially during the pandemic."

"Covid? How was it for you?" Nephi asked.

They walked. She put her hands in her pockets, and took one deliberate step after another, head down, watching her Hunter boots, lost in memories she never wanted to share with anyone, ever.

Here goes. She glanced up at him. He was mirroring her, his hands in his pocket, eyes down.

"You all were getting married and having your happily ever afters. Esther had Parker and their foundation. You had Paisley, her castle, and the entire staff. I ended up alone in an off-campus apartment at Harvard when the shutdown began. They closed everything—dorms, housing, all of it. Sure, I had keys, but I am not usually a rule breaker," Ivy said.

"Ha!" He looked down, smirking at her. "You broke some beauties when we were young."

She couldn't help but smile as she remembered sneaking into Esther and Nephi's second-story window over and over again. "All of my friends went home to their families or friends. My parents were in the middle of a huge project across the country. It felt like I was a lone survivor in a post-apocalyptic world. Even when I braved the streets and saw people, I was too shy to connect."

"You? Shy?"

"Hey. Who's telling this story?" She knew he was looking at her, but she couldn't make eye contact, or the tears resting in her eyes would escape. Her stomach rolled, and she wished she hadn't eaten Aggie's peach cobbler roll. "It was different. I was different when we all lived on the same street. Necanicum is a tiny town. We knew everyone, and everyone knew us. We felt like big fish in a small pond. At Harvard, surrounded by brilliant minds, I felt like plankton, or krill, just waiting to be eaten by

153

someone higher up the food chain than me. I thought they were all better than I was."

"Is that when you left and came here?" Nephi asked.

Ivy shook her head no. "No, but that is when I met my ex, Ian."

"I remember hearing you had a quiet Covid wedding," Nephi said quietly. "We would have come, you know? Covid wouldn't have kept us away. Paisley would have chartered a flight, something."

"I didn't even think about asking. Besides, I was so in love, no one else mattered. He was a new detective living in Cambridge. He told me that in the past, he'd led a military group assigned to do humanitarian work in Africa. That's where he met his close friends."

"He sounds like a great guy. What went wrong?" Nephi asked.

"We weren't married long before I realized a lot of his life was a black hole of secrets. You know how curious I am? I can never leave a mystery alone. I learned that while he was in Africa, he was caught up and sucked into sex trafficking by an extremely dangerous black ops group. I'm still afraid of being found and killed by someone from his world and I always will be," Ivy said.

"What Conner said makes it sound like they already found you."

"My ex and his close buddies did. They took Conner's boat from him during a charter and sank it, so I don't know if they got the word out or if it just stayed with them. He might have been trying to cover up the fact that he'd lost control of his wife who knew too much."

"Is it safe to stay here if they found you before?" Nephi asked.

"Who knows? That wasn't the worst of it."

"There's more?" Nephi asked.

They walked, matched steps on gravel, her short legs stretching while he adjusted automatically to match her stride, as if they'd never left high school or were still children on the beach, building forts in the sun.

Ivy lost her battle with her tears. The dam broke. She said, "He murdered my parents. He ran them off the road on a mountain. It was horrible. He made sure I watched them die in their burning car." Her voice quivered. She stopped walking and burst into uncontrollable sobs.

He picked her up and held her like a baby, while they both cried as he walked toward the cabins with her in his arms.

Finally, she was in a place that was safe to let go and grieve with a person who knew and loved her parents almost as much as she did, who'd spent his childhood with them.

"I'm too heavy," Ivy said, but continued to cling to his neck, wet with his own tears.

He stopped and looked into her eyes. "I don't... I can't..." He took a jagged breath. "Nothing I can say..." He pulled her close, safe in his arms.

They looked at each other and he leaned in. In a flash she knew he wanted to kiss her, just as if they'd never been apart and were as intimate as she had wished for years.

She put her hand over his mouth. He pulled back. Guilt and history wrestled inside her. "I can't. I am going out with Xander."

The sound of tires on gravel broke the spell. They stepped off the road and he put her down carefully. She wiped her face with the back of her sleeve. He turned and hid his red face while a station wagon full of children passed them.

When the car was gone and the dust was still settling, he looked up the road, instead of at her and said, "I'm sorry. I... shouldn't have." They walked a little further in silence before he implored, "I don't want to ruin my favorite friendship."

She smiled up at him, sadly. This was the moment she waited years for and now all she could think about was Xander.

"What is the plan, Miss Marple?"

"I'm going to invite Charlotte to take a walk on the beach."

He nodded and took a deep breath. His eyes pulled the shades down and hid his emotions. She could read him like a book and knew he was putting it all–his history, her history– neatly into a box to contain it.

He squared his shoulders, readying himself for any-thing that came his way. His strength and courage were some of the reasons Ivy loved and deeply respected him.

She reached up and lightly patted his back. He jammed his hands into his pockets, and they walked on.

20

MULTIPLE CHOICE QUESTION

It was noon before Ivy and Nephi walked through the gates of the Sanctuary and put on their best game face. Ivy walked straight to the Knightly House door. She put in her code, opened the door and called, "Anybody home?"

No response.

Ivy's phone chimed. She looked at the notice.

Text from Xander: "I love you. Almost dying puts life in perspective."

She wanted to cry. She felt guilt and joy all at the same time. This was the first time he'd used those three little words to tell her he loved her. She wanted to write back and tell him that she loved him too, but she wasn't alone.

Ivy looked up from her phone to see Nephi reading the text over her shoulder.

"Nephi, I..."

He interrupted her. "You don't have to explain anything. I was wrong. I got caught up in the moment. Two friends mourning family. I understand."

He turned and walked toward his cabin, leaving Ivy on the porch with an open door. She closed her eyes. *Friend zoned. Back to normal.* She felt so torn. She'd spent so many years chasing Nephi and wishing he would kiss her and now that he had tried, even though she stopped him, the kiss still hung in the air, a mess made up of sweetness and crushing guilt. *I need to get a grip on reality. Friend. That's what I have. Accept it, Ivy. Friend.*

A noise inside the house startled her. *Wake up, Ivy. Pay attention. You're talking to yourself.*

Of course I am.

She slid silently through the door and slipped out of her boots before she walked in her stocking feet towards the open library door. She peeked inside the room and gasped in shock.

Brett and Petunia were sitting on the couch, locked in an embrace and kissing. Their heads whipped around in Ivy's direction. They jumped apart. Brett put his hands in his pockets. Petunia's eyes were as round as saucers.

21

COMFORT FOOD

"Please don't tell anyone!" Brett said.

Both their faces were ripening like strawberries on the vine. Silently, Ivy looked from one face to the other, and back again.

Petunia took a step back like a frightened deer. Brett's arm shot out. He pulled her to his side.

"How long have you two been... an item?" Ivy asked.

"An item?" Brett looked truly confused.

"Together."

"Oh." He looked at her. His hesitation made Ivy sure he was thinking about lying and looking to get her permission to talk.

"I won't tell your mom." *Just your brother.* She folded her arms around her waist and watched him squirm.

"Are you sure?" Brett studied her face.

She gave a quick nod.

"Okay," he said. "We've liked each other off and on since we were kids. When I would visit, we would run into each other. Her mom hated me, so we kept it a secret. Gladys hated anyone who wanted to date Petunia."

"Does she know Xander was supporting you financially?" Ivy asked.

Brett shrugged. "Why would that matter? I've worked and saved a little of my own." She smiled at him; he held her hand. "Now, Petunia has more money than I do."

Ivy tilted her head and looked at Petunia with questioning eyes.

"Mom controlled my accounts and spending. I've worked in the garden shop all my life. She started paying me when I was sixteen but wouldn't let me spend it."

"I opened a savings account for us," Brett said.

"Doesn't a minor need an adult signature or approval when they open an account?" Ivy asked.

"Yes. I signed her dad's name," Brett said.

Ivy closed her eyes and shook her head. "How much does she have?"

"So far, we only have about ten thousand. We needed more to leave this place." Brett stood up to his full height.

"Oh yeah?" Ivy asked. "Where do you plan to go?"

"We'd planned to go to Portland. But now we don't need to leave," Brett said.

"Does your mother know about you two?" Ivy asked.

Brett's face clouded over. "So, what if she doesn't? Petunia's mother hates my mom. They have a long history of nasty arguments."

Ivy thought for a moment and decided to change the subject. "Did you hear about the accident?"

Brett nodded.

"They should be home soon. Anderson went to pick them up," Ivy said.

Petunia's eyes opened wide. "I have to go," she whispered and ran past Ivy and out the patio door.

Ivy called after her. "Do you need a ride?"

"She has her dad's truck hidden down the road outside the gate. She isn't ready to have Mom know we're dating. Mom sued Gladys. Petunia's still angry about it."

"I heard about that. I hear the truck is nice. How did he come up with the money?" Ivy asked.

Brett didn't answer.

She was losing ground. "Brett, I worry about Petunia. Do her parents abuse her?"

He frowned, but he didn't leave. She waited patiently and watched the wheels in his head spin while he stared at her and bit his lip. After what felt like a long game of chicken, he was the first to speak.

"Her mother was awful. The best thing that ever happened to Petunia was having Gladys's die. Someone should have killed her long ago."

Ivy gave away her shock with a gasp. "Do you think she was murdered?"

"We all do. Who wouldn't want to do her in? I mean, I wouldn't actually do it, but I understand it." Brett chuckled low and slow, shaking his head.

"Would Petunia do it? Was it that bad? I mean if she was abused, a judge might be lenient or understanding. Did she report it to anyone?" She didn't move. It was like talking to a skittish deer.

"Petunia wouldn't report it. I've wanted to, but our moms would kill us if they'd found what we were planning."

Ivy decided to be blunt. "Who do you think killed her mother?"

He looked down but smiled. "No clue."

She didn't believe him. "Brett, I will think about keeping this from your mother, but only if you tell me who gave Reginald the money for the truck?"

"I honestly don't know. The night she died, someone dropped a manilla envelope on the garden store's counter with a note that told him to cremate his wife without further investigation or an autopsy, and they would make it worth his while. He did what they asked. Another manilla envelope showed up and it was full of cash. He bought the truck from the corner gas station owner that day."

"Hello!" Rhoda bellowed from the front door. Brett looked panicked and ran toward the front door to meet his mother, while Ivy slid out the patio door and jogged to her cabin.

Ivy's cabin seemed empty after the chaos of the morning. She stood just inside the doorway, scanning the clean space, when her stomach growled loudly. *Comfort food. I need comfort food.*

She remembered Aggie's latest creation, opened her cabinet door and found just the thing: a can of peaches.

Knowing it was a long shot, she called Aggie. "Hey."

"Are they back yet? Do we know if Xander was hurt or Rhoda? I am really concerned for the two of them. The mountain roads are deadly," Aggie asked.

"They really are. I did hear from Anderson. He said Xander has some angry looking contusions, and Rhoda may have broken a bone in her leg and possibly her arm. I was just wishing for a snuggle from Judy when I remembered the second-best thing," Ivy said.

"Little Miss Judy sure loves you. What comes in second?" Aggie asked.

"Trying out a new recipe and comfort food," Ivy's voice went up as she turned her statement into a question.

"I get it now. You don't want a friend to talk to. You want my secret recipe." Aggie laughed loudly.

"I do love talking to you, but you know baking puts me in my Zen space," Ivy said.

"Yes, I do. I know because I am the same way with baking and my cat. I'll be right over." Aggie hung up before Ivy could protest. She put water on to boil, loaded up her French press with pumpkin spice cacao, and got out her selection of herbal teas.

By the time Aggie's car pulled to a stop in front of the cabin, Ivy's hair was up, and she was wearing a white apron over her black shirt and jeans.

Aggie let herself in, carrying a wicker basket of supplies. "I didn't know if you had the right kind of peaches and ingredients, so I brought you some home-canned peaches. I went all the way to Hood River last year and picked some of the sweetest peaches I've ever eaten."

"Yum!" Ivy put away her tin can of peaches.

"We need your biggest bowl for my quick roll recipe," Aggie said.

Ivy got out her large four-quart vintage yellow Pyrex mixing bowl. "Is this big enough?"

"No, but we can half the recipe," Aggie said. She turned on Ivy's warm tap and began her lesson. " Do you have a candy thermometer? The water needs to be 110 degrees to make the yeast happy. They love their pool warm, not hot. Do you have honey?"

Ivy got out the small jar of meadow foam flavored honey she'd purchased at the Saturday Market and a thermometer.

"Lovely. Meadow foam is my favorite flavor. It's mellow and doesn't overwhelm the rolls." She put three tablespoons in the water and gave it a quick swirl. "I like my bread sweet. You can also use a quarter cup of white processed sugar, but why ruin quality rolls?" She winked at Ivy. "Now to add the yeast. Here you go, fellas. I hope you love the pool. Remember, they love a warm pool, not a hot tub."

Ivy chuckled and measured out the yeast from a bag in her freezer. "I'd like a hot tub, a warm pool, anything with water."

"Especially a pool like Xander's, with a view," Aggie smiled. "Alas, I am past public swimsuits."

"Do you ever really get past swimming and swimsuits?" Ivy asked.

"Me and Jessica like to take our wrinkled skin suits and swim in our undies and bras by the moonlight in Pirates Cove."

Ivy's mouth fell open, and her brows shot up. She covered her mouth, trying not to laugh. "I'm getting a visual."

"Oh, tosh. There is nothing wrong with it. We bring the littles who once swam in their PJs. It's a family tradition we started years ago."

Ivy bit her lip, but a giggle snuck out. "Did Conner and Jenny join in the fun?"

"Jenny still does, but Conner says he has to maintain his dignity as a law enforcement officer. He can't be caught swimming in the moonlight in his underwear. I told him he'd be fine as long as he didn't wear his Snoopy boxers."

That was all it took to send both women into peals of laughter and wipe away the stress of the day.

22

— · —

MIDNIGHT BOOK CLUB

Conner and the chief pulled up to Nephi's cabin just as Aggie and Ivy arrived. Aggie held a tray of warm peach cobbler rolls and Ivy knocked on the door. The chief got out and caught up to them.

"Evening, Chief," Aggie said.

"Aggie. Ivy. I have solved a mystery. I know exactly what is under the foil on that tray."

Nephi opened the door and his brows rose. Without missing a beat, he said, "What am I smelling? Peach rolls?" He swung the door wide open. "Come in. I'll pour us all glasses of the hard stuff, milk. That's all I have to offer." Nephi laughed at his own joke.

The chief didn't smile. He and Conner pushed past Nephi.

"Ivy. Aggie. I've been thinking. We all feel safe in Balefire, but you shouldn't be out alone, walking at night. We've got a killer in town," the chief said.

Nephi's hands curled into fists. "I would never hurt them! We're ..."

The chief held up both hands, motioning Nephi to sit down on the living room couch. "No one said a word about you."

Ivy sat down on the couch, and Nephi sat next to her. The chief remained standing. "The rental car was rented with Rhoda's husband, Ashley's, credit card and ID."

Ivy's brows met in the middle. "Ashley? I'm surprised. He's too smart to rent a car and use it in a crime."

"I agree," the chief said. "Turns out it was done online with deskless service. In other words, no one got a good look at him and the airport security that was supposed to make sure his ID matched the name on his rental receipt was on the phone when he let the driver through. He tried to tell me that the driver hid his face from the camera when his boss asked if he'd been on his cell again. He confessed to being distracted, so we sent for their CCTV. You can't see the person's face. It's a man, I think, but they have a hood, hat, and jacket on, with dark glasses."

Ivy threw herself back against the couch and looked up at Nephi. "Great. Another dead end."

"Is it? I talked to Ashley, and he said he was with Brett watching the dories because it looks like, and I quote, 'Jolly good fun.' Brett confirmed they were together talking to the dory owners."

"So why isn't it a dead end?" Ivy asked.

The chief took his hat off, scratched his head, and said, "I think it narrows things down a bit. There aren't many people that would have access to his credit card.

I think it shortens our list of suspects right down to the Knightly House."

"Don't you think anyone could get his credit card number online and use it?" Nephi asked.

"The car was rented with his passport. It appears to be authentic, or not fake. They have a photo of his passport that matched the one used at the airport," Conner said. "I think it rules out Gladys' family. They wouldn't have access to Knightly House and Ashley's passport. If he'd lost it in town, he would have reported it stolen."

Ivy bit her lip and slid forward on the couch. "Well... as it turns out, they have had access to the house. I just walked in on Brett and Petunia in a lip lock in the library. No one else was home. If Ashley left his passport at the house, she might have been able to use it or get a photo. I promised not to tell his mother, but knew I would tell you."

"Criminently, it puts us right back where we started," the chief said.

"Not exactly," Ivy said. "Brett said that the money for the truck was delivered after Reginald cancelled or stopped the autopsy. Brett said it started with an envelope of money and a letter instructing Reginald to stop the autopsy. If he did, he would get more money, and if he didn't, he would regret it. Brett said they don't know who made the payments or why. It proves that Reginald's money came from the killer. The perpetrator knew you could confirm it was murder with an autopsy. By paying Reginald, they stopped you from finding out what killed Gladys and bought themselves some time to kill Rhoda. The only other explanation would be that Reginald and Petunia lied to Brett. The money shows they aren't the killers; the killer is paying them. They could also be blackmailing the killer."

"I agree. We can drop Reginald and Petunia as suspects. We have no evidence Gladys died of anything other than natural causes, and they weren't on the boat," the chief said.

"It also means that whoever paid them off has enough liquid cash to pay someone else to do their dirty work," Ivy said.

The chief took off his glasses and cleaned them for a moment. "How do we know that isn't you, Nephi?"

Nephi shot forward on the couch and frowned. "I could have taken off at any time after I was dropped here. When will my cooperation buy me some respect?"

"Don't stew. Vera checked your finances. You had money once. Now you owe money. She couldn't find a way for you to pay off Reginald or afford a rental. Boy, you are so poor, you owe your ex a lifetime of hard work. However, murderers have been known to help in the search for their victims or insert themselves into the investigation to interfere with it."

The chief held his glasses up, checked the lens, and said, "Call Anderson. We need him to help us with our little setup. Ivy, I need you to invite Charlotte to go for a walk on the beach and see what you can learn. Take Conner with you." He put his glasses on and pocketed his off-white handkerchief.

"Won't she think it's odd if I bring Conner? Nephi would be more natural and Xander even better," Ivy said.

The sound of nails scratching the door made Ivy smile. *Finally, someone I can love and who loves me back.* Judy scratched the door while someone knocked. Nephi opened the door and stood back. Judy sprinted across the room and leapt into Ivy's arms and licked her face.

Ivy turned her head away, trying to avoid Judy's wet tongue. "How are you, my lovely?" Ivy said. Judy licked her nose. She laughed and wiped her nose off with her sleeve and wrapped Judy up in a warm hug. Then she looked up.

Anderson and Xander filled the doorway. Xander leaned against Anderson's shoulder with his mouth open, breathing heavily, his brows meeting in the middle over a bruise across his swollen nose. Anderson had his arm around Xander. He walked him to the sofa. Xander put an ice bag on his nose and winced.

"Ivy?" Xander patted the couch next to him and reached out, motioning for her to join him.

Ivy's entire body relaxed. He looked awful, but he was going to be okay. "You look terrible. Why aren't you home resting?" Ivy sat down by Xander. Xander's sad smile and brave face touched her deeply. She held his hand, afraid to hurt him if she hugged him.

Nephi frowned, shoved his hands in his pockets and leaned on the far wall.

Xander pulled her into a tight side hug, winced in pain, and said softly, "I am so glad you weren't in the car with us. It was awful. You don't mind if we use the Rover, do you?"

Ivy smiled to herself, knowing everything would be fine and wondering when her car would arrive. "Not at all."

The chief sighed. "Tell us what happened?"

"I hate to sound cliché, but it happened so fast I was more focused on not going off the road and down a steep embankment, rather than getting a description of the driver. It could have been fatal. I think the car is a total loss."

"I can't tell you how happy we are that you didn't die," Vera said.

"Me too," Xander said. "Don't make me laugh. It hurts too much."

"Can I get you something to eat? Milk?" Aggie asked.

Xander looked at her and smiled. "Thank you, but I'm not hungry."

"We identified the rental car that hit you," the chief said. "It was rented by your new stepfather. I think he's our man."

"That's wrong. I've spent time with Ashley. He isn't a killer, and he isn't organized enough to pull off something like this." Xander shook his head, his brows furrowed. "I don't believe it. My mother doesn't deserve to have another marriage fall apart. Someone has to stand by her. I guess it's me."

"He could have had help or even hired someone," the chief replied. "We have to look at all possibilities, including considering the possibility that it might be one of us."

Xander's face clouded over. "For all you know, it was a random drunk." The room was silent.

"We have the plates, witnesses," Conner said quietly, shaking his head.

Xander struggled to get to his feet. Ivy helped him stand. He walked proudly but slowly toward the door, pushing gently past Anderson. Anderson opened the door and held it for him. He turned and looked over his shoulder at Ivy. "Are you coming?"

Ivy shook her head, no. "Aggie, and I made everyone rolls." It was a lame excuse. They both knew it.

Xander's chin trembled. His lips pressed hard together while his eyes narrowed. "I recognize a book club meeting when I see one. Now I know what it's like to be on the other end of your scrutiny. Is that why I wasn't invited? Sometimes people and relationships are more important than solving a crime, Ivy. Anderson! Are you coming?"

"I want to, but I honestly think I can do you more good here."

He spun around and left, slamming the door, rattling the windows.

"Well," Aggie said. "He has a bit of his mom in him, after all. Let's have some rolls."

Ivy stood facing the door, frozen, her heart aching, and arguing with herself. *Go after him. You don't know*

172

him as well as you thought you did. He's exhausted. You are not making excuses. You didn't lose control. You made a choice and are breaking Xander's heart. If you don't go now, it will be too late. She looked over her shoulder at Nephi, who looked back, right through her soul. Everyone was sampling the rolls when she turned and, with Judy at her heels, quietly went out the door and closed it.

Judy barked at Xander, running to catch up to him. He hadn't gone very far. Xander stopped in the moonlight and was leaning on a tree. He saw her and folded his arms, eyes narrowed. Ivy wanted to help him, but hesitated. She felt his angry energy crackling in the air.

Ivy didn't know what to say. *What can I say? He's right. We were meeting without him.* And then she remembered the moment she'd allowed herself to get too close to Nephi. The moment her heart betrayed Xander.

He turned and continued hobbling toward the house. She caught up to him and reached out to help him walk. He flinched and pulled away, slowly, determined, moving toward the patio doors to the library.

She followed him inside, passed him, and while he limped to the leather couch facing the ocean, she locked the library door to give him some privacy. As he dropped onto the sofa, she went to the fireplace near the patio doors and put a match to a fire Anderson had carefully laid in readiness for some future need. She blew on it for a moment until it was burning steadily before she turned to look at Xander.

Xander sat silently on the couch with his head in his hands. Judy curled next to him, with a paw on his leg.

Is he crying? She sat next to him and quietly waited. When he finally looked at her, his eyes glistened above his firmly pressed lips.

"Why are you even here?" Xander asked. "Why haven't you two driven away?"

"Why would I? I love our life here."

"I felt there was something between you. You have history. Years of it." His hands clenched into fists and his voice broke when he said, "Everyone in the room knows what you felt about him when you were in school."

Ivy quickly looked down, sure he was looking through her soul, not knowing what to say.

He tried to stand up, groaned in pain, and fell back on the couch.

Without words, she turned to him and wrapped her arms around his neck and pulled him to her. He laid his head in her lap and wept.

23

WHEN THE FIRE DIES

The fire was embers, the moon was full. A million stars lit the night sky. Xander's breathing was as steady as the waves against the cliff. Judy and her new friend, Sandy, slept intertwined in the wicker dog basket by the fire.

Somewhere in the quiet moments of holding Xander, her heart burned, filled with feelings for this strong man with a tender heart.

She looked at Xander's beautiful but bruised face, "I love you," she whispered. She kissed him softly, wanting to reassure him. She pulled a blanket over him and left him resting while the sea continued rolling in and out, the same and yet ever changing.

She closed the patio doors and checked the time on her watch. She'd been there two hours. Although she was sure they were done meeting, she headed towards Nephi's cabin. The moon shone bright enough to light her way to the forest's edge, where she used her cell flashlight and followed the short path to Nephi's door.

Conner's car was still parked outside the cabin. She knocked quietly. Nephi opened the door and without a word or expression like a serious poker player, stood back and waited, locking eyes with her until she was inside.

"I should be going," Conner stood.

"Wait. Stay," Ivy said. "Tell me what I missed. Did you learn more?" She wanted Conner to update her. She knew he would cover everything thoroughly, and she trusted him not to pull any punches or hold anything back.

Conner nodded. "Nephi and I are going to set up an illegal poker game on the boat. We are going to wire the whole boat and see if we can get George talking before the game. Aggie is taking peach rolls to Reginald at the garden store and is going to try to get him talking. After that, you and Aggie will make a roll and soup delivery to the house to check on Rhoda and chat. Then the chief wants you to take that walk with Charlotte and learn everything you can about her husband before the game."

"Bagels. I've never seen the chief ask for help like this. He must be positive that George is our main suspect," Ivy said.

Ivy's phone chimed, making her jump. She read the text; a broad smile spread across her face. For the first time that night, her heart lifted. "Do you two want to have some fun?" She wiggled her brows, beaming.

Nephi's eyes rolled. "If I remember correctly, your idea of fun either includes test tubes and protective eye wear or chasing a serial killer."

They laughed together, dispelling the heaviness in the room.

"So she wasn't that different when she was a kid?" Conner asked. "Did she ever follow the rules?"

"Get your coats, men. We're going for a ride," Ivy said.

Conner raised one brow and cocked his head. Nephi folded his arms.

"Do you still drive like you did in high school?" Nephi asked.

"What? I was a great driver. Esther was the one that drove like a granny." Ivy went out the door with the laughter following her.

They crossed the lawn in the dark and walked down the drive to the gate. On the other side of the gate, her new Jeep idled. The auto transport truck driver turned it off, took her I.D., had her sign for delivery, and did some basic paperwork before he turned his flatbed around and drove away, leaving them with Ivy's new ride.

"Well, what do you think?" Ivy asked.

"When did you buy this?" Nephi asked.

"Online while you all slept. You can buy anything online, almost," Ivy said.

"Can I drive it?" Conner asked and tried to snatch the keys.

"Hey! I call dibs on the first drive," Ivy said. She looked at Nephi, hoping he would approve.

"See what I mean? I'm a church goer and my life is falling apart and you have everything. You don't even know if there is a God and you can order a car online," Nephi said.

"I don't have everything," Ivy said. She waited until his eyes met hers. "I don't have my parents. I've missed you and our friends, and until Balefire Bay, I've felt more alone in the world that you can possibly understand. You may question God, but the way I see it, he gave you everything. You have a mother and sister that would do anything for you. Hart and Esther and all our friends would go to the ends of the earth for you. You just have to talk to them."

He looked at his feet, his face shadowed in the dark. He didn't move. She couldn't breathe. *I can't stand the silence. Way to go, Ivy. Your sharp tongue has gone too far again.*

If you two are done with your mutual pity party, I would like to take a ride. Conner snatched the keys. "The Lord giveth and I taketh away!"

"Hey!" Ivy tried to get the keys back, and the mood lightened.

"Shotgun," Nephi said softly.

"That's more like it, dude. Get in and let's try out my new Jeep." Conner laughed and made Ivy get in back.

"You two are the worst," Ivy said. But she smiled broadly as she climbed in back, buckled up, and smelled that new used car smell. She took a deep breath and sighed. "Freedom at last."

Conner opened the sunroof and windows, spun the vehicle around and roared down the mountain, throwing Ivy back and forth in the back seat and pasting a silly grin on Nephi's face.

"Boys!" Ivy shouted over the motor. "If you wreck my new car by hitting an elk, I'm never baking you another cake!"

Conner slammed on the brakes, throwing her forward. He turned in his seat with a mischievous grin. "You wouldn't."

"Test me." She folded her arms.

"Alright, mom. I'll slow down." He rolled respectfully the rest of the way down the hill until he turned onto the highway and the moonlit bay opened up on the right.

It didn't matter how many times Ivy saw this view; it still made her heart burn with its magnificence. "Wait. Stop."

"Never," Conner chuckled.

"No, seriously. Stop." Ivy pointed to the garden store, the first business after the residential neighborhood.

Conner turned the lights off and coasted into the nearby driveway of a bed and breakfast.

"What time is it?" Nephi whispered.

Conner looked at his cell. "Crap. It's almost one am. I have a shift at seven. We should go. They probably forgot to turn the lights off. Who knows? Gladys isn't around to tell them what to do."

"Some police officer you are. Let me out," Ivy said. Conner got out and held the door for her. She quickly walked closer to the shop. *Glad I'm wearing black, but why am I bending over? I'm already short and it's not going to keep them from seeing me.* She smiled at her silliness. *I am probably wasting all our time.*

Her mother's voice suddenly interrupted her thoughts. "Trust yourself. A scientist first makes a hypothesis. Use your instincts, find patterns, and think outside the box and you will solve the mysteries of our world." It was something her mother told her often.

Ivy felt if she looked over her shoulder, she would see her parents standing behind her.

Melodic laughter, followed by a loud snort and more laughter, made her halt. Conner ran into her back. Nephi ran into his. When she looked over her shoulder Conner gave her a cheesy grin and Nephi shrugged smiling. If they could have seen her face in the dark, they would have seen her roll her eyes.

Slowly, they crept closer and stood against a laurel bush by the large front windows.

Ivy's head jerked back. She didn't know what she expected to see but this wasn't it.

A candlelight dinner was set in the middle of the flower section of the store. There was an opened wine bottle and half eaten dinner. Desdemona, wearing one of her notorious hot pink dresses, was sitting in Reginald's lap and they were friendly enough. Ivy backed up, tripping over Conner's feet.

"I can never unsee that," Ivy whispered as they trotted back to the Jeep.

"What did you think you'd see if you investigated a single man at night? Try being a patrol officer checking on Lover's Leap every shift." Conner laughed.

"You're laughing at me?" Ivy said.

"If he isn't, I am," Nephi said. "So, what did that prove?"

"Reginald may not have killed Gladys, but he isn't exactly the mild-mannered man I thought he was," Ivy said.

"Did he know Desdemona before Gladys died?" Conner asked.

"I kind of introduced her. I had flowers from the garden store at the Saturday Market. I showed her where their booth and shop was. I saw her give them the full Desdemona intro," Ivy said.

"There's a motive. Did she and Reginald spend time together before the death?" Conner asked.

"I doubt it. Gladys died a short time after that. But I have seen people jump into relationships quickly after a death," Ivy said.

"Do you think Reginald is that cold?" Nephi asked.

"There are men that get married fast after losing a spouse. Reginald is a catch. He has a successful business, or it looks that way. But I can't see him going after her," Conner said.

"I can see her going after him. She is bold," Ivy said.

"How do you know they haven't been connected before? She could be an old high school flame for all we know," Nephi said.

"I think I'm going to get my nails done tomorrow and have a chat with Desdemona," Ivy said.

"Let me know if you hear anything that the chief should know. Are you sure that's safe?" Conner asked.

"I guess... My turn to drive!" Ivy said and sprinted for the car.

"Shotgun," Conner called after her breaking the spell of quiet on a beautiful night.

Ivy pulled out and drove 101, still as amazed by the view as the first time she'd taken the drive at night.

24

— · —

BEST SAID IN THE DARK

Conner pulled away in his squad car, leaving Nephi and Ivy standing outside her cabin. Ivy should have felt the weight of a sleepless night, but she didn't. She felt as alive as a kid on Christmas morning.

"Ivy?"

"Yes."

"Can we talk for a minute?" Nephi said.

"Sure. Let's go on the back deck," Ivy said. He followed her around the side of the house and plopped in the Adirondack next to hers.

"I want to apologize again for trying to kiss you. You are obviously in some kind of relationship with Xander."

She chewed on her lip before exhaling loudly. "I am. But it's my fault too. I got too close. I gave into old feelings. When we were young, you were the handsome hero in my story."

"Yeah, I was pretty handsome, wasn't I?" He joked, wiggling his brows, but his face was bright red.

"Things were simpler then too. But you've met Xander. He is... There aren't enough words to explain how I feel about him and my respect for him. I know you felt the same way about your wife and probably always will. I feel guilty, because I never want to do anything I'm not proud of."

"Look. You deserve every happiness in the world. You are... well. You matter to me and you're a part of my family and have been since we were kids. It won't happen again," Nephi said.

She smiled but stayed silent, wanting to let him get everything off his chest he could.

He sighed heavily. "I'm sorry about your mom and dad. You reminded me that everyone has their trials. You're right. I need to wake up and stop feeling sorry for myself. God didn't do this to me. I did this to me."

"What if no one did it. What if it was a series of events, an accident?" Ivy asked.

"Then the universe is chaos and everything is a massive, stinking risk. I keep thinking if I hadn't pushed us to drive to the coast that night, or if the weather was different, or what if... You know?"

"I do know. If I hadn't married my ex, my parents would still be alive, so it's my fault, right?" Ivy said.

"No. It's his fault, his choice."

"I can't say that I am religious or know God, but I have often wished I had the connection you did, because when it happened, the first thing I did was fall to my knees and ask your God why. Why me? Why them? I begged for help," Ivy said.

"Did it come?" Nephi asked.

"Yes, ironically. Almost immediately, I remembered flyers in the bathrooms at Harvard and the women's shelter. Everything seemed to fall in place. When I got on the bus with Aggie, I ended up here."

"Aggie." Nephi chuckled and shook his head. They knuckle bumped. "Maybe she is an angel."

"She is in my book," Ivy said. "At least she and this town were the answer to a prayer uttered long before I arrived, if you could call it a prayer. The only way I learned to pray was at your family's dinner table. I almost closed with blessed food. Then I just stopped and listened. I didn't know what to say."

"You had to pray before you ate my big sister's cooking," Nephi said. They laughed softly together at the memories of his sister, Grace's, failed attempts to cook Sunday dinners.

"I should let you go to bed," Nephi said.

"Nephi? Maybe I don't know about God, but isn't a miracle something that couldn't or shouldn't have happened and changes everything?" Ivy asked.

"I guess," Nephi said.

"Could our bus rides with Aggie qualify as a miracle meant to bring us to this place at this moment in time," Ivy said.

Nephi stood up, looked down at her, and said, "Maybe there is a God after all."

25

NAILED IT

Ivy worked silently for several hours in the Knightly House Library. Her last task was valuing antiquarian books the Crow had dropped by earlier, hoping Xander would buy them. Xander always wanted to know the authenticity, value, and provenance of anything he chose to purchase.

The first book presented a challenge. She translated enough words with a translation app to know it was a Hebrew Bible. She decided to ask Xander if he was interested before she did any more work on it.

The next five books were in German. She planned to use the translator to find as much information as possible. She was certain the oldest Bible was dated 1829. There was also a prayer book in German dated 1890.

A handwritten note in German slipped out of the prayer book. She typed the note's text into the translator app. After only a few lines, she realized it was a love letter to a Nazi soldier dated 1945, January 7, before the Germans surrendered to the Allies in May1945.

Ivy sat back looking at the books on her desk. She got online and dove into that period of time. The books troubled her, but she couldn't put her finger on what was bothering her.

She picked up the last book. It was newer than the others. Pages were stuck together. There were wear marks that led her to feel the pages. There was something pasted in between them. Brown paper was pasted inside the front and back of the book. The glue on the back cover was so old and dry it was pulling away on the right-hand corner. She gently pulled the paper back.

There was a black and white photo hidden under the brown paper. Ivy gasped, put her hand over her mouth and stood up so fast, she knocked her chair over backward. The hair on the nape of her neck raised. She held out her hand. It was shaking as she slammed the book shut.

She didn't know what concentration camp was in the photo, but she did know she never wanted to see it again, or any other photo hidden in the book.

Where did the Crow find these books? The truth surfaced and fell together like a puzzle. She knew where the Crow found the books. She was sure he'd found them in the church basement when he broke in and killed the caretaker. And if she was right, the caretaker's death had nothing to do with Gladys' death, or the attempts made on Rhoda's life.

I should leave the church break-in alone until we figure out what's happening with Rhoda. Even as she thought it, she knew she couldn't do it. Something about

187

having an unsolved mystery or murder made her feel like the universe was chaos and that was a terrifying thought. When she solved a mystery, the world had reason and logic again. It felt safer and predictable.

She thought about texting the chief, but decided she should talk to Xander first. He agreed to look at the books, and she worked for him. He might know more.

She called Xander and got his voicemail. She left a short message asking him to call her back. She set the books back in their box and put them under her desk and out of sight.

She needed a break.

She usually had some kind of music playing while she worked, but the entire house had been so still when she slipped in the back door, that she couldn't bring herself to break the spell. The only sign of life was Judy, who had decided to act as a footwarmer, sleeping soundly on her left foot.

Ivy had hoped to see Charlotte, so she could invite her to go on a walk with her. She smelled coffee at one point and heard some chatter on the other side of the library door, but she felt apprehensive. Last night had been a raw and intimate moment for Xander.

She didn't know quite how he would feel in the light of day. Before, she'd always been happy and content here, feeling his presence even when he traveled. They texted often. Today, she couldn't feel him nearby at all and her phone was silent.

At lunch time, Ivy scooped up Judy, waking her. "Well girl. This is as good a time as any to get my nails done, don't you think?"

She looked up Desdemona's shop and called. "Hi Desdemona. Would you do my nails today? Do you have an opening?"

"Sugar, it's crickets here. Come on down. Maybe I'll throw in a massage just for the practice," Desdemona said.

"Thanks. I'm on my way." Ivy cracked the door open and listened to the sound of Anderson and Brett talking in the kitchen. She put Judy in the hall and pushed the door shut. Judy was scratching at the door when she left by the patio doors and wished desperately to be invisible. Everything felt so fragile.

As she walked closer to her new SUV, the happier she got. "My first solo trip."

Ivy studied Desdemona's shop from the car. The amount of work Desdemona had done to the old dockside kite shop to turn it into a spa was actually quite impressive.

The front glass doors had a wooden frame. The building was painted white. White blinds were down in the two front windows. *The Babes by the Bay Spa* sign was over the door in scrolling hot pink letters.

Ivy had to smile when she realized Desdemona had bedazzled the wooden doors. The frame around the window looked like it was covered in sequins. When she got closer, she realized every inch was covered in various sized small mirrors glued to the wood, which was painted silver behind them. The creativity surprised her.

A bell tinkled when she entered the spa waiting room. The room was also white, white floors, walls, ceiling, couches, and even white flowers on the receptionist's desk. The only colors in the room were the silver side tables and coffee table and the hot pink spa name on the wall behind the front desk.

Ivy felt the simple decor was tastefully done.

Then Desdemona emerged from the back in a hot pink jumpsuit with chandelier earrings large enough to light a four-person table at a restaurant. "Darlin! Come on back."

The back was similar to the front. Desdemona sat on one side of a table with what looked like a Dremel, lights, and safety goggles to Ivy. She stopped in her tracks, surprised at all the nail polish on the wall behind the table.

"I didn't realize nails were like an industrial art."

Desdemona cackled. "Oh sweetie, anyone who says they are a natural beauty is either you and Jenny, or lying. It takes power tools and work to keep a body up like mine. I told you, I am no spring chicken. Stick with me and you will look this good when you're a grandma."

"I didn't know that you're a grandma," Ivy said.

"Oh, not yet. But there is a baby on the way that will call me Nana someday."

"Congrats. Does the baby's family live close to you?" Ivy asked,

"Sort of. They live in Portland. Now, what color would you like?" She handed Ivy a metal ring with a hundred or so fake nails on it of just as many different colors.

Ivy picked it up, completely overwhelmed. "I was just thinking natural looking, you know, with square tips, short."

"You mean exactly like they are now?"

Idiot. "Well, no. I mean pretty. Mine are always chipped and ragged from typing and baking, you know?" Ivy said.

"I can certainly make them stronger, whiter, and healthier looking, but you are not putting my talent to its best use." Desdemona held up her hand displaying long pointed nails painted pink and silver to match the salon.

"They are definitely on brand," Ivy said. She smiled. "I type for my job and work with books. If Xander saw pointed nails touching a book from the dark ages, he would panic."

Desdemona threw her head back and laughed lightly. "I've been dating someone who likes to work in a garden. I had to order leather gloves in black. Can you imagine me in black? I met him while he was still married. Now that he's available, I'm ready to dig in the dirt."

"Do tell. Who is your new love interest?" Ivy said. She smiled broadly and winked. She was surprised to see

191

Desdemona's cheeks turn a shade that matched her pink lipstick.

Desdemona looked her in the eyes and sighed. "Can you keep a secret? I'm not quite ready to share it with the world, you know? One never knows if it will last."

"I am a great secret keeper," Ivy said. She immediately felt guilty. *I'm awful. It's too late to avoid sharing this secret.*

"Reginald. You know. He owns the garden shop."

Ivy feigned surprise. "Reginald? Really? He is always so quiet."

"You know what they say. It's the quiet ones you have to watch out for." Desdemona's eyes twinkled above her pink smile.

Ivy laughed. "Hey, now. I'm a quiet one."

"Exactly. Look at that handsome man you have all tied up in a pretty bow. You're going to end up in a castle overlooking town as a Mrs. instead of a librarian," Desdemona said. "I've watched a few others circling around him, waiting for him to make a mistake."

Ivy felt gut punched. "Is it that obvious?"

"It is to me," Desdemona said.

"It isn't to me. I don't trust my picker at all."

"I heard about the ex who came to town and sank Conner's boat."

It was Ivy's turn to be embarrassed. She felt her cheek and wasn't surprised when it was hot and probably red. "Everyone was so kind. I felt terrible that he'd followed me here."

"Hey now. It's not your fault, sweetie. I haven't heard one bad word about you. Anyone who shared it was telling me to keep an eye on you. This town loves you."

Ivy's brows rose while her heart warmed as much as her cheeks. "Really?"

"Oh yeah, baby girl. Everyone keeps their eye on you. The day your ex came to town was the day you became this town's girl, and they plan to protect you from any of his friends still floating around." Desdemona opened a drawer and took out a pair of pink cat eyeglasses and put them on, turned on a bright light, and gently took Ivy's hand and began filing her nails.

Get it together, Ivy. This is about her. "How did you meet Reginald?"

"He was hard to miss after his wife died. I had set up a standing order for white and pink hydrangea, daisies, or roses for the waiting room. I love flowers." She worked quickly and expertly on Ivy's right hand, followed by her left. "I went in to drop off a casserole and share my condolences. Petunia is such a shy little thing. I asked her to come down sometime and have her nails done for free. We chatted while Reg sat silently watching. When Petunia left, he took the casserole without saying a word. I was all the way to the door before he invited me to dinner to share the casserole with them. It was shepherd's pie and pretty large. He said they needed help eating it." She chuckled softly.

"It was nice of you to take them food."

"It's what you do when someone you know passes on." She brushed Ivy's fingers with a clear substance and then dipped them in pink powder, white for the tips, and placed them in and out of a light.

Ivy was silent, hoping Desdemona would say more.

"Petunia missed dinner. She was out with that Brett. She is so smitten." She looked up and winked at Ivy. "He's your boyfriend's brother, right?"

Ivy nodded and matched her smile.

"She's gone more and more. I love her but I did like having Reg to myself. The first thing he did was buy me this." She held out her arm. A silver cuff with one larger diamond in the middle and two small diamonds on either side. "Don't be impressed. He was very proud of the fact that it was authentic cubic zirconia." She threw her head back and laughed. "The folks at the jewelry store saw him coming miles away." She shook her head in disbelief. "I had a chat with them later. No one treats Reg like that."

"I saw he bought a brand-new truck," Ivy said.

"It looks new, and he calls it new, but it was gently used. Once again, they tried to take him, but this time he held his own. He knows vehicles. He's always wanted a truck like that," Desdemona said.

"It's beautiful. Did Gladys leave him money or life insurance?" Ivy knew this was a very personal question, but Desdemona seemed to trust her.

Desdemona sighed. "That woman. He is so beaten down. I had to help him sort her accounts. She left a will giving everything to him. She actually called Petunia a stupid girl in the will and said that's why she would need her father to manage her money for the rest of her life. Can you believe it? He hasn't received a life insurance payment yet. Leland, a local lawyer, is working on straightening things out. Everything was in her name. He didn't sign on a single account."

"That's awful. Did he even know what insurance or money there was?" Ivy said.

Desdemona stopped and looked at Ivy. It was the first time Ivy had seen her frown. If her brows could move, Ivy guessed they would have, but Botox kept them in place.

"He doesn't know how to handle his own money. But he can learn. Luckily, he told me he played cards and won some cash for the truck and basic expenses."

"I can't imagine winning that kind of money," Ivy said.

"I didn't really believe him and did a little snooping. I know better than to take someone at face value. He did go to a bar one night and play cards." She giggled. "He said it was the first time since he was in the military. I believe his story about meeting an Englishman there, mainly because of Xander's visitors. Besides, there are plenty of tourists in town. He told me the winnings paid for the truck."

"An Englishman? I wonder. Was it Ashley? Rhoda's husband?" Ivy tried to sound casual.

She tipped her blond head. "No. It was his daughter's husband."

"George?"

"That's the name the bartender gave me. But he wasn't sure he remembered right. I bet his wife was upset when he threw away so much money. Anyway, I encouraged

Reginald to get on with life. He didn't even want a funeral. After I listened to him talk about how Gladys treated him, I just wanted to kick her ash off the dock!" She laughed softly.

Ivy waited, silent, hoping for more.

"He promised me that he wouldn't gamble again, and as far as I know he's kept his promise." She cleaned the powder and table before she put a clear coat over Ivy's nails and put them under the light again. "I'm with him almost every night, so he hasn't had time. But let me tell you. One trip to a bar to play cards and we will have our first and last fight. There. All done."

"They're beautiful! My nails have never looked so good," Ivy said.

"Depending on how fast they grow they should last almost a month. If they grow fast, you can come in and get fixed up in two weeks." She stood up and led Ivy back to the lobby. "Thanks for listening to this old lady rattle on. It's nice to have someone to trust and talk to." She swept Ivy up in a hug.

Ivy knew Desdemona shouldn't trust her, but she couldn't help hugging her. "Funny how you can get to know someone as nice as you are over nail polish."

"You come back now," Desdemona said.

"I will." Ivy meant it.

26

Murder Seriously

The small silver bell attached to the door at the Balefire Book & Tea Shop rang, announcing Ivy's arrival. Jenny looked up from the newspaper she was reading at the register and Aggie waved at Ivy.

Ivy settled herself in a soft chair by the fire, facing Aggie. Jenny leaned on the back of Aggie's chair.

"What brings you in?" Jenny asked.

"I have just had the most unexpected conversation with Desdemona. Did Aggie tell you she was going to take rolls to Reginald?"

"Do tell," Jenny plopped herself on the love seat.

"Aggie, you can cancel the roll order and your trip to the garden store," Ivy said.

Aggie tilted her head and leaned forward, frowning. "What? I thought that was what the chief wanted us to do. Why?" She scratched her head, pulling a tuft of grey hair out of place.

"I have the scoop, without the bribe. Well, it did cost me these." She modeled her nails.

"They look nice," Aggie said.

"This is the first time I've had them done. Desdemona did them for me," Ivy said.

Jenny leaned toward Ivy and gently took her hand, looking closer. "Did she dip them? She did a wonderful job."

"Dip? I'm so confused. What has this to do with Reginald?" Aggie asked.

"Let her finish," Jenny said.

"So. It actually started last night. I bought a new car," Ivy said.

"What?" Jenny jumped to her feet, "Why didn't you lead with that? Did you buy a used one from Dudley's Used Drives in Rockaway?"

Ivy beamed. "No. I got it online! I purchased the whole thing virtually and had it delivered. It's a lifted SUV, 4-wheel drive and the cutest..."

"Girls!" Aggie interrupted them. "I am happy about your car, and all but what does this have to do with Reginald?"

Ivy shrugged. "Sorry. I just get giddy when I think about having my own car and my freedom back. So, Conner and Nephi went with me last night on its first drive. Well..." Ivy paused for a second and looked at Aggie. "Conner called first dibs as the first driver, Nephi yelled, 'shotgun,' leaving me sitting in the back seat of my own car."

"Rude," Jenny said.

"Girls... seriously. Back to Reginald. I'm dying of curiosity," Aggie said.

Ivy and Jenny grinned like schoolgirls at each other. Just a glance and she knew she and Jenny would be testing out her new ride.

"Okay. Anyway, It was late and dark. When we hit Highway 101, we saw lights on in the flower area of the garden store. Since we knew that we were looking at Reginald as a suspect in the cover up of his wife's murder, we stopped a little way away and snuck up to the windows. It's like a greenhouse, you know," Ivy said.

"We know." Aggie folded her arms in exasperation. "Give us the Reader's Digest version."

"What? What is the Reader's Digest version?" Jenny asked.

Aggie chuckled. "I forgot for a moment that I was old, and the Reader's Digests was before your time." She looked at Ivy who was smiling and shaking her head. "It means give us the condensed version, the highlights."

"The Reader's Digest was so last century," Ivy said. "You'll never guess what we saw."

"Ivy!"

"Oh. Sorry... again." Ivy grimaced. "Desdemona was in Reginald's lap, and they were snogging. I mean, you know, making out?" Ivy waited to see if her description had spanned the generation gap.

"No!" Aggie said.

Bingo. They understand. Ivy nodded. "Scout's honor."

"No way! You are not a Scout and never were. How could he so soon after his wife's death?" Jenny said.

"I've seen it before," Aggie said. "Some people just can't tolerate being alone."

"So, what has that got to do with nails?" Jenny said.

"Honestly, I wasn't sure if it would get me anywhere, but I made an appointment to have my nails done by Desdemona. Have you been to her shop?"

"Ivy! Get on with it. Honestly." Aggie threw herself back in her chair, laughing.

"Her shop is beautiful. But that's not the story. She fully admitted they were dating, and she told me who gave Reginald the cash for his truck."

"Who?!" Aggie said.

"George. Just as we thought. Reginald told her it was George, and that he was British. Desdemona asked the bartender, who confirmed George's name and accent, but did say he was too busy to be sure."

"It's enough for me," Aggie said.

Ivy nodded. "It's a start. But it does mean Ashley didn't pay off Reginald. The story Reginald told Desdemona was that he won the money in a poker game with George. Although it sounds farfetched, Desdemona wants to believe it. She really likes him. She said that there wasn't a funeral because Gladys was so mean to Reginald that she just wanted to kick her ash off the dock. I like her." Ivy looked around at everyone, watching them digest the information.

"So, he didn't really win the money in a card game, did he?" Jenny said. "Men can be such liars."

"Now, now," Aggie said. "I've known women to spin a few yarns as well. Do you need us to explain what spinning a yarn means?" Aggie belly laughed.

Jenny smiled. "That doesn't answer my question. Why did the chief want Mom to give Reginald rolls?" Jenny asked. "Has the book club been meeting without me and Mom?"

"It wasn't planned. Most of us met last night, up at the cabins," Aggie grimaced and shrugged. "Sorry. I should have caught you up this morning."

"No worries. What are the next steps the chief wanted you to take?" Jenny asked.

"Conner and Nephi plan to set up a poker game. I won't give you the details so that you don't need to worry about letting the cat out of the bag," Ivy said.

"Now you're putting cats in bags. Good grief," Jenny said.

Ivy put her SUV in drive, rolled the windows down, and put her hair up. Her heart was full, and her smile was broad when she turned on her favorite road trip playlist and sang loudly, if a bit out of tune, as she drove back to the cabin.

She'd parked by the Crow's Nest and was admiring her nails on the steering wheel. She realized she was smiling like a silly schoolgirl when she heard Judy barking.

Xander slowly and carefully walked her way, bruised, looking like he was in pain, but smiling.

She climbed out and picked up Judy, grinning at Xander. "There is the smile I love."

"What is this?" Xander asked.

"Just a little something I ordered online," Ivy said. She grinned and wiggled her brows.

"Nice! When we go to the next book club meeting, you're driving."

"Do you want to go for a test drive right now?" Ivy asked.

"I wish. My mother is on the warpath. She insisted I find the coffee girl and send her for more of Aggie's cinnamon and peach rolls. I'm sorry she is such a pain," Xander said.

"I'm not surprised she wants a peach roll; I am also not surprised she is grouchy if she looks anything like you." Ivy opened the passenger door of the SUV revealing an entire box of rolls.

"Brilliant! How did you know?" Xander said.

Ivy shrugged, still grinning from ear to ear.

"You're the best. She was furious and said you weren't at work today. I told her you were, but you make your own schedule."

"I was at work! She didn't look for me, did she? I was in the library all morning. I could hear voices once in a while, but I didn't see a single soul. Do I need to clock in and out?" Ivy said.

Xander chuckled and shook his head. "Don't let her get to you. She doesn't trust anyone. She's still my mother, even though I am a grown man."

"Oh, you are, are you?" Ivy walked beside him to the library doors. "She's right. You trusted me and I applied under an assumed name while I was running from my ex, who nearly killed all of us."

He snorted; his hand shot up to cover his mouth. Red in the face, he said, "That's right. You're the employee that was married to the homicidal maniac."

"Yes I am."

He took Judy from her arms, set her on the ground, and hugged Ivy for more than a few minutes. They walked across the patio to the library doors, arm in arm when he said, "We all know none of that was your fault. Did you go to the book club this morning?"

"When we met last night, we talked it all out. I ran a different errand and then picked up some rolls. But I do have a question for you, and I need you to look at the books the Crow sent you."

"The Crow?" Xander's brows drew together, and he tipped his head.

"Sorry, the antique dealer. The Crow is my nickname for him."

"I think the books he brought you might have come from the church on the hill. He might be the person who killed the caretaker."

"I thought they had the killer in custody?"

"I think they arrested the wrong man. You'll understand why when you look at the last stack of books he delivered. They are from Germany. There are World War II photos hidden in one of the books," Ivy said.

"Did you call the chief?"

"Not yet. I wanted to talk to you first and get your opinion," Ivy said.

Xander frowned. "If you believe the books are stolen, then they are. I won't buy them. I'm going to deliver them to the station, so the chief has a good look at them before he tries to tell you the case is closed."

"I think that's a great idea. It's a relief to know that the caretaker's murder was probably about theft and not part of Gladys' death or the attempts on Rhoda."

"It simplifies things. Did you know the caretaker?" Xander asked.

"No. I haven't been to a church since high school. But I did talk to the pastor's wife. She said they called him Angel. She obviously really cared about him," Ivy said.

"He was a great guy," Xander said. "Whenever I saw him, he had a smile on his face. He loved gardening and I loved walking in his garden, when I had time."

"I am so sorry. I feel terrible. I didn't realize you knew him and here I am talking about checking off a list," Ivy said. She held her breath and waited for his response.

"You didn't do anything wrong. You didn't know we were acquainted. Would you help me set up a donation to cover the cost of his headstone, or whatever will help the church and his family?"

"I would love to help." She gave him a quick hug. "You are so generous. You're a good man."

He smiled.

"I have a question for you on a totally different subject," Ivy said.

"Fire away," Xander said.

"Have you heard anything about George having a gambling habit?" Ivy asked.

They walked quietly, side by side, for a moment.

"Charlotte isn't much of a talker, but I have a feeling she isn't happily married," Xander said.

"She is always weepy. I rarely see her smiling. He's always touching her, and she looks like she doesn't like it. She flinches. Why?" Ivy said.

"Good question."

The library patio doors opened and, in the distance, she could see Rhoda on a small aluminum scooter patients use to get around instead of crutches. Her injured leg had a medical boot on it and rested on the scooter while she pushed herself with her good leg. She looked as angry as storm clouds. A white bandage on her nose and two black eyes was the first thing that Ivy noticed. Her free hand was on her hip.

"Where have you been?" Rhoda bellowed while they were still fifty feet away.

"I went to find Ivy," Xander called back to her.

Rhoda's arm fell to her side. "Not you! Her! And why do you think you own my dog? Put her down!"

Ivy froze.

"Mom. Do not talk to Ivy like that. I brought Judy with me when I went down to see her."

"I don't know what you pay her, but she is never working!"

Xander sighed in frustration. "Yes, she is! She worked all morning before running to town to buy these for us!"

Her face softened. "Are those more of those wonderful peach things?"

"Aggie made them fresh just an hour or so ago," Ivy said.

"I didn't see you working," Rhoda said.

"Did you look in the library?" Ivy asked.

"Yes. Just a few minutes ago," Rhoda said.

"During my lunch hour, I had a manicure," Ivy said. She held up her hands.

Rhoda looked at her silently until Xander handed her the box of rolls. Then without a word, backed up the scooter and turned toward the door.

She didn't ask, but Xander jogged and held the door open for her.

"How long do you have to wear the boot and use the scooter, Mom?"

"I don't know. They want to see me next week after the swelling goes down. Until then, I am not supposed to put any weight on it."

They passed through the door, and it swung shut, leaving Ivy and Judy in silence. She closed her eyes and took a deep breath in and let it out slowly and loudly, trying to let the stress she felt melt away.

The library door opened and Xander returned. Ivy smiled at him. He shrugged apologetically, took Judy out of her arms and left again.

Ivy sat down on the leather couch hard, suddenly exhausted, closed her eyes and once more tried to take a few deep breaths to calm her nerves.

Her eyes were still closed when someone sat down next to her, making her jump. Anderson looked like he had melted into the couch.

Ivy glanced at him and closed her eyes again. "I didn't hear you come in," Ivy said.

"That's because I snuck out of the kitchen and came through the patio doors. You left them open," Anderson said.

"The breeze is nice."

"Yes, it is," Anderson said, "I'm just going to close my eyes..."

The library door popped open again and Xander popped his head in. "Anderson, can you make Mom an espresso and warm up a few peach rolls for her?"

Anderson opened one eye and turned it toward Ivy, lips pressed firm. "No problem."

The door closed. Anderson leaned forward and put his head in his hands. "I forgot how much chaos surrounds Rhoda. I know I shouldn't complain, but she is like a tornado of trouble."

"No worries. I am just glad she didn't bring her flying monkeys," Ivy said.

He chuckled softly. "I told you. You can run, but you can't hide. Remember when you asked how bad could it be? It can be worse than this." He let his hands fall to his knees and groaned while he pushed himself up.

"Are you okay?" Ivy asked.

He tucked his chin in and raised his brows as high as they would go. "What do you think?"

"I don't know how you do it," Ivy said.

"Semper Fidelis. Semper Fi," Anderson said while walking to the door.

"Always faithful," Ivy said to herself after the door closed again.

27

SHE HAS SEASHELLS BY THE SEASHORE

Ivy turned on her playlist and worked for an hour. Indie music drowned out the sounds in the house. Her favorite song was the last one on the list. She hit the back button and played *Three Little Birds* by Kate Rusby again.

She smelled a dusty leather book, put it on the desk, and let it fall open. She loved seeing what page was opened most. It was hand-drawn mushrooms and their descriptions. They were all poisonous.

Her phone chimed.

Text from Conner: *The game is afoot.*

Text from Ivy to Conner: *Afoot, Sherlock? Is the card game and boat prepped?*

Text from Conner to Ivy: *I'm Watson. You're She-lock. Yes. We're ready. We just need to invite him.*

Text from Ivy to Conner: *Let me know where and when. I want to listen in.*

Text from Conner to Ivy: *Will do.*

The library door's code lock clicked, and Ivy's head snapped up. She turned off the music. She hoped it was

Xander so she could bring him up to speed. It wasn't Xander. It was Charlotte.

Charlotte closed the door behind her and spun around. She gasped, her hands to her heart. She stepped back, bumping up against the door.

"You surprised me," Charlotte said.

"Charlotte. Come in." Ivy smiled and motioned for her to come down toward the table where she was working.

Still wide-eyed, Charlotte walked to the table and stood looking down at Ivy.

"Have a seat," Ivy motioned for her to sit at the table. "How are you doing with everything that is going on?"

Charlotte looked at her warily.

"Your dad sure picked a firecracker for his wife," Ivy said. *Who will want Xander to fire me if I walk away from my job again.* She went back to work and waited silently for Charlotte to speak. A full minute passed before she glanced up and Charlotte replied.

"They are complete opposites, like a lot of married couples are. George is very different than I am. You know they say that we are attracted to people that have characteristics we lack?" Charlotte said and gave Ivy a small smile. "I was teaching school when I met him."

"What age?" Ivy asked.

"Five-year-olds."

"What was George doing for work when you met?" Ivy asked.

"George was a bad boy, but I thought he was very handsome. See? Complete opposites."

"That describes me and my ex. He was a homicidal maniac, and I was the complete opposite," Ivy said.

Charlotte looked at her quizzically. "Really?"

"More real than you can imagine. Promise."

Charlotte giggled softly. "Oh well then, I shouldn't bother you."

"Nonsense. I am so tired of work I am cross eyed. Do you want to go for a short walk with me on the beach to the north?" Ivy asked.

"I would love that."

Ivy couldn't believe her luck. She didn't even have to track down Charlotte to spend time getting to know her as the chief wanted.

Charlotte followed Ivy down the rickety wooden steps leading to a small bay and rocky beach north of Xander's house. The bay was fed by two small streams where giggling children played joyfully on the unusually warm spring day. Just beyond the stream, a dory was being pushed out to sea by two hearty men who jumped aboard and expertly navigated the waves as they went out to sea.

A hundred-and-fifty-foot-high rock made of volcanic basalt sat in the middle of the bay, like a giant castle tower, eroded by time and tide. Somewhere in the past, the Pacific and the wind had carved a tunnel though the north side of the rock. The kind of tunnel that, in Ivy's teen years, would have called to her scientific, mystery loving mind. She smiled when she remembered her days in Necanicum, up the coast. She remembered a hair-brained beach adventure she, Nephi, and her best friend Esther had gone on together.

As she walked with Charlotte, Ivy admired the cedar-shingled beach cottages, interrupted by the occasional stone and steel modern monstrosity, that lined the bay. Trails leading to the beach were created and maintained by years of local children, ignoring fences and yards, running over the same path their parents had taken. Pirates Point, a sheer cliff begging to be conquered, ran out to sea on the north side of the bay. It beguiled amateur climbers, who would underestimate it and inevitably need a high angle rescue.

Warm sunshine and a light breeze from the south made it the perfect day for a walk, side by side, along the ocean. Ivy needed to learn Charlotte's secrets but instead found herself falling back in time. Ivy realized she and Charlotte were really not that different. She glanced sideways at Charlotte's fragile and perpetually sad profile.

"I'm divorced, you know," Ivy said.

Charlotte's head whipped around, and she studied Ivy through narrowed eyes.

Ivy gave her a sad smile.

"I've heard Rhoda and others say little things, but I try not to listen to others' private business," Charlotte said.

"There was nothing private about it. He terrified everyone in Balefire. He sank my friend, Conner's boat and was declared dead after the Coast Guard couldn't find his body," Ivy said. "When he drank, it was like his skin peeled back and a demon took over." Ivy waited to see if her honesty about her own life would let Charlotte know she wouldn't be judging her, and she could trust her.

Ivy slipped off her sandals and carried them. Charlotte followed suit. They walked in the wet sand on the edge of the ocean, cool saltwater waved rolled in and out, over their feet.

Ivy rarely shared her own story and when she did, she always steeled herself, expecting the usual judgement or unwelcome advice. She was used to a barrage of questions. Why did she stay with him, marry him, it takes two, and worse. But they still got under her skin sometimes.

Ivy waited. Nothing. No words. Just the waves, the heartbeat of the ocean, her heart.

"I am sorry that happened to you," Charlotte said.

When it was clear Charlotte wasn't like everyone else, Ivy said, "Thanks for not judging me. I thought I would put it out there and if you were judgmental, this would have been a short walk."

"Oh. I would never judge you. How could I? My own life certainly is... " Charlotte shook her head and gave Ivy a sad smile before she stooped to pick up a perfect sand dollar and examine it. "These are so beautiful."

"They have secrets too. If you break it open little doves or angels fall out. I heard a poem about it once. Beauty in the breaking." Ivy laughed softly.

"I like that," Charlotte said.

Ivy glanced at her and went on. "I guess that describes my life. Bittersweet, but more beautiful after the breaking. I feel stronger than before it happened." She looked down at the water washing over her feet, half smiling.

"Was it hard? You know, to leave?" Charlotte asked.

"Oh yeah. But what took forever wasn't leaving, it was finally putting away any feelings of love for him, even though I knew, without a doubt, he was a homicidal maniac. Every once in a while, I catch myself looking over my shoulder, even though everyone is sure he's dead."

"Really?" Charlotte said and stopped walking, looking directly at Ivy for one of the first times during their walk.

Ivy nodded, yes. "But I have an alternate reason for wanting to walk with you." Charlotte frowned. She waited, frozen, for Ivy to tell her more.

Ivy turned to walk side-by-side again. Charlotte followed. A cold wave reached their ankles. "I saw George stand over you. He looked really angry, familiar, and was saying things I couldn't really hear. It gave me such bad PTSD; I didn't do anything to interrupt it. I froze. I've felt worried about you and terrible ever since it happened. Later, I realized recently how selfish that was of me. So many people stood by and said nothing when they saw my bruises," Ivy said.

"I know that feeling. I am shocked when I have bruises on my face even, and no one says anything. It makes me feel like I must be crazy, overreacting."

"Right?" Ivy said.

214

"Everyone loves George, even me. Did you ever feel crazy for loving someone who... well... struggles so much?"

"So crazy. I still don't understand why I loved my ex, even after I saw him do horrible things. I felt totally crazy. It wasn't until we separated that I realized I had actually become a sort of caregiver for him. I always worried about his wounded soul, and felt sorry for him. I even got sucked into his manipulation and tried to be more and more perfect, you know, fix things. Have you ever heard the term gaslighting?"

"Yes. But I don't really know what it means," Charlotte said.

"It's when someone who is emotionally or mentally abusive creates events that make you feel like you're crazy. He had me convinced that his anger was my fault. I still can't understand why I believed him. I'm a Harvard graduate for Frank's sake." Ivy was surprised at how comfortable she felt talking to Charlotte.

"Then I've been gas-lighted, broken, and feel like it's all my fault too," Charlotte said, and there it was. The space between Ivy and Charlotte was gone, and with it shame and fear.

They walked silently. Ivy glanced at Charlotte, knowing she was remembering, sorting, seeing old memories through a new lens, the lens of acceptance and a taste of safety.

"George gambles."

Ivy nodded, but didn't look at her or speak. She felt Charlotte had just given her the tip of the iceberg. She was gauging Ivy's response. Testing her to see if she was trustworthy.

"And he drinks a lot," Charlotte said.

"So did Ian."

"He isn't just physically abusive, although he did strangle me once. I am afraid that he will hurt my father for his money."

"Do you mean you think he might kill Ashley?" Ivy said.

"I don't know about murder. I must sound crazy."

"You don't. He sounds dangerous," Ivy said.

Silent tears ran down Charlotte's face.

Charlotte gulped air, waved a hand in front of her face trying to regain her composure. "I am so sorry. I don't know what's wrong with me."

"You never have to apologize to me. You may not believe me, but crying is good for you. I promise you, there will come a day when the tears stop, and this will be a distant memory." Ivy led her up to a driftwood log half buried in sand, but large enough to sit on. She sat silently beside Charlotte, while Charlotte finally allowed things she had been holding tight inside to wash her face and wet her hands.

Ivy looked around, surprised by how empty the beach was. They were a good quarter of a mile past the children playing in the stream. Off in the distance an older man walked his dog. She looked back and checked the stairs to the beach, hypervigilant, watching for any sign of George. Nothing. She wished she'd checked his location before their walk, and knew where he was, so she could be sure he wouldn't see them.

After some time, Charlotte calmed, and her tears slowed. She wiped her eyes and tried to get her wet curls out of her face. "I am so sorry. I don't know what's wrong with..." She stopped and laughed lightly, if not a little hysterically. "I know exactly what's wrong with me. My marriage started dissolving the day it began and now I'm pregnant," Charlotte said.

"Are you happy about having a baby?"

She looked at Ivy, brows raised. "I am one minute, then I'm worried. You're the first person I've told besides George. He was not happy. Apparently, I didn't follow his schedule and am ruining his grand plan. I'm trapped. He doesn't want a child but already he is threatening to take the baby if I try to leave him. He says I will never find him or our child."

"What if I said my friends and I want to help? The same people that helped me."

Charlotte looked at Ivy, eyes opened wide. "You mustn't tell a soul. He'd kill me if he knew I'd told you."

A thousand ideas for freeing Charlotte ran through Ivy's mind. *Stop it! It's her life. She knows him best. She knows what she wants and whatever that is, you need to support it.*

Ivy rubbed her face, working to wipe away the frustration and concern she felt. "Charlotte. What do you want to happen? If you could have or do anything, what would you do?"

"You'll think I'm wicked and evil if I tell you."

217

"Pinky promise, I won't," Ivy said.

"Pinky promise?"

Ivy nodded and smiled.

Charlotte smiled back. " I've thought about a thousand scenarios and felt guilty about all of them. I have been praying in the chapel on our estate almost every day. I needed help, but how could I ask God to send my husband to jail?"

Ivy laughed. "The only things I know about God, I've heard from my friends. But didn't your God flood the earth to clean up a mess and wipe out dozens of crazy Egyptians chasing slaves after parting a whole sea? It doesn't sound like anything's out of his scope."

It was Charlotte's turn to laugh. "For not knowing much, you picked two times he was very hands on."

"A friend and I were talking. It seems like a small and silly thing, but we both decided meeting Aggie on a bus was a God thing. Too many coincidences. So, who knows. Maybe our meeting wasn't a coincidence either. Can you pray for a targeted bolt of lightning?"

"I don't believe in coincidence. Actually, I think today you are a God thing, something heaven sent," Charlotte said. "I believe in miracles, and I have been begging for one. I've put my life in God's hands."

Uncomfortable, Ivy smirked. "I've been called lots of things, but no one has ever called me heaven sent or a God thing. Seriously?"

"Yes," Charlotte looked Ivy in the eyes without flinching or looking away.

Ivy looked down and shrugged. "God must be desperate. There are better people to send than me."

"I trust you. I don't know why, but I know with my whole soul, you are the answer I've been asking for."

Ivy felt terrible. She'd brought Charlotte to the beach to confirm her suspicions and interrogate her, and now Charlotte saw her as some sort of angel. *Maybe I could be an avenging angel.* She had a quick mental image of herself, dressed as Joan of Arc, carrying a rolling pin. *Get a grip! All I need to do is find a murderer and take Nephi off the suspect list.*

Silently letting go of her hidden agenda, Ivy asked, "Tell me, what do you want to happen?"

"George almost always has gambling debt. I know there have been other women. But what I worry about most is a box full of drugs I found in my suitcase when we arrived at Knightly House. I couldn't believe it. He sent his pregnant wife through airport customs and into the United States with drugs. I opened the box. It was full of powder in tiny baggies. I wanted to throw the box off the cliff by the lighthouse. He rented a car to drive the box to Los Angeles tomorrow. He made a big deal about taking them to California to make me happy, but he probably is going to sell the drugs to someone. That's what we've been fighting about. I don't want anything like that near my baby." She wrapped both her arms around her waist, which still looked tiny to Ivy.

"How far along are you?" Ivy asked.

"I haven't been to a doctor, but I think I'm two months along."

Ivy forced a smile. "I don't know a thing about babies, but I'm sure you'll keep your baby safe."

"What I wish would have happened is that he would have been caught with the drugs before the airport and gone to prison for the next eighteen years. I would be stupid and miss him, but at least my baby would be safe."

"If he was in prison, he couldn't set you up and use you like he did at the airport," Ivy said.

"Yesterday, I checked the box. It looks like he might be using some. I swear some are missing."

"Charlotte, I have to ask... Remember the woman that died in the bakery?" Ivy said.

Charlotte tipped her head and looked at Ivy. "Yes."

"I am going to tell you something I've wondered about. It's only my opinion, I promise. It isn't a fact. It's just a suspicion. Do you understand?"

"Sort of."

Here goes. "I think Gladys, the woman that died at the bakery, was poisoned. I don't think she was the target. She took one of your family's cinnamon rolls and ate it," Ivy said.

Wide eyes, Charlotte put her hands over her open mouth. They dropped to her lap. "And you think George poisoned the roll?"

"I really have no idea and there is no proof she died of anything other than natural causes," Ivy said.

Charlotte took a deep breath and exhaled loudly. She shook her head. "I don't know. I know he is dangerous, but what reason would he have to kill someone else? I've seen Gladys' cute daughter with Brett. She is so gentle.

Brett told me some of the things that the woman used to say to her. If she was poisoned, are you sure it wasn't her own husband?"

"Like I said, it's only a suspicion," Ivy said.

"Brett thinks there is probably a list of people who didn't like Gladys. Plus, I don't think George is stupid enough to do anything in public like that. If he was going to murder someone, he'd get someone else to do his dirty work," Charlotte said.

"You know him best. You're probably right," Ivy said.

Charlotte folded her arms and frowned. "Murder? I don't know, but the drugs... You're going to think I am awful, but after he sent me through customs, I was so angry, I wanted to call the police myself and turn him in. How pathetic is that?" Charlotte said.

"First, you're not pathetic. Second, do you mean it? Would you be okay if he was caught with his drugs and was taken to jail in America? I can't promise anything, but I can ask the chief for help."

Charlotte looked out to sea, closed her eyes for a minute, and twisted her wedding ring on her finger. Softly, she said, "I am awful. But that feels right."

"I don't think you're awful at all. I think you have more courage than I did when I decided I'd had enough," Ivy said.

"Had enough? I can't believe how much had to happen before I had enough. It took my baby for me to be ready to end this never-ending nightmare." Charlotte took in a deep breath and let it out slowly before she looked at Ivy sheepishly, rolled her eyes, and a smile spread across her face.

"Charlotte, will you let me do what I can to help you? I have an idea," Ivy said.

Charlotte studied Ivy's face before she nodded. "What can we do?"

"Not 'we,' just me and my inner circle of very trustworthy friends. I have an idea, but I won't do anything unless you approve and trust us," Ivy said. "Also, if we do anything, you need to be far enough away that you and your baby are safe."

"I can't imagine what you can do. George seems to read my mind and always knows when I plan to do anything like leaving him," Charlotte said.

"I won't tell you anything for him to deduce. He isn't God, and he can't read your mind, but we do have to make good decisions and be wise," Ivy said.

Charlotte looked at Ivy, narrowed her eyes, and said, "You wouldn't do anything illegal or that will hurt George, right?"

"I don't want to hurt George."

Charlotte smiled, "That's good, because you aren't very big and he was a street fighter when he was young. He was a boot boy."

"I'm small but mighty." Ivy grinned, winking at Charlotte.

Charlotte laughed, her shoulders dropped, and she looked more relaxed than Ivy had ever seen her.

"Seriously. What can anyone do? He is always one step ahead of me, that's for sure," Charlotte said.

"I've been thinking about it ever since I saw the way he treated you." Ivy stood and wiped the sand from her jeans. She reached out and pulled Charlotte up. "And if I am going to do this, it has to be before he leaves for L.A."

Charlotte put her hand on her belly. "I can't believe I am trusting you. I've only spoken to my father about George before you. He didn't believe me, so I stopped trying. Trust is hard."

"I still wrestle with trusting people. You'll probably always be slow to trust. But maybe that isn't such a bad thing. Honestly, trusting Xander took an entire murder investigation and a few life and death situations with our friends. But now, I would trust him with my life," Ivy said.

"That's a story I want to hear," Charlotte said.

"What if I told you I am certain that the same people that helped me once would be willing to help you?"

"Who are they?" Charlotte asked.

Ivy hesitated to give Charlotte everyone's names. She was surprised at how protective she felt of her friends and now Charlotte.

"If they are able to let us help you, I will let you know after I get their permission," Ivy said.

"I can't imagine what it would feel like to have friends I trusted like that. That's why I feel so trapped. I've lost all my friends in the last year, thanks to George's behavior in public," Charlotte said.

"There is one caveat. I need to tell them truthfully what George has done, is capable of, and about the baby."

Charlotte looked down, rubbed her baby bump, and frowned. "Are you sure you have to?"

"Yes," Ivy said.

She sighed. "I know it sounds strange, but I feel sorry for George. Don't hurt him. He is my baby's father."

"I totally understand that feeling, except for the baby part. I've never been that lucky. There are no guarantees in life. At Balefire, we help each other when things like this happen. So far, they've kept all of my secrets," Ivy said, studying Charlotte's face to see if she was pushing her too far.

Charlotte closed her eyes and bit her lip.

"Look, forget I offered. I can't guarantee that something won't go wrong. All I can do is promise to work with you and be there for you after things happen and until you don't need or want me."

Charlotte looked directly in Ivy's eyes. "I can't believe I'm saying this, but what other option do I have? I can stay and bring a baby into a dangerous situation or take a leap of faith and leave him."

"You can change your mind," Ivy said.

Charlotte exhaled, looked out to sea and over at the children running up the beach to their waiting mother. "I'm desperate. What can I do to help?"

"Pray. We don't have a chapel in the Knightly House, but you are welcome to pray in my cabin if you need a quiet spot. I may not pray, but I welcome your prayers," Ivy said.

"I'll pray all day if that's what it takes," Charlotte said.

"Remember, I can't make promises, but I can promise to be here no matter what the outcome. We can always hide you at Aggie's. She takes in strays and feeds them."

"I would have a cinnamon roll baby if I stayed with her," Charlotte said.

"Right?" Ivy said. "I can't say no to anything she makes. She is amazing."

"I need to change the subject. I have a question for you. How is your dad doing financially?"

"He has a lot of small businesses. In fact, that's how I met George. George was gambling at one of dad's pubs. He was so funny and kind to me when I met him. He swept me off my feet. It's legal to gamble or be a bookie in England."

"Who inherits if something happens to your father?"

"Dad doesn't trust George. He never says it, but it is obvious. He told me that if something happened to either of them, I was to call his solicitor. He and Rhoda worked with his solicitor to set up a will that leaves Rhoda's money to him and vice versa. They also purchased very large life insurance policies on both of them, so the surviving spouse would be well taken care of," Charlotte said.

"He sounds like he has a solid plan. What happens if they both die at the same time?" Ivy said.

"Honestly, I have no idea. I'd have to ask our solicitor for details," Charlotte said. "If they both die at the same time, I might inherit, but, knowing Dad, his solicitor will be the executor of the will."

Ivy said, "Did you have a prenup?"

"No," Charlotte said. "I worry that George will kill me. I feel it. As soon as I inherit, he'll gamble it away. I have to get this fixed for my child. If he found out you knew," Charlotte whispered. She looked at Ivy, wide-eyed and wringing her hands. "I have just put you in danger."

Ivy remembered feeling similar feelings, but after her parents died, she didn't have another relative or child to worry about. "I can't promise you this won't be hard. I remember thinking leaving was impossible and being sure that every day was my last. But here I am, irritating you," Ivy winked and tried desperately to lift some of the horror she knew Charlotte was feeling.

"If I died, my child could end up alone with George," Charlotte said. She looked at the horizon, silent.

Ivy watched the possibilities sink in. "I can't promise anything, Charlotte, except that if nothing happens, he will gradually tighten the noose, making leaving harder and harder for you. I can also promise to be here to help as long as you want me."

Charlotte bit her lip and finally shrugged. "I have been trying to find a way to end my marriage. A baby complicates everything, but I am having my baby. What choice do I have? I obviously haven't found a way out on my own. Thank you, Ivy."

"I had a lot of help when I left. Aggie and my friends helped me. It's my turn to pay it forward," Ivy said.

"How can you do anything before he leaves for L.A.?" Charlotte asked.

226

"If we can, we will. If you change your mind, no worries, just text me. I'm going to put my number in your phone under Coffee House.

After putting the number into Charlotte's phone, she smiled. "Come on. Let's see if your prayers can make us a miracle."

Two new friends headed back the way they came, arms linked, waves chasing them along, hoping to find a way to invite Charlotte's baby into a different world. A world where children play joyfully on the beach.

28

—·—

THE BEST-LAID PLANS

Ivy texted the book club, being sure to include Anderson and Xander this time.

Text to Book Club: I met with C. We need to meet at Aggie's. Who is available? The gambler is leaving for L.A.

Text to Xander: Can you help keep Rhoda busy while we meet at Aggie's? I'm not ready to share too much with her yet and she will be safer with you. I promise to fill you in ASAP.

Text to Anderson: We want you with the book club but need help. Would you be willing to keep track of George and give us a heads up if he heads this way?

One by one, the book club members responded in the affirmative, except Jenny. She had to pick up her girls right after school.

I can fill her in later. Ivy thought.

Before Ivy drove to town, she left Charlotte sipping warm mint herbal tea, eyes closed, resting in an Adirondack on the deck of her cabin.

Ivy parked in front of the shop, and before she went in, she scanned the horizon. The sky was blue with only a few random clouds in the distance, the water lapped lazily on the rocks, and boats bobbed on small swells as they headed back to the bay.

The seagulls gave away the storm coming their way. They were gathered in what Ivy liked to call congregations, waiting for someone to say amen. The kind of groups that made children want to run through the center and scatter the gulls in the sky. She checked her weather app. A storm warning for later in the day was front and center. She checked the local scanner page and NOAA's weather app. Offshore, the wind swirled toward shore. Still, she wasn't worried. She'd seen forecasts that were far worse.

"Hi Aggie," Ivy said. She sat on the loveseat. It was an overstuffed rose chintz sofa that faced the front window and group. She liked having her back to the wall or bookshelves and knowing what was coming her way.

"It feels good to sit down," Aggie said, as she sat down by the fire. "What did you learn?"

"I learned that I like Charlotte," Ivy said.

"Do tell," Aggie said.

Nephi and Conner came through the doors laughing and a little sunburned. Conner slapped Nephi on the back, before he put a finger to his lips and then pointed at the group.

"Did you miss us?" Conner asked.

"You should. We are about to amaze you with our skills," Nephi said. They knuckle punched each other. "We are ready."

"I don't know how you two get anything done together," Aggie said.

They flopped down on the couch next to Ivy. Nephi threw his arm around Ivy's shoulders.

"P.U." She pushed his arm off.

"Hey now. That's the smell of a hardworking man!" He leaned back and knit his fingers behind his head, smiling, and leaning her way.

"Don't make me bite you." Ivy elbowed him.

He belly laughed. "You haven't changed. You still fight dirty," Nephi said.

That set Conner off. His laughter was loud and contagious.

"Children! This is a business," Aggie said, and pointed her head towards a couple sitting at a table. Both of their mouths hung open and they held their tea midair. That sent Conner, Nephi and Ivy into peels of laughter.

Ivy put her hands over her mouth, trying hard enough to stop laughing, she snorted and hiccupped. "Crackers!" The next hiccup was louder than the last. Aggie tried to look serious.

The man got up and helped the woman to her feet. "Come on, Mother. Let's go to the bar, where it's quiet."

He smirked and frowned at the group before he let the screen doors swing closed.

"Sorry, Mom." Conner bit his lip, trying to gain his composure.

"You're grounded." Aggie suppressed a smile.

Ivy hiccupped and pointed a finger at Conner. "Alright now. This is serious business." That didn't help. They were all laughing again.

When the laughter died down and everyone had a cup of their favorite beverage, they sipped their drinks quietly, waiting for a new shopper in the bookstore to leave.

Ivy leaned forward in her seat, looking at her friends, face by face. "I talked to Charlotte. She needs us. Things are far worse than we've imagined."

"Oh dear," Aggie clucked. "Is he dangerous? Will he hurt her because of something we do?"

"She believes he will eventually hurt her and possibly kill her. Charlotte has asked for our help. I am surprised she trusts us. Her marriage is everything you're now thinking and worse," Ivy said.

"What's your opinion? Do you think he'll kill her if she leaves?" Aggie said.

"Stay or let us help—both options are risky," Ivy said. "He might be some sort of drug dealer. She said he has a box of drugs he might be planning to sell to settle a debt. He's driving the box down to L.A. tomorrow," Ivy said.

"Maybe someone paid him to transport them to the states," Conner said.

"Or just because that is who he is, a flaming jerk," Nephi said.

"What kind of threats is he making?" Aggie asked.

"He said he'd kill her family if she leaves him. He ticks off all the domestic violence lethality markers, meaning there is a high likelihood he would follow through on his threats. He's strangled her in the past," Ivy said. "He also threatened to hurt her father if she leaves him, he beats her, gaslights her, and more."

"The chief needs to hear this. His leaving for L.A. is going to change everything," Aggie said. She opened her knitting bag and nervously clicked away with an angry energy.

"There is one more thing," Ivy said. "She's pregnant. About two months."

Aggie's needles froze mid stitch, the room went silent, and the boys gave her their full, solemn attention.

"He's threatened to take the baby, and worse," Ivy said. "Where are you on the poker game and the boat?" Ivy asked.

Conner beamed. "Today, we wired the boat up so well, we can hear you and see you in every single space, even the door to the bathroom. If you breathe, we will hear you. And..." He paused for effect, wiggling his brows. "You won't see a single camera. Xander bought and paid for the best equipment available and for overnight shipping."

"Good job," Aggie said.

Conner smirked. "I asked Nephi if I could wire up one of the chairs at the card table and make an electric chair, but he said no."

"At least one of you had some sense," Aggie said.

Ivy smiled. "Sounds like a good idea to me."

"All we have to do now is find out where he is and invite him over for a play date," Nephi said.

"And we need cash for the buy-in," Conner said.

"How much?" Ivy asked. "Would ten thousand do it? I can get out $9,999 in cash the same day if I can get to the bank before it closes. Anything bigger sets off an alert and the bank will make me wait for special approval. I better get that done before they close."

"Sounds good to me," Nephi said. "I can throw in ten bucks."

"There is one more thing, Conner. Where is the chief in all this? Is he up to speed?" Ivy asked.

"He's on his way, with Vera," Conner said. "I'll text him and let him know we're all here."

"Well then make yourselves comfortable. This needs to be shared with him first," Ivy said.

Aggie pushed herself out of her deep overstuffed chair and to her feet. "Ask him if he wants chocolate or coffee, would you, Love? Who wants rolls and cookies?" Aggie asked. Every hand in the circle shot up.

The chief and Vera joined Ivy and Conner at a table in the bakery, while Nephi entertained Aggie by the fire with stories about wiring the cameras in the boat. Apparently, this was their first effort and Nephi was proud to say he was only shocked once.

"I talked to Charlotte today. I told you he is leaving for L.A tomorrow? We have other complications to our poker plan I thought you should know about before we go forward," Ivy said.

The chief took off his aviators and rubbed his watery blue eyes. He slipped off his jacket, took off his hat, and rubbed his short hair vigorously before leaning forward. "Give it to me straight and fast."

Ivy took a deep breath and told the chief what Charlotte had shared. "So, as you can see, George is a very serious gambling addict as we suspected. He might be delivering or selling the drugs to pay debts. He knows Charlotte is...pregnant...that's right, pregnant, and he is still physically abusing her. He doesn't want the baby."

The chief fell back in his chair and closed his eyes for a moment. "Keep going."

"He hid the drugs in Charlotte's suitcase without telling her and then sent her through customs when they entered the country. She said the box was full of small baggies of powder," Ivy said.

"Powder could be anything, fentanyl, cocaine, or who knows. It only takes two milligrams to overdose and die," Vera said.

"She also thinks he may be using some of his inventory. But after talking to Charlotte, I am convinced he used them to try to kill Rhoda, but Gladys died instead," Ivy said.

The chief smacked the table with the flat of his hand and swore. "Not in my town. Why don't losers like this overdose on their own drugs?"

"I would rather he sat in a cell for the next 18 years, or time enough for Charlotte to raise her baby without having to worry about him," Ivy said.

"Without an autopsy, we'd need a confession. No one gets a sentence like that, unless it's for murder. Did the boys invite him to poker yet?" the chief asked.

"Better. He saw Nephi when we ate lunch at the local bar and grill. Nephi asked him if he knew where any action was. We said we did, got his cell number, and promised to text him the deets," Conner said.

The chief looked at Nephi through narrowed eyes. "Why would he trust Nephi?"

"Because the boy needs a haircut and looks like the sort who'd be willing to blow his money playing cards," Vera said.

Nephi sat back and folded his arms. "I need more tattoos."

"This is serious business. I don't know if I will let you be on the boat. You're a civilian," the chief said.

"I'm going to front Conner about $10,000 of my personal money for the game," Ivy asked.

The chief's head jerked up. "Can you do that?"

"If I get to the bank soon. Yes. I opened a local account."

"I have to think about it. I could work with our county drug task force to get the money but that will take more time," The chief said.

"Sometimes it's better to get forgiveness than permission. We don't have time. I'll give the money to Nephi as a gift. You'll have nothing to do with it," Ivy said. The chief didn't give her any push back.

"I have been talking to the drug task force officers about joining the party. They look like a bunch of thugs, but they're experts in just this sort of thing. I guess we better put together a pretty solid sting. We can get him for drugs. But to get him for Gladys' murder or attempting to murder Rhoda is going to require a confession. Let's go catch ourselves a killer," the chief said. He pushed his chair back, stood up, and put his aviators back on. The meeting was over.

"Yeehaw!" Vera jumped to her feet. "Can I play poker?"

One of the chief's bushy brows rose above his aviators.

"I take that as a no. Well at least let me be in on it," Vera said.

The chief nodded. "Come on. Conner, get your buddy Nephi. I want you to take me on a tour of the boat. The drug boys can help us set up a command center at the Marina. We've got a lot of work to do. Meet me at the station and I'll gather the team so we can plan our strategy."

"Can I help?" Ivy asked.

The chief immediately shook his head, no. "Not on your life. But you can sit in the command center if you don't interfere. We wouldn't be doing this without your uninvited and constant input, Miss Marple. You can also help Vera make sure Charlotte is somewhere safe tonight. We can't put this off another day."

29

— · —

MOTHER DEAREST

After delivering the cash, Ivy asked Xander to get Anderson and meet her in the Knightly House Library. She opened the glass doors on the patio and caught Judy as she jumped into her arms, and Sandy wagged her tail at her feet.

"Hi girls." She hugged Judy, feeling stress drain from her body as she looked into her chocolate brown eyes. "Where are your grownups?" She put Judy down and texted Xander, letting him know she was in the library.

It wasn't long before Xander joined her, gathering her up in a tight hug. Ivy let herself melt into the feelings, the smells, and the place she loved, his arms. She breathed him in, as the stress of the day simply faded away. His tall frame engulfed her.

Xander and Ivy held each other until Anderson came into the room. Xander kissed her forehead before they sat together on the leather couch. Anderson sat in an armchair facing them. The view from the window behind him had gone from serene to threatening. Rolling clouds in dark grey tones were fast moving and as ominous as the coming events.

"Where is everyone?" Ivy asked.

Anderson sat back in his chair. "Brett is gone, working. He told me that Reginald hired him to help with the garden shop. I'm sure he's there for a single flower, Petunia."

"Still, it gives him work experience," Xander said.

Anderson nodded. "I have no idea where George and Ashley have gone."

"George plans to drive to L.A. tomorrow. I don't think he realizes how long the coast is. They might be renting a car for the trip," Ivy said.

"Can the chief pull this thing together before he goes?" Xander asked. "If he doesn't, we lose the leverage of charging him for the drugs. That would at least keep him in custody long enough to hopefully get a confession for Gladys' death. There isn't enough evidence to charge him without a confession."

"It's a tight deadline. If the chief goes forward, it's going to be a long night," Anderson said.

"Where is Rhoda?" Ivy asked.

"Rhoda is shopping online in the kitchen and Charlotte is taking a walk after a nap in her room. I worry about that girl. She sleeps a lot," Anderson said.

"There is a reason for that," Ivy said. "She's expecting."

"A baby?" Xander said.

She smiled at his startled face. "No, puppies."

"Seriously, Ivy," Xander's worried eyes look straight into hers.

"Serious as a heart attack."

Xander exhaled sharply. She could see the wheels turn in his mind as this new piece of the puzzle worked its way into this nightmare they were all living.

Anderson leaned forward and looked into Ivy's eyes. "I've seen bruises on her that looked suspicious. Is that... is he abusing her, and does he know she's pregnant?"

"Yes, and yes. Charlotte and I had a long conversation. She realizes if she doesn't find someplace safe before the baby's born, she will be putting it in danger. Vera has a plan and will meet us at my cabin with an advocate to move Charlotte to a shelter tonight, if she is willing to go."

"A lot of victims won't leave," Anderson said. He fell back into the leather chair.

"She told me she was ready. All we can do is offer her safety. She knows him best. She needs to be the one to decide what's best for her. She's made it this far without help. Trusting us after her experiences with George will take incredible courage. She could change her mind. It might be a risk she isn't willing to take," Ivy said.

"I remember how hard it was for me to trust anyone after one of mom's boyfriends. He was controlling and took a swing at her once," Xander said.

"I didn't know that she's a survivor?" Ivy said.

"I don't know if I would use that term. Luckily, Mom can hold her own." He was silent for a moment and then unexpectedly smiled. "I will never forget their first and last fight. She sent him packing. But she's my mom, you know?" He looked back and forth from Anderson to Ivy.

She nodded silently. Anderson rubbed his face, frowning.

"It's history," Xander said. "I should have called you, Anderson, but it never occurred to me. I was used to keeping Mom's secrets." Xander looked up at Anderson. "Sorry. I know now you would have come and helped us."

Anderson shrugged. "What's done is done." He folded his arms and crossed his legs.

Ivy worked at staying in the room, grounded by touching the leather couch and looking at him while she was triggered. She leaned into him.

Not knowing what to say, she said something an advocate had once said to her. "I'm sorry that happened to you."

He shrugged again. "I try not to think about it. Having George and Charlotte in the house takes me back there. I've had suspicions, but she is so quiet. I didn't know how to bring it up. I'm just glad Mom doesn't know about Charlotte... "

"Doesn't know what?" Rhoda stepped inside the door, walking on her medical boot, in all her angry glory, hands on her hips, ready to go to war. Ivy had been so engrossed in their conversation, she didn't hear the tell-tale sound of the hinges warning them of company.

Xander jumped to his feet. "Mom."

"Xander." Then she melted. Tears fell on her cheeks while she crossed the room and hugged him like only a mother bear can. "I heard what you said about my abusive boyfriend. I wasn't the best mother, but I tried. Can you ever forgive me?"

"Forgive you? I love you, Mom. Okay, sometimes I am a little afraid of you, but..." And they were hugging again.

Rhoda's arms dropped. "Okay. You all are too easy to sneak up on. I've been listening at the door the entire time." Her face lit up. "I'm going to be a grandmother!" She clapped joyfully.

Ivy's heart lifted and a smile took her face over.

Rhoda's hands went back to their usual position, on her hips. "Now, what are we going to do to clean house and get rid of that... that jerk, before I start shopping for the baby? I am not letting my grandbaby be raised by an angry gambler."

Anderson stood up. "Rhoda, your job is to treat Charlotte, Ashley, and George like you don't know a thing. If Brett returns, take him to the grocery store or do whatever it takes to get him out of the house and anywhere George isn't. Don't tell him what is going on, yet. You can text us or call us if you need help. And please ask for help before you kill the man. Okay?"

Rhoda rolled her eyes and folded her arms. "Fine," she said, softly.

Ivy left Judy with Xander and crossed the lawn to her cabin to meet Vera. As she walked up the stairs, lightning flashed, and thunder rolled.

Vera saw her coming and let her in just as heavy raindrops began pelting her back.

"Heavens to Betsy!" Vera said.

Another flash of lightning and thunder. Ivy fell onto the sofa. "Phew! It sounds like the lightning is just outside. There's almost no time between the flash and thunder."

Charlotte was curled up on the other end of the couch, pale and wringing her hands. "We've been waiting for you. I didn't want to go anywhere without talking to you first."

"Good. I want to be sure this is your decision, and no one is pressuring you," Ivy said.

"I offered her a ride to a hidden shelter just down the coast a bit, until we have things cleaned up here. An advocate is on her way to transport her if she is willing to go," Vera said and popped a piece of gum in her mouth before she sat down at the kitchen table.

"What do you think?" Ivy said

"If I don't like it, can I call you or text you? Would you come and get me?" Charlotte asked.

"Absolutely. I will drop everything and pick you up," Ivy said.

There was a soft knock at the door. Ivy and Charlotte turned to see Vera pull back the curtain on the small window in the door.

"It's my friend. She's here," Vera said. She unlocked the door to let her in.

A small woman with red and grey hair came in, dripping water on the floor. "Holy cow! That came up fast. I think I saw a waterspout on my way up here."

"Rosemary? This is Charlotte," Vera said.

Rosemary drug a kitchen chair across the room and sat on it, facing Charlotte. "Hi. It's a pleasure to meet you, Charlotte. Vera has filled me in, but I want to hear it from your lips. Do you feel like you're in danger? Are you afraid?"

Charlotte looked at her hands. They were shaking. She jumped to her feet and began pacing back and forth in front of Rosemary. "I am terrified. He's going to kill me if he finds out I've talked to any of you," Charlotte said.

"What makes you think that?" Rosemary asked. She leaned forward and sat silently, waiting for Charlotte to find her words.

"He says he will if I leave him or tell anyone. He's needy, you know? He is terrified of losing me, but if I stay, I'm going to die."

"Has he threatened you with a weapon?" Rosemary asked.

Charlotte leaned forward, closed her eyes, took a deep breath and let it out slowly. With her eyes closed, she said, "He has threatened me with a gun and strangled me. I thought I was going to die the last time he choked me. He killed my cat and said he'd do the same to my father and me if I left him."

Rosemary sat back and waited until Charlotte opened her eyes, left her past and returned to the present. Rosemary made eye contact with Charlotte and said, "Well, that's enough for me. We have everything you need at the shelter including clothing, toiletries, food, pet food, entertainment, and most importantly an umbrella."

Charlotte's entire body relaxed, she sat back down on the couch, and smiled. She was still shaking and pale, but Rosemary was reassuring. "So, just like a dorm at college, but with perks."

Rosemary smiled back, reflecting Charlotte's relaxed body language. "Absolutely. You may have to clean your own room, but one of our residents is from another country and she makes the best food I've ever sampled. It makes me want to move in. I think you'll like the other women living there. But you will have your own private room and bathroom."

"I'm ready to move in," Vera said, laughing.

"Me too," Charlotte said.

"Alright, get your coat and let's go," Rosemary said.

"I don't have a coat," Charlotte said.

"No problem. I have a dozen in our boutique for survivors. My pickup is parked right outside the door. It's warmed up and ready to go," Rosemary said. "Ivy, do I need a code to get out, like the one Vera gave me to get into the Sanctuary?"

"No, the gate should open as soon as you are close," Ivy said. Surprised at how proud she was of Charlotte, and melancholy about letting her go, Ivy hugged her and stood at the open door until they drove away.

"Alright Girly, let's get to work," Vera said.

30

SWIMMING WITH THE SHARKS

The wipers on Ivy's SUV worked furiously. It was all she could do to see the taillights of Vera's police car. The storm hid the moon, and tall pines lined the winding coast highway. Without any streetlights, Ivy was left to drive, white knuckled, using the reflectors and yellow paint to stay on the road.

When they pulled into the Marina parking lot, Vera drove across the lot and behind Iverson's Dry Dock offices. Ivy followed her. Lightning flashed; thunder rolled.

They parked under a carport behind the building. Vera took two black rain slickers out of her trunk and handed one to Ivy.

When they rounded the building and could see the Marina parking lot, Vera pointed. "That's the police van. It looks like an old delivery van. It's parked close to the dry dock with the best view of Conner's boat and the pier. It's going to be crowded with the chief, and one of the drug boys, Frank." She smiled broadly, her blue chewing gum showing. "He likes to be called Frank, but sometimes I call him Franklin just to annoy him."

"You're so bad," Ivy said. "You just want to get under his skin."

Vera laughed. "It's such nice skin. Let's go." Vera motioned for Ivy to follow her across the lot and through puddles of standing water in the black night. They pressed their bodies against the back of the van. The windows were tinted black. It looked abandoned.

Ivy anxiously watched for headlights or any sign of George.

Vera knocked, "It's Vera," she said softly. The side door slid open an inch and then opened fully. A tall, lean man with flaming red hair that mirrored Vera's stopped chewing his gum long enough to say, "Look what the cat drug in," in an unmistakable southern drawl.

"Hello, Frank." Vera said. Vera motioned for Ivy to go in first.

The chief was sitting next to an officer, manning a large microphone and looking at a wall of screens showing different parts of the boat, inside and out.

"Ryan. What is going on?" the chief said. He pointed two screens top right. The picture was fuzzy enough it was hard to tell what he was looking at.

"Because of the wind, the bow and stern views aren't great," Ryan said. "They won't be totally available unless the wind and rain stop."

As if on cue, lightning flashed and thunder rolled across the bay.

"Lightning is rare in these parts. We've had some sheet lightning out over the ocean and a few strikes on shore," Frank explained to Ivy.

"What if the power goes out?" Ivy asked.

"We're battery powered and have back up options. As I understand it, the boat has an onboard generator. See on the small screen on top?" He pointed. "That is the engine room. The boys really have the boat wired for sound."

Larger screens showed the main living space on the boat. You could enter the room from the main deck through sliding glass doors.

The bar which Conner normally stocked with Coke Zero, root beer, and goodies was in the far-right corner. Tonight, there were whisky and wine bottles and a small keg of what she guessed was beer, along with red plastic cups on the counter behind the bar.

Next to the bar was a short stairway that led to the sleeping quarters and a small bathroom, as well as the engine room.

A couch was anchored to the floor. A round table was set up next to the couch and three folding chairs were on the opposite side of the table. One camera must have been anchored somewhere in the ceiling. It allowed you to see the top of the table.

Ivy was looking at the green felt and boxes of cards on the table when Nephi's face filled the screen.

"Check. Check. Check. How's our sound?" Nephi said. His face left the screen, but his laughter was loud and long.

The chief bent over Ryan to get close to the mic, and bellowed "Nephi! You better not be sampling the whisky. We need you to take this seriously. I'm going to yank you out of there! They could be armed."

A jolt ran through Ivy. *Guns?* "They won't bring guns to a card game, will they?"

The chief looked at her and shook his head. "Just when I start to think you're a genius."

"Here." Frank rolled a stool in her direction. She sat down, her stomach in knots.

Vera cackled at something Frank said. She sat on a stool in the corner near him. He had a clip board and was adjusting the sound board. Vera was in full uniform. Both the chief and Vera were armed.

"We have a car pulling into the parking lot," Ryan said. George pulled in, driving Xander's black SUV.

The driver's door opened, and a man in a hat and coat got out.

"Is that George?" Ivy asked, softly.

The chief shrugged.

The passenger door opened, and another man got out. The chief jumped to his feet and once again shoved Ryan out of the way. "We've got a wild card, boys. George brought a friend and they are coming your way."

The back passenger door of the SUV opened, and a smaller man emerged.

"Make that two friends." The chief growled and fell into his chair, folding his arms.

"When are the rest of the drug boys going to arrive, Frank?" the chief asked.

"They're on their way. Shouldn't be long now, They are coming in two different vehicles, so it doesn't look like they know each other," Frank said.

"The rain is slowing down," Vera said.

"I wish the wind would stop," Frank said. "I'm getting seasick just thinking about them being on the boat."

"Shush! Who are the other men? We need to know. Vera, as soon as we get their names, call the station and get their background. We need to know who we have. I hate surprises!"

The energy was so high, and Ivy was so anxious about the outcome, she tried to melt into the van's dashboard.

"Hiccup." Ivy was mortified. This was too small a space for hiccups. She looked at her hands and realized they were shaking. She hiccupped again and Frank snickered.

"They are on the wooden dock. Don't forget. Get him to talk about the drugs or get him so broke he has to offer them to pay. We can't arrest anyone for being a gambling addict. And if you can get a confession for Gladys' murder, even better!" The chief took off his aviator style glasses and hat. He wiped his brow with a wrinkled handkerchief he'd pulled from his pants pocket.

Ivy couldn't look away from the screens. When they reached the boat, the three men carefully climbed the plastic stairs up and over the side of the boat. Ivy wished she could catch a glimpse of their faces, but they were hidden deep in their slicker hoods.

All three of the men walked carefully. The boat's deck had sand in the varnish, so it wouldn't be slippery when it was wet. The tallest man reached out for the other man's elbow, like he was trying to help him. The man yanked his elbow away. Conner opened the door, and they filed in. *Why is he treating the other man like he is older and needs to be helped? Is it respect? If George is the larger man, who would he treat that way? An older man? Woman?*

In a flash, she knew. Ivy pointed at the screen. "It's Ashley."

The chief's head spun around.

The larger man's face flashed in the camera as he took off his slicker.

"George! You know you're welcome," Nephi said. He nodded toward the two other men.

George grinned like a cat about to eat a mouse and slapped Nephi on the back.

"Let me take your coats. It's crowded in here," Nephi said.

"I'll keep mine here." George threw his coat into the corner. "I might need to go out and smoke if you are as good as Conner says you are."

The other men's backs were to every camera except one, and it wasn't a good angle.

Ivy had to know if she was right.

George and the other two men took off their coats.

Vera gasped. "You're right, Ivy. It's Ashley."

"Why didn't we see this coming?!" the chief barked.

Ivy didn't move. She was shocked. "We should have known."

251

The last man to remove his coat, pulled back his hood to reveal short, black hair. They couldn't see his face, but no one needed to. It was Brett.

"Brett? Ashley?" Nephi said. "If we'd have known you were bringing a minor, we would have stocked up on energy drinks and candy." Although he was trying to hide it, Nephi's coloring gave him away. He clenched his teeth and anger oozed from every pore. He turned quickly and went down the stairs with their coats.

"George," Conner said. "You promised this was on the downlow. I could get fired and fined for serving a minor alcohol, not to mention this game isn't exactly above board."

Ivy had been so fixated on Nephi, she had forgotten to look at Conner. She trusted Conner to keep his cool, and that is exactly what he was doing. He was trying to take back control of the situation.

"Brett's with me," Ashley said. "We're going to make a man of him tonight. Well, in one way. We can discuss the other ways later. Right, my boy?"

"I brought my own money," Brett said.

"It's a ten thousand dollar buy-in. Where did you get that kind of money?" Conner asked.

"I've been collecting cash from Mom's purse for a long time. Honestly, she probably won't even notice. Ashley gave me the rest," Brett said.

Conner's eyes got wide, but after a beat he was as calm as water. "He's right. We are going to make a man out of you by teaching you a lesson you'll never forget. I'm taking every cent you brought to the table home with me." He took a step and leaned over Brett. "And if word of this game gets out, I will know you went whining to your mommy."

"You won't hurt me," Brett smirked.

"No, but I will, kid." A tall and broad-shouldered man filled the sliding glass door. Ivy had been so fixated on what was happening, she'd missed seeing him get on the boat. He wore a very expensive Grunden rain slicker. He looked like a Pacific Islander. He had tattoos on his neck and up one side of his face that looked tribal. Black braids cascaded down his back.

"I am John Doe. Are we going to play or what?"

"And I'm in love," Vera said. Ivy suppressed a smile.

"Please tell me he's one of ours," Ivy said.

"He is and his name isn't John Doe," Frank said. His face was as serious as a heart attack. "And if anything goes down the wrong way because two people joined the game, he is the one we'll all answer to. He's the highest-ranking detective of the three of us. He is a Temporary Field Officer or TFO with the DEA. He broke records at the police academy for the hostage shot. They will be sorry they messed with Sam. I mean, John Doe."

"I feel better," Ivy said. "Go John Doe."

"I got my cash. Let's play," John Doe said.

Watching more closely, she spotted the second officer walking to the boat. What was left of his hair could be described as a toilet bowl cut with a ponytail. He had a wet brown t-shirt and dress pants that were two sizes too big. Instead of climbing the ladder, he put one hand on the rail and leapt over it to get onboard. He didn't knock, he opened the door, at which time, Ashley pulled a gun and pointed it at him.

"Chillax, Dude. Conner, what is with the antique pistol?"

Conner snatched it from Ashley's hand so quickly, Ashley didn't have time to relax. "Why, this is a Luger P08, World War II era. It only holds eight rounds, old man." Conner emptied it.

Ashley bristled, "That's why a smart man carries an extra magazine."

"How did you get this into the States and past customs?" the wet officer asked. He smiled and one tooth was missing. The tooth next to it was gold. His remaining teeth were crooked.

"When you have money, you can do what you want," Ashley said. He pulled himself to his full height, nose tilted in the air.

The officer put the gun on the table. "This is a dead man free zone."

Ashley didn't respond. He snatched the gun from the table and put it back in the holster under his sweater. "I am not that kind of man. I am a well-respected leader in my community."

The wet officer laughed and snorted, before he held out his hand to Ashley. He mimicked his English accent. "Name's Carl. Who might you be, your highness?"

Ashley said, "You can call me Ash."

"Call you a what?" Carl threw his head back and laughed maniacally. He looked at George and Brett, standing silently by the bar. George held a whiskey, and Brett held an unopened beer.

"You're drinking tonight, little man? Why don't you just give me your cash and skedaddle." Carl held his hand out to Brett.

"I'm not little." Brett put his chin up defiantly. Carl turned to George, and Brett put the bottle back in the fridge and took out a root beer.

"Good decision, Brett," Ivy said to herself.

The chief looked at her, but didn't respond.

"Ivy!" Vera moved closer. "We call him Crazy Carl, because..."

The chief interrupted her. "I think she can tell for herself. I doubt there is a record in the States for Ashley P. Bruce." The chief took out his cell and made a call. "Bruce. I need you to call Scotland Yard and see if Ashley P. Bruce and George Taylor have a criminal record. No, I don't have DOBs for either man. Ashley looks to be about sixty, and George is probably thirty but lives in the fast lane, so he looks around forty. Vera will text you with physical descriptions and photos from the screens in the van. Call me the second you learn anything. Oh, and good luck. You're going to need it."

Vera used her cell to take pictures and texted them.

"Alright blokes. Everyone is here. It's time to let me win all your money," George said and lit a cigar.

Conner got up, snatched it from his mouth, walked out the glass doors and tossed it in the bay. "Not on my boat. No one smokes."

George stood up. "Hey. That was an expensive smoke."

"Sit down, George. I've got dozens. You can have one after the game," Ashley said.

Ivy looked at Vera, eyes wide and moved close enough to whisper. "Who is this guy? He is a completely different Ashley than the one Rhoda introduced us to."

"All I know is that if Xander was here and could see Brett sitting at that table, he would have ruined the sting and thrown Ashley and George in the bay," Vera said.

Ivy's brows raised and she nodded in complete agreement. "Can you imagine if Rhoda walked in on all of this?"

"The only person to leave the boat alive would be Brett, and she would be dragging him out by the ear," Vera said. "I better focus. They're playing their first hand."

The cash had been banked and locked in Conner's safe. Stacks of poker chips lined the table. Ivy wasn't a card player and had no idea what they were playing, other than Conner and the chief calling it poker. She didn't care what it was, she just wanted it to be over.

Nephi lost big time on the first hand.

Vera leaned close to Ivy. "Don't you worry. They all need to lose a little to be believed. Crazy Carl is cheating. You've never seen anyone better at it."

The lightning had moved out to sea. The rain was lighter, but the wind was worse. While they prepared, they checked the radar.

Anxious and worrying about every possible way things could go wrong, Ivy got on her weather app and checked the radar. She passed it to the chief. He swore under his breath. Currently the wind was doable with gusts of thirty-five miles an hour. Two gales were traveling toward them. There was a wind warning. If Ivy was a weather person, she would have predicted the storms merging one massive super storm with winds over eighty-five miles an hour.

"What else can go wrong?" The chief got on the mic. "There is a windstorm headed our way, boys. I figure we have about three hours before it makes landfall."

Nephi had no idea how he did it, but he finally won a hand. In the meantime, George and Ashley were cleaning up. They drank whiskey and celebrated their wins.

"It's going to be a short night at this rate," George said.

"How did you two meet?" Conner asked.

George laughed loudly, and somewhat inebriated, slapped Ashley on the back a little too hard.

"Now that's a story!" George said.

"We don't have to tell it," Ashley said. He frowned and took a big swig of his drink.

"We met at a poker game in a warehouse in the Cotswolds. Ash here owned the pub. I invited him to join the local boys for a game," George said. He laid down his cards and pulled back a pile of chips, including Ashley's and Brett's.

"By the time the game was over, Ash here was into me for a quarter of a million quid," George laughed loudly. "I wasn't about to let him drive away until I had my money,

257

so I made him take me back to his manor house. Phew! What a home. Then I met his daughter. She was smoking hot."

"Leave it," Ashley said. His lips were pressed in a firm line. He stared down at the table.

"This is the best part. I married Ash's daughter!" George threw his head back and guffawed like a donkey.

Vera frowned and shook her head.

"Fudge Biscuits!" Ivy growled.

"We are going to take this son-of-a-gun down if it is the last thing I do as a chief." The chief slammed his fist down on the table, causing Ryan's coffee cup to fall to the floor.

Ivy glanced up and noticed John Doe's biceps twitch. He glanced at George through narrowed eyes. "You won't have to if John Doe gets a hold of him," Ivy said.

It wasn't long after George's love story that the tide changed. In the beginning, George had tripled his buy-in. The game progressed and he kept losing. He was close to broke. Ashley won back most of his buy-in.

"What just happened?" Ivy asked.

"Just you watch," Vera said.

In a matter of minutes, all the chips were in front of Nephi. George had run his debt up to fifty thousand. Crazy Carl was making card magic. No one was the wiser. Even Ivy couldn't tell how he was doing it.

Carl and Nephi looked over their cards at each other. Nephi had the bulk of the chips. Nephi looked at his hand and smiled, like he'd been dealt winning cards.

George looked at his cards. Ivy saw a micro expression. He smiled for a split second. Nephi leaned back in his chair smiling like he was sure he was going to win. George was already deep in debt.

"Give me fifty thou in credit," George said.

"You don't have that kind of money," Nephi said.

George looked at Ashley, winked, and said, "We will soon. I'm driving to L.A. and coming back with cash."

"Give me your passport and I'll give you the credit. If you don't pay it, you won't get it back," Nephi said.

"And if you even think about getting a forgery in this town, I will know. Local forgers owe me and will be on the lookout for you. I will get your picture out to my friends and put a price on your head. I will also report you for sex trafficking. Even if you're not a trafficker, the feds will go through your entire online history."

George didn't flinch. He blinked rapidly and frowned before he fished out his passport. He threw it on the table. Brett's mouth fell open.

George pointed at Nephi. "I will take that back and more. I'm taking Charlotte and leaving this sad little town." George's face relaxed into a smile, and he laid down a full house, three nines, and a king.

One of Nephi's brows rose. "Say goodbye to England for a while." He laid out his cards. He spread out four sevens and an ace. Nephi took the passport, waved it at George, and handed it to Conner who put it in the safe. "Game over, fellas."

George leapt to his feet, almost knocking the table over. His fists and his teeth were clenched. He growled.

John Doe slammed the table like he was angry. One of Carl's eyes looked at John, the other wandered over to George. He laughed low and frighteningly long.

Nephi pointed at George. "Unless you have something else to pay me with hidden in your pockets, your life is mine," Nephi said. "Try to skip out of town and my little friend, John, will send you to your final resting place after our host takes this ship a hundred miles out to sea."

"Boat," Conner said softly.

Carl's eyes crossed, he passed gas and laughed louder.

The façade that was George finally began peeling off his face. He tossed the table over.

"Start up the motor, Conner," Nephi bit his lip, trying to suppress a smile without success.

Conner shook the boat keys in George's face. Ashley tried to take them without success. Brett slowly backed behind the bar, shaking, and wiping his eyes. He crouched down out of sight.

"I have something better and worth more money," George roared, silencing the room, except for Carl, who burped loudly and long. "Shut him up." George pointed at Carl who tried to bite his finger.

"I'll toss you overboard before I will lay a hand on my buddy, Carl," Conner said.

"Just listen!" Now desperation was creeping into George's voice. The room fell silent. With his hands up, palms out, like he was trying to push everyone back, George said, "I have twice that amount in fire, it's quality Fetty. It's top grade, packaged, and ready to sell. I have a buyer in the city. We were supposed to meet tonight.

The drugs are in the car. I'll help you meet the buyer and give you your cut, or you do what you want, just give me my passport tonight."

"Not happening," John Doe said. "We won't let you out of sight until we have the Fetty. We know what to do with it. We don't need your buyer."

"What is fire or fetty?" Ivy asked.

"Names for Fentanyl," Frank said.

All the color went out of George's face. For the first time, Ivy saw panic in his eyes. He stepped back, away from the table.

"How do we even know how good the Fetty is or if it's something we can sell until we see it?" Conner said.

"It's good, okay?" George said.

"It was good enough to kill that old bat in the bakery, wasn't it?" Ashley said.

Ivy gasped. She had hoped for a confession, but was shocked by Ashley's callousness.

"You killed Gladys?" Nephi said. "Did you push Rhoda off the boat too?"

George's smile spread, his eyes narrowed, and he laughed softly. "So, what if I did? Watching you try to resuscitate her was more fun than I've had in a while."

"We got him, boys. Bring them in. All of them," the chief said quietly into the mic. "Frank, call in the troops." Frank got on his cell phone.

"Not Brett, please?" Ivy said.

Two county squad cars quietly pulled alongside the van.

261

"Move, Ryan. I need the mic from here on out," the chief said. Speaking into the mic, he said, "Give them time to get on dry land."

George turned his back to the screen. He picked up his coat, fumbled with the pocket and dropped it.

Ivy jumped to her feet and pointed at the screen. "Chief, he's got a gun."

When George turned around, he was pointing a snub-nosed revolver. He swung it from side to side and man to man.

"Throw my passport to me," George said.

Nephi did as they were told. It landed at his feet.

"Come on, man. I thought we were friends." Crazy Carl smiled wickedly, but did not laugh.

George backed up against the glass door. He pointed the gun at the silent room, using his other hand to unlock and open the sliding doors. The wind filled the room. He backed out of the doors and onto the wet deck.

John Doe took a step toward George. George fired a shot that embedded itself in the wood near John's head. While they all looked at John, George leapt overboard. The splash was muffled by the sound of the wind.

Conner, Nephi, and John ran to the rail, but the wind-blown camera didn't show any sign of George in the choppy water.

"Go! Go! Go! Get that man before he gets on another boat!" the chief shouted into the mic.

Lights and sirens on, the squad cars sped toward the boat. A squad car parked sideways, blocking the path to the floating dock, the other stopped at the spot where

George would be more likely to emerge if he was swimming. They swung a rooftop spotlight back and forth on the water and boats.

No one was looking at the screens.

"Gentlemen," Ash said.

Ivy looked up at the screen and a shiver ran down her spine. Ashley had Brett in a one-armed choke hold with the Luger pointed at his temple with his other.

"Brett!" Instinctually Ivy lunged for the van door. Vera grabbed the back of her shirt.

"There is a gun out there. You stay here," the chief said.

All they could do was watch it play out. All eyes were on Ashley, the wild card in the game.

"Toss me the boat keys," Ashley said.

"Not again," Conner's shoulders fell. "This boat is new! My last boat sank." He frowned, fished in his pocket, distracting Ash while Carl tried to move around behind him. Conner threw his keys on the deck.

But Ash was too smart for Carl. He swung out and pistol whipped him, opening a gash in Carl's forehead. Carl swayed, but didn't fall.

Ash shook Brett once and said, "Pick up the keys, nice and slow." With his arm around Brett's neck, Ash pushed him closer to the floor.

Brett picked up the keys.

"Everyone off the boat! Now!" Ash barked.

"We're not going without the boy," Nephi said. John stood next to him, his arms folded.

263

Ash tightened his chokehold, while Brett clawed at Ash's arm uselessly.

"I've killed before and will not hesitate to send you all straight to the bottom of the ocean. Now back up!" Ash barked.

"Let him breathe, man!" Crazy Carl lunged at Ash again. This time, Ash caught him on the cheek.

"Oh, man," Carl said and spit his gold tooth into his hand before pocketing it.

Ivy was so glued to the screen and the unfolding drama; she jumped when the mic clicked.

The chief quietly said, "Conner, get your men off the boat."

"Everybody off the boat like Ash says," Conner said.

One by one, they backed onto the deck. Crazy Carl was the last to go.

"It's okay, Carl. Get off!" Conner barked. He pointed at the dock.

Once they were off, they all watched helplessly as Ash pulled Brett across the boat's deck and threw him overboard on the open water side, away from the dock. Brett screamed as he went in and then it was silent.

Ash locked himself in the cabin and charged up to the helm. John jumped back onto the boat, crossed the bobbing deck, and expertly dove into the choppy water. Ivy lost sight of him in the churning waves. All she could see or hear was the wind blowing the surf on the water. In less than a minute, he surfaced with Brett and swam towards shore.

"Ashley is getting away," Nephi shouted and began climbing back onto the boat.

Conner grabbed his belt. "Stand down. I gave him my car keys. He's going nowhere."

A gunshot passed through the acrylic window on the helm before a string of swear words.

"I'm going to kill you all! Stay back!" Ashley was clearly as panicked as he was angry and dangerous.

The lights on Xander's SUV came on.

Ivy jumped to her feet. "Chief! George! Someone started Xander's car!"

They'd all been so fixated on the drama unfolding on the boat, no one saw George come on shore. The motor fired up and the tires spit gravel as the car flew out of the parking lot and turned south on Highway 101.

Ivy grabbed her fob and began running to her SUV.

"Stop her, Vera," the chief yelled from the van.

Ivy didn't look back. She was almost to the Jeep when she heard Vera breathing heavily beside her.

"I'm driving," Vera said. "Get in back, Conner's coming. And buckle up, buttercup."

Ivy smiled broadly and climbed in the back seat.

"Shotgun!" Conner shouted, making Ivy jump.

"You drive!" Vera yelled and threw him the keys before getting in the passenger side.

Nephi picked up Ivy, pushed her to the other side of the SUV, and climbed in beside her.

Conner pushed the button to start the motor. There was no sound. "What's wrong?" he bellowed.

"Hybrid," Ivy shouted.

Conner backed out and hit the accelerator, spraying gravel. "Oh, yeah." Conner laughed hysterically.

Dismayed, Ivy shook her head, but felt adrenaline wiping away all her common sense.

George was well out of sight. Conner took every twist and turn on the winding highway so tightly, they hit the gravel roadside more than once.

"Watch it! That's a hundred-yard drop! I don't want to get my hair wet," Vera yelled over the noise of the motor.

"Taillights! There he is." Nephi pointed ahead.

Conner slammed on the brakes, hit the steering wheel, and said, "It's an RV. The driver is probably ninety and can't see over the steering wheel."

"Hey now. I have one of those," Vera said.

"Yeah, but you live in yours, so it stays put," Conner said, and smiled.

"If we're stuck in traffic, so is he. What's the hold up?" Nephi said.

"I'll check with dispatch," Vera said.

Before Vera got her call to connect, they rounded a bend and got their answer. Half a dozen cars were blocked by a massive tree, rock, and mud slide covering more than fifty percent of the road. Xander's vehicle was stuck in the middle of the line of cars.

An older man, Ivy guessed was a local volunteer fire-fighter, held a stop sign. Another man was putting up a sawhorse with flashers and a road closed sign.

Suddenly, Xander's SUV pulled onto the right shoulder of the road. One of the firefighters frantically waved him away. George hit the gas, the firefighter jumped out of the way as George spun his tires and mowed down the sawhorse. He rounded the rock pile on the edge of a twelve-hundred-foot drop to the Pacific and drove out of sight. The firefighters gave up trying to stop him. Their shoulders slumped. They put the barricade back up, and walked around the rubble and out of sight.

Conner turned off the car. He and Vera jumped out with Nephi and Ivy on their heels.

"We have to get around this and find him," Conner said. He flashed his badge at the firefighter. "You need to let us through!"

"No can do."

"Police, now move!" Vera barked.

"Volunteer Firefighter and I don't care who you are, you aren't moving. Not unless you want to die," the firefighter said. He pointed behind him. "Go see for yourself. But be careful, officer. It's a long way down."

The firefighter stepped aside, and Ivy gasped. Little known to out of towners, large chunks of Highway 101 and the cliffside occasionally slid off the side of the mountain. On the other side of the slide, a massive half-circle of the road and mountain was missing.

Ivy reached out and grabbed Conner's arm to steady herself. "George must have gone over the edge of the cliff." Her heart was pounding in her ears at the horrifying thought of anyone falling that far.

Just beyond that, there was another barricade and a bulldozer clearing the rockslide. At the speed he was going, George had nowhere to go but over the edge.

"Was that your friend that went over?" the firefighter said. He looked at Conner, blinking rapidly. "I'm lucky he didn't take me with him. I've notified dispatch."

Conner shook his head. "He is a suspect in a case I am working on. Here's my card. His name is George Taylor. I'll notify dispatch. They have his details."

"Did he fall all the way down? Is there any chance..." Ivy asked.

"I'm sorry. It would take a miracle for your friend to survive a fall from this height," he shrugged. "This will be all over the Facebook scanner page. When we find him, you'll know if you follow the local page." He picked up his stop sign and went back to work.

31

PULLING A VERA

Conner drove carefully back to the Marina. "Have you been able to reach the chief, Vera?"

"I can't get a call or text to go through. As soon we get cell service, I'm going to check with dispatch," Vera said.

Ivy reached across the seat and touched Nephi's hand. "John was a hero."

Nephi nodded. "Most beautiful dive I've ever seen. Definitely better than your cannonball."

"Are you kidding? My cannonball was epic." Ivy smiled, remembering.

"You looked more like a ping pong ball than a cannonball." Nephi squeezed her hand and smiled, his eyes laughing.

A squad car and officer blocked the entrance and exit to the marina. He recognized Conner and Vera. He motioned for them to drive around the car and enter the parking lot.

The officer approached the window. "Stay behind the van." He pointed. "Park there and keep your head down. We have a shooter."

"Thanks, man." Conner expertly took them around the squad car and parked Ivy's car behind the van between her SUV and the boat.

Armed officers were behind parked cars surrounding the dock and keeping Ashley from leaving the boat.

Conner turned, looking at Ivy and Nephi. "You should go home. If you stay here, don't get out of the car. Let's go, Vera."

"What's happening?" Ivy asked.

Vera turned in her seat. "Isn't it obvious? It's a standoff. He's right. Go home and get some sleep. I'll come to your cabin before sunrise. I'll ask the chief to let us collect Charlotte and bring her to Knightly House, where we can tell her about George with some support. Tomorrow's going to be a paperwork nightmare."

"Crepes. Where's Brett? Someone is going to have to tell Rhoda and Xander. She'll be out for blood," Ivy said.

"Don't you worry about Brett. I am sure he's back in Balefire Bay, safely locked in our interview room and someone has called his mommy," Conner said.

"Then he's not safe," Nephi said.

Vera slipped out of the SUV and followed Conner to the van. They both emerged wearing bulletproof vests, helmets, carrying a shield and big guns. They crouched down and jogged over to the chief, hiding behind a minivan.

She and Nephi didn't move. Finally, she opened her phone and the Facebook scanner page for the county.

"It's already on the scanner page," Ivy said. She showed Nephi her cell. "I don't know how they got a picture that fast. There is a photo and post about the slide and the report of a car driving erratically and falling off the cliff." She refreshed the page. "Here's the post of the standoff with a picture of the marina. The person who posted it must have taken the picture from the highway."

"What does it say?" Nephi asked.

Ivy scrolled. "Nothing we don't already know. They talk about the standoff. They say the shooter is on a pleasure boat. Pleasure. Conner will love having his fishing boat described as a pleasure boat."

Two shots rang out. Surprised, they both jumped. Ivy's heart pounded in her chest. Ash screamed, "Back off!" Or at least Ivy thought that was what he said. The words were muffled by their vehicle and the wind.

"That's three shots, unless we missed one while we were gone," Nephi said. He got out and scrambled to join the chief, Vera, and Conner.

"Chief's going to love this," Ivy said. She slipped out of the car and ran to join the others. Another shot made her jump before she got to the chief.

"Do you know how to follow directions, Miss Marple?!" the chief bellowed. If you get yourself shot,

I'm going to shoot you twice more, just for good measure."

Ivy grinned sheepishly, shrugged, her brows rose to new heights. "Sorry, Chief."

Nephi's cell phone rang. He jerked his head back. "You don't suppose... "

"Answer it!" the chief said through gritted teeth. "Put it on speaker."

Nephi did as he was told. "Hello?"

"Is this the fisherman's servant?" Ashley said.

Nephi rolled his eyes. "How did you get this number?"

"It's taped to the dash by the wheel. Put your constable on the line," Ashley said.

"Constable?" Nephi said.

"Give me that." The chief took it from Nephi.

"We know you're almost out of ammo. You can't kill us all before we drag your sorry little royal body off that boat. We've called Scotland Yard. We have your number. You won't be safe anywhere in the US," the chief said.

"Can he do that?" Ivy whispered to Vera.

"Doesn't matter as long as Ashley believes him," Vera whispered.

"You don't know how many bullets I've got. All I have to do is get this boat started and I will be on my way. Either tell me where a set of keys are on the boat or have someone bring me the keys," Ashey ordered, like he was ordering a gardener to shovel horse manure.

"Not happening. You come out, hands up, pockets turned out, and lay on the dock," the chief said, through clenched teeth, sounding more like he was growling than speaking.

"Then you better put your head down." A shot ricocheted off the family van they were crouched behind.

"That's eight, isn't it?" Vera said.

"I count eight," the chief said. "But the second I send someone charging in there, he'll reload. We can't take the risk." He pointed at Ivy and Nephi. "You two. I guess you aren't going to listen, are you, Miss Marple? Take your buddy back to the van and wait until we have him in custody."

"He could try to swim," Ivy said.

"I'm not going to jump in to save his sorry life," Vera said.

The chief tried to talk Ashley into surrendering. After some time, Ashley's cell went silent. They tried to reach him, and it went straight to voicemail.

The chief wiped his forehead with a handkerchief. "His phone's dead. It goes straight to voicemail. Everyone, let's head back to the van."

Conner held his position with Nephi. The chief, Vera, and Ivy scrambled back to the van.

Everyone held their positions, silently watching the monitors.

The sun peeked over the mountains in the east, lighting up the parking lot and exposing officers who fell back.

"I need coffee and a bookstore bakery," Vera said. "We need to end this."

One of the chief's brows rose as his eyes looked like they'd burn a hole in Vera's forehead. "Okay, Vera. How are you going to make that happen?" the chief said.

Vera pushed her way past the chief, stepped out of the van, in full view of Ashley and shouted, "Shoot me, you sorry excuse for a man!"

The chief reached out and grabbed her by the arm and yanked her back inside. "Are you crazy? I ought to write you up and fire your fanny!"

Vera put her hands on her hips. "See, I told you! His Luger holds eight rounds. He was bluffing, and he's too much of a coward to jump in the water. He ain't smart enough to start the boat without the keys, and if he did, I'm sure he can't drive the thing."

The chief rubbed his face with both hands. "Well then, why don't you go out there and get him?"

Vera turned and took a step toward the door before the chief pulled her back, again.

"Seriously, Vera. Sit down!" He motioned to the chair. "For the love of all that is holy!"

"Hey!" Ryan turned in his chair to face everyone until he had their attention. Then he pointed at the screen. "You don't have to go out there. Crazy Carl and John are already there."

There he was, Crazy Carl, yelling obscenities at the boat. His forehead was still bleeding as he walked up the dock and easily jumped onboard. John emerged from the water just like a scene out of a movie, and hung on the side of the boat, holding onto the rail. Working hand over hand, he made his way toward the bow.

Carl climbed to the top of the helm and was kicking the broken window when John emerged like Aquaman, gently moved Carl over, and with one kick, pushed in the entire front window. They heard Carl yelling and Ashley screaming for help.

Ashley ran out the sliding door to the deck. Carl took a hold of him, while John stood by, grinning from ear to ear.

"What is Carl doing?" Ivy said.

"Why, he's giving him a wedgie. I need to ask Carl out. What a man," Vera said. She folded her arms and grinned, winking at Ivy.

Sure enough, Carl had a handful of white underwear and was pulling it as hard as he could, lifting Ashley off his feet.

"I'm going to get a complaint of police brutality." The chief sat down.

"I'm going to get a picture." Vera had her cell phone out before the chief could stop her.

"Hey! My boat!" Conner ran down the dock to salvage what was left of *Never Again II.*

32

Book Club Meeting

"Are you up?" Nephi said. He took the steps to her deck two at a time and plopped down in the chair next to her. Ivy quickly turned her back on him and cupped her hand around her cell so he couldn't see the name of the person she was talking to.

Ivy whispered into her phone. "Okay. Okay. I've got company, so I need to go. Great to talk to you too."

"Are you keeping secrets?" Nephi asked.

Ivy chuckled. "Of course, I am. I am a mysterious woman."

"Let me see the phone." Nephi reached for her cell.

She quickly covered the phone and put it in her hoodie pocket.

"I want to go down and see what is happening with George and the slide," Nephi said. "What do you think?"

"You don't need to. I checked the best online source for breaking news. Do you want to see?"

"You're talking about your Facebook group again." He rolled his eyes.

"The area is closed as they put together an incident report and recover Xander's car. You're not going to see pics like the group's anywhere else online. Read the comments for up to the minute details." Ivy opened one of her favorite groups on social media, *Believe It Balefire Scanner Page.*

The top post had photos of the slide in the early morning sun and an ambulance standing by. Men in harnesses stood a foot back from the edge looking down.

"I bet this shot was taken with a drone," Ivy said. It was a video that went from the men on Highway 101 and followed the cliffside past a climber and down to the rocks. More pictures were sprinkled throughout the comments. Another climber was already at the bottom of the cliff, studying Xander's SUV, which was resting with the wheels up and top crushed.

"Has Xander seen this?" Nephi asked

"I don't know. How did they get this picture of the county sheriff's department boat with a diver going over the side and into the water?"

"Any sign of George?"

Ivy was silent for a minute. "I can't see how he could survive this."

"I wonder if it will take the Jaws of Life to get into the vehicle. Can't we ask Conner?" Nephi said.

"Maybe, but it's still an open investigation. Conner has rules to follow."

Nephi winked. "I am certain you can get him to abandon his principles, Miss Marple. I know, ask Vera."

She laughed lightly. "Maybe, but I am saving my charms for a serious emergency. Besides, even you should know George isn't in the picture anymore, literally. Hopefully the drama is over. I saw the chief leave Knightly House early this morning. I am pretty sure he was delivering the bad news to Charlotte and Rhoda," Ivy said.

"Is it bad news?" Nephi smiled and tipped his head.

"Rhoda must have been so shocked. I wondered about Ashley, but had no idea he was so evil he would sell his daughter to pay a debt," Ivy said.

"Do you think the chief told Charlotte about her father using her to settle a debt?"

"I don't know. She'll find out eventually," Ivy said.

"Maybe it's a good thing George had the accident, and Ashley is in jail. If Rhoda could have gotten her hands on them, there'd be another murder." He sighed. "I would like to have seen that."

"Not me! But I do feel terribly sad for Charlotte. I need to go see how she is," Ivy said.

"She's lucky to be rid of him. I doubt she will even miss him," Nephi said.

Ivy let out a heavy sigh. "You'd be surprised. No matter how awful things get in a marriage, it is still an ending, a loss. I had to grieve the loss of a dream, of what I wished it would be."

He surprised her by standing up and pulling her into a hug. "You're right. Sorry." His arms dropped and he looked intently into her eyes.

Ivy looked down. "I know you understand."

After a moment, he gave her another quick hug. "Do you want to go to Aggie's?"

Ivy walked to the rail and looked down on Balefire. It was a sunny morning with her favorite eagles fishing in the bay. It looked like any other day, but Ivy knew that it was a day Charlotte and Rhoda would never forget. Brett would no doubt remember last night and today too.

"I want to find out what happened to Brett and see how everyone is doing," Ivy said.

"I was pretty sure you would want to stay here. I called Aggie to ask if she would deliver. Jenny said Aggie got up early and made soup, sandwiches, and cinnamon rolls for everyone. She asked if we would pick them up. Can I borrow your car?"

"Not on your life. And I will drive."

Ivy pulled into Aggie's back parking lot before they walked around the building to the Balefire Bay Book & Tea Shop's entrance.

The chief was sitting by the front window with his morning coffee. Aggie was knitting in the chairs across from him.

The screen door slammed, and Nephi said, "Honey, I'm home!"

"You're not my honey, young man," Aggie said, smiling.

"Great," Jenny said.

He stood next to the chief. "I wasn't talking about you." He leaned over and kissed the chief's bald head.

"Hey, now!" The chief used a napkin to wipe his head.

Grinning, Nephi sat next to him. Ivy sat by Aggie.

"You're in a chipper mood this morning, young man," Aggie said and knit a few more stitches.

"Yes, I am! Does anyone else want a kiss or a hug?" Nephi held his arms out.

"Shouldn't you ask the chief for his consent?" Jenny said.

Aggie fell into a fit of giggles.

"What wound you up?" the chief said.

Nephi's eyes twinkled over his crooked smile. "Let me tell you all about it." Nephi leaned toward the chief until he had the chief's full attention. "I am no longer a person of interest, a suspect, George's patsy for every crime he committed. And there is plenty of work for me to do on Conner's boat. Soon, we are going to be at sea in the sunshine making money and catching fish. It doesn't get any better than that."

The chief nodded, smiling. "I guess you're right. It's a great day for you. It's also a good day for Ivy. When we interviewed Ashley, he admitted he was responsible for the note in Ivy's pocket that said, *stop or die*. He was trying to scare her away. He regrets not following through on his warning. He thought you were too feminine and nice to be a real threat."

"He got that wrong," Aggie said. She sat up proudly. "We should all be thanking Ivy. Without her complete incapacity to give up when she's made up her mind, they

280

might have killed Rhoda, collected on her life insurance, and who knows what would have happened to Brett, Charlotte, or Xander. Ivy, your obsessive nature is a gift to us all." She leaned toward Ivy and winked. She pulled on her yarn and kept rapidly working.

One corner of Nephi's mouth turned up. "She is a little like a bloodhound, isn't she? No. She's more of a Shih Tzu."

Ivy turned her nose up at Nephi. "I've given up a lot of things, like ballet, dieting, and true crime mysteries to be the best Shih Tzu you know. You're welcome."

"I bet you watch true crime documentaries," Nephi said.

"No doubt," Ivy said. Ivy leaned closer to Aggie and studied her project, trying to change the subject. "What are you making?"

Aggie said, "I am making baby booties in yellow, and a matching hat in an adorable light green." Aggie held up her partially finished bootie for Ivy to see.

"Jessica is making matching hats for Charlotte's baby," Jenny said.

"That is so nice of Jessica. Your stitches are incredibly even. I could never do anything like this," Ivy said.

"Tsk. Tsk. Tsk. You and I both know you can do anything you set your mind to," Aggie said.

Nephi pointed at the bootie. "No. She can't do that. I'm sure." Nephi laughed at his own joke.

"So, you know about Charlotte's baby?" Ivy said.

"The chief was just filling us in, poor girl," Jenny said.

"Poor girl and poor Rhoda. She thought she finally had her prince charming," Aggie said.

"Xander is with his mother. One minute she is furious and the next minute she is crying like her heart is broken," Ivy said. "Who wouldn't be upset?"

The chief put down his cup. "I never saw that one coming. Ashley was an unexpected player."

"I agree," Ivy said. "It was Brett that blindsided me. I knew something was going on with him, but didn't expect to see the three of them together like that. Do we know any more about how he got there?"

The chief wiped his glasses with his handkerchief. "He wouldn't talk last night. I finally got answers today. George gave Brett two milligrams of Fentanyl to put on the roll that was meant for Rhoda. He said it was crystalized marijuana and would knock her out, giving Brett a break from her. Not being familiar with drugs and thinking it was a prank, because marijuana is legal in Oregon, he put it on the roll that Gladys took without asking. At some point he panicked, changed his mind, and knocked the plates onto the floor."

Aggie put down her knitting and pushed herself out of the overstuffed chair. "So, it was all about getting Rhoda's money, even if Brett went to prison for life?"

The chief nodded. "He was set up to take the blame. That's why they kept him close. They were spooked and were threatening to hurt Anderson or one of the family if he told anyone. They were telling him he was a man and grooming him as a patsy. Turns out Ashley had a large life insurance policy on Rhoda."

"I would like to give those two a real piece of my mind and the bottom of my shoe in their backside," Aggie said.

"Don't you worry," the chief said. "They are going to pay for their crimes. Scotland Yard had a thick file on both men, but have never had enough evidence to charge them. Ashley married at least three other women for their money. Unfortunately, one is missing, and the other two were frightened and didn't report his theft of their money. He is a real Lord, but his family's money ran out years ago. He runs gambling establishments throughout the UK. We're piling on all the charges we can. We will prosecute them before they are deported, or the Yard comes to escort them back to England. That way, if he returns to the states, he will have to serve the full sentence without early release."

"What about Brett? I know he did the wrong thing, but he is so young," Ivy said.

The chief nodded in agreement. "That he is. I visited with the prosecutor by phone as soon as I knew the whole story. Brett agreed to testify against George and Ashley. As long as he cooperates, he will likely get bench probation and some community service hours. His attorney will work with the District Attorney and settle out of court."

"Well done, Chief. Does Rhoda know?" Aggie said.

"I phoned her before I came here," the chief said.

"We should go home and check in to see if Rhoda or the family needs any help," Ivy said.

"Before you go, I want to apologize to you, Miss Marple. The books Xander shared made me look into the caretaker's history. He had an uncle that came to Balefire after serving honorably in World War II. That and the fact the uncle was stationed in Germany toward the end of the war made me wonder if he'd left the books behind with his brother and they were in storage with other memorabilia, like Ashley's Luger. If that is where Ashley got the gun, the antique dealer is in hot water."

"I'd be happy to go through the antique store's inventory," Ivy said.

The chief chuckled. "I'm sure if he sold the gun, it wasn't listed on his records. We have enough for a search warrant letting us go through the store, his apartment, and vehicle. It went to the judge this morning."

"He hasn't been paid for the books yet. What do you want us to do if he calls Xander?" Ivy asked.

"Stall. I have the books the antique dealer gave Xander and Vera researched the antique dealer's criminal history looking for aliases. There's plenty of evidence to convince the judge to let us take a peek and see if he is dealing in stolen goods and also killed the caretaker."

Ivy exhaled loudly. "And you were right. The murders weren't connected. Thank you for telling me. I was beginning to think everyone was right, I see murder in every mystery. I seriously questioned myself."

"You weren't wrong. You do have a nose for murder, and you have twenty-twenty vision. That's why I listen to you even when it might land me in hot water. Thanks to you, we know Ashley and George had a motive: money from the life insurance policy." The chief winked at Ivy.

"That's why her death needed to look like an accident, not suicide or homicide. The insurance would have investigated her murder, delaying a payout," Ivy said.

"Yes Ma'am. I am sure they thought being in a small town like Balefire would make getting away with her murder easier, and that a country bumpkin police force wouldn't spot it. What they didn't count on, was you, Miss Marple."

"Poor Rhoda," Aggie said. "She lost all her dreams of a happy ending all at once."

"Poor Rhoda? You've got to be kidding me." Jenny threw her hands up in the air. "She lives in a massive house with her perfect sons. There is nothing poor about Rhoda. She will bounce back."

"I believe you're right. She always has. Ivy, I made soup for Rhoda and the Knightly House," Aggie said. "I put the soup and sandwiches in a transportable warming tray, so they should be fairly easy to carry as long as you don't go on another high-speed chase."

"I can't promise a thing," Ivy said.

Ivy and Nephi followed Aggie to the backroom of the store. The hot box was on a desk by the back door. "Here, young man. You carry the box. Ivy, here is a box of my peach cinnamon rolls." Nephi reached over to open the box lid. Aggie slapped his hand. "If Ivy tells me, you ate a single roll before you gave them to Anderson, it'll be the last roll you eat." Then she winked at him.

Nephi picked up the heavy box of food. Aggie held the door open for him.

"Then I better make sure you don't hear." Nephi laughed loudly while he trotted to the SUV.

"Don't worry. I'll keep him in line," Ivy said, smiling.

Aggie waved goodbye. "See you, love. You let us know if we can do anything else, and please send our love and condolences to everyone."

33

EGGS AND BEGINNINGS

Ivy parked near the front door to Knightly House. She looked at Nephi. He looked back, lips pressed firm, determined to go in.

"Are you okay going in?" Ivy said.

"I never know what to say to people when someone dies or this..." Nephi stared at the house.

"I don't either. When I lost my parents, the last thing I wanted was for someone to try to make it better by saying things like, 'at least they didn't suffer,'" Ivy said.

"I know. People said my son was in Heaven waiting for me, and it was meant to be." Nephi continued looking straight ahead. "That one always infuriated me. Was that God's will? Does God let children die? I should have died with him."

"Ouch. I would hate that, and I don't even know if there is a God," Ivy said.

"You," Nephi said, looking in her eyes.

She didn't understand what he meant. She waited for a full minute until she said, "Me?"

He nodded but didn't make eye contact. "You and Aggie."

Her brows drew together, and she waited for him to explain.

Still staring at the front door, he said, "You saved me after Aggie found me. You're my evidence of God, a higher power who cared enough about me to put me where I was. It felt like a miracle."

"I remember feeling that way about Aggie. It was magic, unbelievable luck, or whatever. It was beyond a co-incidence. But God?" Ivy said.

"Exactly. But God. I was lost. I wouldn't have been found, but God. I should have killed myself, but God. I was alone and in need, but God."

Ivy thought for a minute. "I guess. But a real miracle? Magic? I wonder what the mathematical odds would be for both of us, old friends, to meet Aggie on the same coast bus and be convinced to come to Balefire Bay for a job she knew she could get us? I still don't understand why He doesn't save people like your baby boy. If my comparative religions course and research is correct, He's raised people from the dead, so why not save all of us?"

"He did." Nephi opened the door and got out, waiting for her on the stairs.

"I don't get it," Ivy said.

"I do, finally."

Ivy got the box of rolls from the back seat. They walked quietly, side by side up the stairs and knocked on the door.

Anderson swung the door open wide, smiling from ear to ear. He took the rolls and motioned for them to follow him, "Come in! We're in the kitchen." He looked completely different to Ivy compared to the day he was polishing the counter for Rhoda. He sat the rolls down, threw his hands in the air, and bounced on his toes,

"Everyone! Food's here," Anderson announced. They placed it on the bar and unpacked the soup and sandwiches.

Rhoda was actually talking softly. She and Charlotte were at the table. Brett and Xander were first to dish up their plates.

"I'm starved," Charlotte said. She and Rhoda got in line for food.

"Finally. They didn't feed me at all at the station," Brett said.

"My poor baby boy," Rhoda hobbled over to Brett and gave him a kiss on his cheek.

"Mom! I'm not a baby."

"You'll always be my baby, just like your brother. I think I will make letting me kiss you a part of your family community service plan." Rhoda went to give him another kiss. He ducked.

Xander's eyes twinkled as he stuck his tongue out at Brett.

"What are you, twelve?" Brett said.

"Better twelve than a hundred and twelve," Xander said.

"Alright, you two. The mother-to-be should have been allowed to dish up her food first. Make way," Rhoda said.

Ivy caught Xander's eye and joined him at the table, "How is Charlotte?"

"Doing better than I expected her to," Xander said. He put down his bowl of soup and pulled her into a warm embrace. "You smell so good." He kissed her. "I was so worried when I heard what was happening. Then I was furious that the chief let you be there at all. Now, I am relieved."

"I'm my own woman. I go where and do what I want." Ivy squared her shoulders.

"You definitely do what you want, and I love you for it," Xander said. "But maybe you should be required to do family community service too."

"What did you have in mind?" Ivy said.

"I think a back rub would be a sufficient punishment." Xander winked.

Ivy got on her tiptoes, pulled him to her and kissed his cheek. "I better get a peach roll before they're all gone," Ivy said.

Ivy was filling her plate when Nephi walked over to Brett, sat by him, and asked him how he was. His kindness melted her heart. Soon, things would go back to the way they were and the electricity she'd felt between them would need to end and be packed away. He looked up, serious, and met her gaze as if he'd known she was staring at him.

Charlotte tapped Ivy on the shoulder and surprised her with a tight hug.

"How are you holding up? It must be so hard. And I'm so sorry about your dad, too, Charlotte," Ivy said.

"He will bounce back. He isn't that old. It will be nice to know where he is, even if it is in prison, and have some space from the chaos. I was feeling guilty for leaving George and terrified at the same time. Father loved him more than me, or at least I thought so. I also knew George would take my baby away from me or worse. He was already threatening me with it," Charlotte said.

Ivy hugged her back and sat down at the table, inviting Charlotte to sit next to her. "Did the chief tell you what happened?"

"Not all of it. I saw some of it when Rhoda and Xander were looking online. The chief told me George had died and that he couldn't comment on an open investigation. He's coming over tomorrow for a full interview."

"I'll let him fill you in after he takes your statement," Ivy said.

Nephi put two small rolls in front of Ivy and Charlotte. The rest of the group finished eating and gathered around the island talking, and glancing their way once in a while.

"Is it wrong that I felt a huge weight lift when I knew he was dead for sure?" Charlotte said.

Ivy thought for a moment. "I know I haven't told you my whole story, but no. I remember feeling the same way. I had been hypervigilant for so long, I was exhausted. I still catch myself looking over my shoulder."

Charlotte nodded. "It's a habit. Sometimes, I start crying when I think about George and me. I always thought I would raise my children in England with my father. You know? The dogs, the horses, and room to play. Now I don't know where life will take me," Charlotte said. "That's the only thing that makes me sad, really, really sad. I didn't think I would end up so alone."

Ivy noticed Xander was listening to Charlotte. He joined them at the table. "You're welcome to stay here as long as I can have one of these rolls." He smiled at Charlotte. "Ivy will tell you, there are a lot of little cabins and houses hidden in the woods with room for you."

"Thank you, but I don't want to impose."

"Impose? Impose!" Rhoda said and sat at the long table with them. "You're carrying my first grandchild. You are not an imposition. You are a gift from God. Please don't leave." Rhoda reached across the table and took Charlotte's hand. "No one was there for me when I was a young mother. Poor Xander will tell you what a rotten mother I was. I never want you to feel like I did. You always have me. Anything I have is yours."

Charlotte squeezed Rhoda's hand. "Thank you, Rhoda. Forgive me for misjudging you. You're a treasure. I would be so grateful to have a family like this surrounding my child and helping me raise my baby."

Ivy couldn't get over the change in Rhoda. The only explanation Ivy could think of was the news she was going to be a grandmother.

"Then it's settled. Let's find a few cottages together in the Sanctuary, and if there isn't one to your liking, Xander will build one, won't you dear?" Rhoda said.

Xander's mouth was full. He glanced at Ivy who nodded yes back to him. He swallowed and said, "Absolutely."

"That is too generous and costly," Charlotte said.

Xander wiped his mouth and looked around the table. "When I had all the money in the world, the success, and the fans, it was just Anderson and me. I don't know if you agree, Anderson, but it was lonely sometimes. What is the point of being successful if you don't have a family to share it with? You are now our family, and your baby will be loved. Do you want to stay here? It's your choice."

The room was silent while Charlotte looked from face to face. A single tear ran down her cheek. She wiped her nose with a napkin and softly said, "I choose you."

"Even me?" Brett asked.

Contagious laughter broke the spell and made a magical memory. The kind that binds families together.

At the end of the day, Ivy was sitting on her deck waiting for the sunset when she heard Judy bark happily. Judy ran to her and jumped onto her lap.

Xander was right behind Judy. He gave Ivy a quick kiss and sat in the chair next to her.

"The sky is as beautiful as you are," Xander said.

"Awe." She smiled at him. "I've missed this quiet time, just you and me and the sea."

"Me too. Listen, I came down to apologize. I have been so busy trying to make Mom and everyone happy, I neglected us. I never want to take you for granted. I told Mom, nicely, that she would have to solve some of her own problems from now on," Xander said.

"And I need to apologize to you. Something happened when my life and ex were a mess. I blamed myself. I stopped trusting my own judgement, which made trusting anyone else nearly impossible. I've been thinking about you and about us. I've gone over and over my time with you," Ivy said. She leaned toward him. He ran a shaky hand through his hair. "I want you to know that I trust you."

He breathed a sigh of relief and smiled at her.

Ivy shrugged. "And I probably need a boatload full of therapy."

"Beautiful Ivy, that's a boat ride I would be happy to take with you." He kissed her sweetly.

She stroked Judy and the sky began to turn purple with a touch of gold on the clouds near the horizon.

"Now, back to my mom. I don't know why, but she got over Ashley fast. I thought she'd rant and rave until he was hung. But she is happier than I have seen her since before Dad died."

"You're kidding, why?" Ivy said.

He shook his head no. "Strangely, out of the blue, she and Anderson have become friends. They spend all their time together."

"Which frees you up to watch sunsets?" Ivy asked.

"I am telling the truth. She even said she feels guilty about how lost she was when my dad died. She keeps thanking Anderson for being like a father to me and Brett."

"That's amazing," Ivy said. "I wonder if becoming a grandmother has something to do with the change?" Ivy said.

He chuckled. "Hang on. There's more. I came down to deliver a message from her. I think she is nervous about telling you herself after the way she's treated you. She said to tell you that she's sorry for calling you Coffee Girl. She said she missed the obvious—us. She also wanted me to give you something."

Ivy looked at him and tipped her head. "A gift?"

"She said she really has her hands full with Sandy and would be honored if you would be Judy's mother, as long as she and Sandy can visit sometimes. She wants you to have Judy."

Ivy threw her hands in the air. "Judy! Did you hear that?" She scooped Judy up and laughed with joy while Judy licked her face. "I am your mom." Tears welled up in her eyes.

Xander laughed with her. "I'll let Mom know that you liked her gift and don't mind parenting Judy."

"Don't mind? I am ecstatic. I don't know what has come over your mother, but I like it."

"We all do," Xander said.

"My mother always taught me that if I wanted to know if a man was a good man, look at how he treated his

295

mother. She was right. You are a good son and a good man."

34

THE SECRET IN THE GARDEN

Ivy stood close to a tree in the church garden with Xander, but hopefully out of sight of the group of church members gathered around a large fountain with an angel at the top, pouring out water. Ivy thought the sound of the fountain and the sparrow that drank from it were perfect for the garden.

"It's perfect. I can't believe you put this together so quickly," Xander whispered.

"The pastor's wife is wonderful. She put today together. I just had the fountain shipped. You were the one that sped up the process. When the artist who had created it heard you were the one buying it and the reason you wanted it, he moved heaven and earth to get it here quickly."

"I love this," Xander said.

Ivy's heart burned with love while the church choir sang *Amazing Grace*. When they were done, the pastor's wife got up to speak.

"We are gathered here in memory of Angel and to celebrate this beautiful and anonymous gift in his honor.

Look around you and know that he lived. His life mattered. He was quiet and invisible, but his work touched anyone who walked in his garden."

35

— · —

Balloons and Babies

Six weeks later, Rhoda hobbled up the gravel trail between the cabins at the Sanctuary with Charlotte and Ivy like they were old friends.

Ivy wanted to shout for joy. "Charlotte, I can't believe you came up with the party idea and that allowed everyone to hijack your gender reveal."

"I wanted to thank you. I'm so excited for today. I hope it all goes the way you want it to. I love sharing the party. I am looking forward to making you happy and eating cake. We've planned a great surprise within a surprise."

Ivy's stomach knotted. "I still worry it might not be the happy occasion we envision."

"Never give up hope," Charlotte said. "I believe in miracles, and I've been praying you have one. I know I am. My baby will be safe and our home will be full of love. That feels like a miracle." She rubbed her tiny tummy.

"Everything is decorated and ready to go, but you can't go in the library until Anderson brings you in. Okay?" Ivy said.

"I can't even peek?" Charlotte asked.

"No!" Ivy said. "We have surprises for you and guests I don't want you to see. That is, if everything arrives on time."

"I can't wait for the surprise I know about," Charlotte said. She picked up a sand dollar and another small clam shell and tucked them in her pocket with the other shells she'd already found.

"Aggie made a pink and blue cake for the shower," Rhoda said. "We can put them both out, like you said, and then cut only one. Will you tell us if it is a girl or boy before the party?"

Charlotte stopped, tapped her chin, looked up at Rhoda, bit her lip, suppressing a smile, and said, "No."

Rhoda's shoulder dropped. Ivy fully expected her to demand an answer, but she didn't. Something was softening inside Rhoda and changing her into Nana Rhoda.

Charlotte linked arms with Rhoda. "Okay, I give. It's a girl."

Rhoda hugged Charlotte and squealed with joy. "I can't wait to buy her dresses!"

"What if she hates dresses?" Charlotte asked.

"Of course she will love them," Rhoda said.

There's the old Rhoda we all know.

"Whatever she likes and looks like will be perfect," Charlotte said. Then she stopped walking, "Unless she looks like her father."

"I bet you'll love her no matter what she looks like," Ivy said.

"No betting!" Charlotte threw her head back and laughed musically. Her joy was growing by leaps and bounds. "George wasn't all bad, just mostly bad. But I guess I will always love parts of George," Charlotte said.

"That's because you have a soft heart," Rhoda said.

Ivy's cell phone rang. "Uh huh. We aren't too far away. Got it." She hung up. "It's time. I'm actually nervous. What if I made a huge mistake?"

"Then you made it with the best of intentions," Rhoda said.

"Let's go. I can't wait! I'm starving," Charlotte said. Ivy and Rhoda had a hard time keeping up with Charlotte's long legs as she rushed back to the house.

Ivy wiped the dirt from her feet before opening the front door of Knightly House. She stepped in and listened as they walked toward the library. Her heart filled with joy.

"I can't wait," Rhoda limped past her and went into the library. Ivy could hear Anderson's deep voice. She heard Xander's and Jenny's voices followed by Aggie's and Rhoda's loud laughter. She was surprised that Rhoda's loud laugh had become something she loved about Rhoda. Her laughter was almost always followed by Anderson's. They seemed to be joined at the hip lately.

Brett ran down the stairs, followed by Petunia.

"Did the warden let you out?" Ivy asked. "Does she know you're fraternizing with a girl?'

Petunia's cheeks turned pink, and she giggled.

"Mom knows. She said I could come to the party and that it didn't matter what the law says. She is the law in my life. Then she gave me family community service hours. I have to help Anderson clean up tonight," Brett said. "Petunia's going to help me."

"That sounds like a pretty short sentence to me," Ivy said.

"I don't know what I was thinking," Brett said. "I should have gone to my mom that day at the bakery. She would have killed George, and possibly Ashley, and I wouldn't have been in trouble."

"Why didn't you?" Ivy asked.

"They threatened to hurt her. I didn't care if they hurt me." He sounded brave. But to Ivy, he sounded young. "They pushed and pushed, and I gave in. I was an idiot," Brett said.

Charlotte walked ahead of them.

"You are a teenager. You were also lucky to survive. Are you interested in gambling with the men now?" Ivy asked, suppressing a smile.

Brett stopped, looked at her and said, "I never want to see another playing card as long as I live. I didn't realize what Mom meant when she said you could be addicted to gambling like George. I've had my fill."

"Petunia, I'm sorry about your mom," Ivy said.

"Thanks," Petunia said, looking down at her feet.

Anderson poked his head out of the library and motioned for Brett and Petunia to come in. He looked happy, but a little anxious like he usually was before a dinner or event. They passed him and went into the library with Charlotte.

Anderson came out. "Follow me." He went through the kitchen to the back to the porch.

"Is she here?" Ivy said.

"Really? Seriously? Why didn't you tell me she was bringing friends!" Anderson said. "I don't know if we have enough food."

Ivy's brows drew together. "Friends? I didn't know. Who did she bring?"

"I don't know who they are. There are a bunch of them." Anderson took out his phone. "I got Nephi to share his location with me a few days ago when I sent him to town on a fool's errand so we could get some things ready without him. He's close."

Anderson opened his house security app and showed her CCTV of Nephi driving up to the gate. The gates opened. Nephi was driving her SUV. It was full of pink and blue balloons.

Ivy snickered. "Has everyone arrived?"

Anderson gave her a quick nod.

Ivy grinned, bouncing on her toes. "I am so excited and nervous. It will be great or a disaster."

"Think positive. You've already proven you can do hard things," Anderson said.

Nephi parked by the house and wrestled the biggest balloon bouquet Ivy had ever seen out of the car. Ivy and Anderson waited at the door.

A balloon popped. "Crepes!" Nephi yelled. He took the stairs, still yelling. "Anderson, don't ever ask me to get balloons for you again. First this and now I have to eat tiny sandwiches and sit through a baby shower. I told you I wasn't coming."

"Bring them this way," Anderson said.

Ivy followed, elated like a kid on Christmas morning. She wanted to jump up and down. Instead, she bit her lip and followed Nephi and Anderson.

The balloon bouquet was so large, Nephi couldn't get close to the door. He tried twice before he used his foot to kick the door open. The weight dropped off the bottom of the balloon bouquet.

Suddenly there were balloons everywhere in the house. Nephi's mouth fell open as he watched them float to the ceiling. The room filled with laughter. Jenny's kids chased balloons with Aggie and Jenny, Desdemona giggled, Reginald laughed with her and stood on his tiptoes trying to catch one.

Then Ivy saw her.

"Mom?" Nephi said quietly. Mable, an older but timeless woman with flaming red hair threw her head back and laughed as she ran to her son and gathered him into a tearful hug. She had always been one of Ivy's favorite people.

"Why didn't you tell me you were living here?" Mable asked.

Nephi's head dropped but he was still hugging her. "I didn't want you to see me this way."

She pushed him out to arm's length, tilted her head and scratched her cheek before she said, "See you what way? There isn't a single way you could be or have been that I wouldn't love. You know that."

"I couldn't bear what happened. It was all my fault," Nephi said softly. The room and time stood still as everyone watched their exchange.

"Oh, so you're God, now? In control of everything? Nephi, stop punishing yourself and let yourself be happy and remember the good times. Shame is a waste of life," Mable said.

Nephi cried and laughed at the same time. "I missed you, Mom." And that was it. The heaviness lifted from his eyes and shoulders.

Ivy hugged them both. "Grandma Mable, you need to meet our friend, Aggie," Ivy said. "Make room, big guy." She passed them and opened the patio doors.

A flood of people hugged, chatted, and overwhelmed with love. Nephi walked his mother over to meet Aggie.

Ivy let go. She felt like one of Nephi's balloons, free and bumping along on the ceiling. All the people she and Nephi had left behind, lost due to their own shame, were embracing them.

"Esther!" Ivy screamed and jumped into her tall friend's arms, laughing, crying, and overwhelmed with joy. "Parker! Oh, look how happy you two are." She patted Esther's husband, Parker's little tummy, while his knuckle rubbed her head.

"My mom's here." Esther pointed. Grace Hart, Esther's mother, and her stepfather Joe Hart who were hugging Nephi and talking excitedly. It was a reunion like no reunion Ivy had ever experienced before.

Then Esther and Parker turned toward the door. The room became silent. Ivy searched everyone's faces. They were fixed on one thing.

Paisley, Nephi's ex, was standing, not in a wheelchair. She was at the patio door with her father, weeping and scanning the room, hesitant, biting her lower lip.

Nephi crossed the room and picked her up like a baby and held her. Paisley kissed his salty face and then, like they'd never been apart. He kissed her back. Then he pulled his head back and said, "I'm sorry. I'm so sorry." Ivy held her breath waiting, terrified knowing Paisley could crush him with a single word.

Paisley took Nephi's face in both her hands. "I'm sorry. I blamed you and it was never your fault. I pushed you away because I was sure you wouldn't want me this way–broken. Forgive me."

"I pushed everyone away. There is nothing to forgive that isn't forgotten now," Nephi said.

Paisley smiled and pushed his shoulder gently. "Put me down. I want to show you!"

He set her down. Her twin, Parker, handed her two canes.

She beamed. "Surprise." She took two wobbly steps before he was holding her again.

"It's a miracle," He said.

And suddenly Ivy knew that Nephi and Paisley's love would last longer than time. He was exactly where he belonged.

She found Xander and hugged him. They stood by the door, watching. Ivy stood up on her tiptoes, and he bent over. She whispered in his ear, "I love you too." He hugged her and kissed her.

"Can we make it official?" Xander said. His eyes twinkled.

She tingled all the way to her toes. "Yes, please." He kissed her again.

She was waiting for the usual knot in her stomach when it came to commitment and trust. It was gone, replaced by the warm sensation of hope.

She took Xander's hand and looked around the magical library and realized she too was exactly where she belonged. Her two worlds had collided and become one. If there was a God, she hoped heaven would be exactly like this.

The End

– · –

PEACH ROLL RECIPE

ACKNOWLEDGEMENTS

Special thanks to:

My Heavenly Father, eternally the best storyteller, creator, and caregiver, for sending me miracle after miracle in my times of need, for inspiring my stories, and for always being with me.

To my BFF, Author Deb Goodman. She listens, keeps me formatted, and cleans up my messy author's life.

To my daughter, Erin, for being there and sharing her condo when I needed a place to write in Utah, for reading my books without a bribe or threat, and for keeping me laughing all day long.

To my six children, who love and care for each other, their spouses, my fifteen grandchildren, ten or more chickens, two goats, their eight dogs, cats, and organic gardens. You bring me joy, the information on the best poisons to use, and endless fun to add to my tidy murder mysteries.

To the Lassies, for your lifetime of love and constant connection no matter where in the world we are.